STING IN THE TALE

THE NOVEL

There is a new player among terrorist factions in Kashmir: Ghazni Baba. And Inspector General Dashamlav has vowed to stop him at all costs.

The infamous Amaso, leader of the terrorist group responsible for the 9/11 bombings, and thus the key target in the American anti-terrorism campaign, has been spotted in the Kashmir area, and the Americans will stop at nothing to get him.

Mili, the spoilt reigning Bollywood actress, refuses to become "fodder for terrorists" when she discovers that her latest film is to be shot in Srinagar, Kashmir. However, the prospect of co-starring with Milind Kumar, Bollywood's superstar icon, is enough persuasion.

These three groups are drawn together in Kashmir. Mili and Dhruv, a friend of Milind Kumar, are kidnapped by Amaso, and are held under cover of the worst snowstorm in living memory. It is under these circumstances that Amaso, Mili and Dhruv play out a modern version of the Arabian Nights. Dhruv, a professional storyteller, has three chances to tell a tale with an unforeseeable twist, to win his and Mili's freedom. But can he do it before the snowstorm blows itself out?

THE AUTHOR

Rajeev Sharma has been writing on issues related to terrorism, intelligence and diplomacy for over two decades. This is his seventh book, but first English fiction. He started his creative writing career with a Hindi novel. He has published five non-fiction books also.

STING IN THE TALE

A Thriller

Rajeev Sharma

Kaveri Books
New Delhi • India

ISBN : 978-81-7479-092-7

This book is a work of fiction. Names, characters, places and incidents are products of the author's imagination or are used fictionally. Any resemblance to actual events or locales or persons, living or dead, is entirely coincidental.

Originally Published in Paperback by
Kaveri Books
4697/5-21 A, Ansari Road, New Delhi-110002 (India)
Ph.: 011-23288140, 23245799 • E-mail : kaveribooks@vsnl.com

Typeset in Nebraska Font by
Vaishnav Graphics & Systems, New Delhi-110 055

Printed at
Salasar Imaging Systems, New Delhi

PRINTED IN INDIA

This book is dedicated to two most important women in my life (in chronological order as they came): sister Sarika and wife Pratima.

Acknowledgements

I have no literary pretensions for "Sting in the Tale", nor is a thriller meant to be as such. I have always believed that a thriller should meet two barest requirements: one, it should flow from the writer's heart and involve the reader; two, while reading it, the reader should feel that he or she is watching a film.

The reader is the final judge of my triumph or failure.

I started writing this novel in April 2006 and finished it within hundred days. For this reason, the connoisseur may find it stilted writing. It was my conscious effort to write the kind of English as it is spoken in the Indian subcontinent, not as the critics would want it to be. Blame it on me, if you find the language pedestrian.

During the course of writing, scores of my friends chipped in with precious advice. My sessions with diplomat-writer Vikas Swarup, were of immense help. My friends in the intelligence community, who gave extensive briefings on operational matters, would be embarrassed if I were to name them.

I want to make a special mention of my South Africa-based literary agent, Christa Martin of Cellar Door Literary Agency. Her contribution to the novel is immense. She tried her best to give me an international breakthrough in my maiden creative writing venture in English, but could not. I look at her efforts in only one way: her triumph and my failure.

I am also indebted to Paris-based literary agents - Marc Parent, Paul Muller and Anne Confuron - who pored over the manuscript, but could not go beyond.

There are many close friends who helped me in one way or the other. Following is a small list, in alphabetical order, of those who have promised to promote the book :

Ajit Doval, Amit Varma, Anand Gupta, Anil Jindal, Anil Nagpal, Anil Patni, Anurag Srivastava, Ashish Aggarwal, Ashwini Gupta, Chitleen Sethi, Dinesh Bhatia, Dilip Sinha, Dr Pulkit Khurana, Dr Ravi Gupta, Dr Sunil Gupta, Iftikhar Gilani, Jeetan Singh, K J S Sodhi, M K Laul, Navtej Sarna, N K Singh, Om Arora, P N Andley, Pragiya Tiwari, Prashant Sood, P Harish, Rajiv Bahl, R K Vyas, Robinder Sachdev, Rashmi Kant Dave, Ratika Mehrotra, Raj Kumar Singh, Rajiv Rastogi, Rajnish Verma, Rupak Kumar Datta, S Satyanarayanan, Sandeep Chakravorty, Sandeep Vyas, Sanjay Anand, Sanjeev Chauhan, Satish Misra, Shambhu Kumaran, Shalabh Kumar Sharma, S S Negi, Sunil Sharma, Suresh Verma, Suvir Sharma, T C A Raghavan, T R Ramachandran, Vinayak Sharma and Vipul.

Contents

1

Cat and Mouse

The gates of the sprawling double-storied white mansion in the heart of New Delhi were flung open by an alert sentry, who had spotted the familiar car from a distance.

Diwakar jumped out of the car and rushed to his room on the ground floor. The room was conspicuous in one way: there were no wires visible in the 20 by 10 foot room. Beads of sweat were visible on his forehead even though December was more than halfway through. The Joint Director (Operations) of the Intelligence Bureau summoned his steno immediately and dictated a top secret note for Inspector General Dashamlav about the outcome of his interrogation of a suspected terrorist. Diwakar was just returning from Red Fort where the IB had kept the young man, after he was picked up the previous night by India's internal intelligence agency. After finishing his dictation, Diwakar looked at his watch. It was 10.15 am. There was time to have some coffee after hours of hard work.

Around the same time, in downtown Srinagar, a well-built man in his late thirties got down from a taxi in a crowded bylane and melted into the crowd. He walked briskly, a walk that could signify to any observer that he was not a stranger to Srinagar. However, nobody noticed the man as he crossed several lanes and finally stopped in front of a nondescript house. He knocked twice.

"Salaam Zahir Bhai," beamed a young man as he peeped out of the half-open door.

The man, wearing a dark overcoat and a hat, ignored the greeting and walked in. The young man took his visitor to an antechamber and sat in front of him, speechless.

"Where are the others?" Zahir Bhai asked in a measured tone.

"Mir, Osman, Haider and Pasha are in Srinagar and should be coming any moment. Janesar, Suleiman, Ali and Manzoor have gone to Kupwara and will be coming back tomorrow. You have met them already. You have not met Hanif, Qadir and Aslam who have gone to Delhi for recce."

"How are you doing in your studies?"

"Very well."

"Have you received all the books?"

"Yes, Zahir Bhai."

"Your examination date is fast approaching. Are you fully prepared?"

"Yes, Zahir Bhai, Will you have some kehwa or breakfast?"

"No. I had it courtesy Indian airline. What about the dog and the Baz? "

"The Mir group has done something about the dog. They are expected here any moment. The other party has gone to Kupwara for the Baz..." he left his sentence incomplete to answer the knock on the door. The four men had arrived. All four greeted Zahir Bhai reverentially.

Without wasting time on acknowledging their greetings, Zahir Bhai got up and said, "I have to go now and tie up a few things before catching my flight back to Delhi. But tell me, have you got the dog?"

"Yes, Zahir Bhai. It's of good breed," Mir replied.

"What about the dog handler? Have you found somebody suitable?"

"Yes, Zahir Bhai. He is a retired head constable of Jammu and Kashmir police," Osman informed.

"Okay, now listen carefully," said Zahir Bhai, looking at his host. "I need the Baz for this exam. If 100 are not available, have 50; but not less than that. Keep me informed. Khuda hafiz."

Seconds later, Zahir Bhai swung back and said, "Remember the precautions. Do not call me on my mobile unless the heavens are falling. Call up from a public phonebooth on my usual number. Use only coded language."

Zahir Bhai did not turn back this time.

Mili was no longer listening to the script. She smelt a rat when she heard a reference to Srinagar the seventh or eighth time. She jumped off her sofa and asked the producer, "Mister Satish Bhimani, are you suggesting that the location for the film would be Srinagar?"

"Madam, please be patient to hear the script first," said Bhimani, aware of the actress's notoriety for throwing tantrums.

"No, but I must know whether the location is Srinagar or not; because if it is, I am not going to act in your film."

"Madam, I have already paid you two million rupees in advance, which you have accepted and you have no business..."

Mili cut him short with another one-liner. "But I am not prepared to go to a place like Srinagar and be fodder for terrorists."

There was a minute's silence in the room occupied only by the producer and the reigning siren of Bollywood.

Mumbai's pleasant weather had just turned very stuffy.

"You did not make any such precondition while accepting the signing amount," Bhimani said, his voice now trembling with anger.

"If that is so, then I am prepared to return the advance right now. Nevertheless, I will not go to Srinagar, come what may. You must understand Mister Bhimani that I am only 28.

I am not ruling Bollywood for the past six years to get my career and life snuffed out because of a film being shot in a place like Srinagar. You will have to change the location."

"The location will not be changed; it cannot be changed. Only the heroine will be changed. I will tell Milind Kumar about your attitude," said a defiant Bhimani as he folded up his file and got up.

"How does Milind Kumar come into the picture?" Mili asked, perplexed.

She did not quite understand the reference to Milind Kumar, who was the most popular superstar Bollywood had ever produced. At the age of 35, Milind Kumar had already become a living legend, an actor whose rumoured price per film was anywhere between fifty to a hundred million rupees. His mere presence in a film was considered a passport to success at the box office and every heroine worth her salt dreamt of teaming up with him, once at least. Mili had not been fortunate thus far.

Bhimani looked at Mili, said nothing and started walking towards the door.

For once, Mili thought she had bitten off more than she could chew. She ran after Bhimani, held the producer by his coat sleeve and said apologetically, "I am sorry Bhimani, but please tell me how Milind figures in this?"

"He is the hero of the film." Mili was dumbstruck, as Bhimani continued, "and it was Milind's suggestion that I sign you as the leading lady of the film."

"You mean Milind recommended me?"

Without waiting for his reply, she said, "You should have told me that earlier. Of course, I will do the film. I will go anywhere for the shooting."

"Shall we resume the script where we left it off?"

"No need for that. I will hear it in Srinagar. When do we leave for Srinagar?"

"Next week."

On a moonless, cloudy night, a ship cast anchor on the high seas in the Bay of Bengal. The Commander of the 100-tonne, 80-foot-long ship trained his nightvision binoculars southwards over the vast seascape. A Cyprus-based company had booked the vessel. It had originated from Greece. The declared cargo was timber. After sighting a tiny speck on the horizon, he handed over the binoculars to a tall, fair-complexioned man in flowing robes and snow-white beard.

"Sheikh, this is the island I had mentioned to you," the Commander told the authoritative-looking man.

"Hope your boys are on the job?" the Sheikh asked in a heavy Arabic accent.

"Yes, indeed. You yourself can see."

Eleven speedboats were darting towards the ship. Within minutes, the speedboats surrounded the ship, switched off their engines, and several muscular men started shifting the ship's cargo on to the boats. The exercise was over in about twenty minutes. The Commander himself supervised the transfer of cargo.

The boxes, wrapped in polythene for protection from heat and water, were loaded on ten boats. Then the Commander helped the Sheikh to get into the more distinctive eleventh boat, instructed the skeletal staff on the ship to stay put quietly until they returned, and ordered all the boats to move towards the island.

The clouds had grown denser and blacker. Having been a seaman all his life of four decades and a half, the Commander knew that there was no way that any spy satellite could track their movements for the next two hours at least. Their destination – the island – was full of tall palm trees, so thickly interwoven that the island remained dark even during daytime. Jaffna was not very far.

The mid-sea operation did not go unnoticed, nevertheless. A reconnaissance plane of the Indian Navy sighted the foreign vessel in its waters and radioed a command to the vessel to identify itself. The communication staff, already nervous about the unexpected development, reported the matter to the Commander. He heard the disturbing news quietly and ordered his staff not to respond to the radio message.

He knew the nearest Indian naval base was at Rameswaram in southern India and an Indian armed patrol vessel could not reach the spot in less than 12 hours. The

Sheikh, with the Commander in tow, briskly walked towards a small mud hut, apparently built a few hours ago. Ten men and a young woman were waiting for the high-profile visitor outside the hut. The woman was stunningly beautiful, dressed as she was in black robes. Each one of them bowed respectfully to the Sheikh and made way for him to enter the hut. There were no tables or chairs. In the name of furniture, there were twelve cushions made of grass, neatly arranged on the mud floor. The Commander remained outside the hut, well out of earshot.

Inside, the Sheikh addressed the small gathering.

"We have gathered here for our plenary review meeting of operations of The Green Jihad. You are aware that such review meetings are held strictly as per operational demands, which can be twice in a year or once in three years. Each one of you present here is an important spoke in the wheel of our organization. In the coming years, we need to target our biggest enemy, the United States of America, like never before. I need to pick your brains on how best to complement and supplement our efforts so that we have situations where there are not too many people dying, but too many people watching. Let us start with our Egyptian unit head. Remember the ground rules. Nobody will address anyone here by name."

The Egyptian immediately grabbed his chance. "Sheikh, I beg to differ with your policy of creating situations where there are not too many people dying but too many people watching. My argument is that if we kill a large number of people in one strike, the world will have to watch us."

"But this can alienate us from the masses. Can we survive without support from the locals?" Sheikh asked.

"Sir, we can continue to have the support of the Islamic Ummah as long as we target the infidels only. Agreed, there can be no insurance against self-goals where our own innocent brothers and sisters are killed. But we should look at the long-term objective."

"Fair enough; the point is accepted. Now let's turn to our Iraqi brother. He has something to say."

"Yes. We need to step in, in a big way, in West Asia. Poor Palestinians have been waging a just and noble war for their homeland against Israel for over half a century. The Palestinian brothers and sisters have launched so many Intifadas but to no avail. We have to engineer a jihadi twist to the Palestine-Israel conflict which has not happened so far."

"Okay. I think that is a valid point. I accept it. I hope you all agree?" the Sheikh said.

All present thumped the mud floor as a token of their prompt approval of the suggestion, which was passed unanimously. This was followed by brief presentations by the Somalian, the Turkish, the Chechen, the Saudi, the Filipino, the Afghan, the Uzbek, the Uighur, and the Spaniard, as well as the Pakistani woman. Each one stressed taking the activities of their respective local jihadi theaters to a new pitch.

The sole woman in the group, who was the South Asian head of the organization, gave the longest and the most passionate presentation where she emphasized the need for The Green Jihad to put Kashmir on the same pedestal as Afghanistan, Palestine, Middle East and Chechnya. The Sheikh looked around, found most others as skeptical as him and asked, "Any takers?"

There were blank faces all around. The Iraqi was the bluntest in his rejection of the Pakistani woman's suggestion.

"Sir, my considered opinion is that we should bite only that much we can chew. Kashmir is a political issue between India and Pakistan and has never been as close to the hearts of Muslims of the world as the issue of Palestine."

The woman protested. The Sheikh could see the ship's Commander signaling from outside the hut to conclude the meeting immediately and the woman seemed bent upon converting this plenary review meeting into a chaotic discussion.

"Alright. The woman should not have any reason to suspect gender discrimination here. I propose that we take up a select few cases in India-held Kashmir. These should be strictly experimental and we would review our strategy at an appropriate time. What do you say?"

This time, everyone concurred.

"Now we come to the last point. All of you have already been briefed about the consignment of arms and ammunition that I have personally brought for your respective needs. The goods would have already reached our safe house in Jaffna. I must place on record the help given by the LTTE in this operation, though they have done it only on an one-off basis. Let us see if we can win them over in the near future. You will be notified as and when, and where, our next meeting is convened. I declare this meeting closed."

The Sheikh's reference to the LTTE– the Liberation Tigers of Tamil Elam, a Sri Lankan terrorist outfit fighting for a separate Tamil homeland in the small island country since 1980s – was significant. A tie-up between The Green Jihad and the LTTE could mean a coup of sorts in the world of terrorism – the former being an Islamic jihadi organization while the latter was an out-and-out Hindu unit. Besides, the two terrorist outfits getting together had the potential of emerging as the world's most lethal terror group.

The LTTE is the only terrorist organization in the world that has an air force of sorts, a fleet of ships, anti-aircraft guns, surface-to-air missiles and even a submarine. The LTTE runs offices in about 40-odd countries with sizable Tamil population. The half a million Tamil expatriates in Canada, Germany, Switzerland, Britain, Italy, Australia, Singapore and Malaysia are forced to contribute at least five per cent of their salary to the LTTE, thus adding approximately 25 to 30 million US dollars to the LTTE coffers annually.

As the Sheikh paced towards the shore, he asked the Commander, "Your boys took the necessary precautions about the meeting place?"

"No need to make any efforts, Sheikh. The sea will do the job for us in a matter of hours. The whole island is going to be submerged. There will be no trace left of the meeting venue."

Dashamlav extended his hand to welcome Diwakar. He was one man Diwakar always looked forward to meeting. Everyone in the profession regarded Dashamlav as the quintessential intelligence man.

Dashamlav relit his cigar and said, "We have received several wireless intercepts suggesting that Ghazni Baba is in India and planning something nasty."

"Sir, I do not really understand who this Ghazni Baba is! It is only for the last six or seven months that we have been hearing of him, through the intercepts, of course. Do we know anything about him? Do we have his photograph or computer sketch?" Diwakar asked.

"I am afraid not. Apparently, he is an important cog in the ISI wheel as far as this Republic Day is concerned. So please keep an eye on that. Dashamlav's reference was to the all-powerful Pakistani intelligence agency, the Inter Services Intelligence. "Anything further on the Hanif front?"

"Yes sir, Hanif has led us to two more of his accomplices. I have talked to them also. They are all singing like canaries."

"What has come of their interrogation?"

"That they all were frequenting one particular phone booth in the city not only for making calls but also for receiving them. Agent 71 B reported their activities as suspicious. We have taken necessary action."

"Anything else?"

"Yes, their conversations have several references to a dog and a hundred Baz."

Qurban Mian was a popular man in the Jama Masjid area, though he had arrived and settled there less than a year ago. The public phonebooth he ran belied his financial status. He was a sharp and happy-go-lucky man. However, on the Ides of December, he was not his usual bubbly self and glanced outside every now and then. Bang opposite his phone booth was a scooter automobile repair shop. Normally the customers would come, leave their vehicles for repair and return later to collect them. For the past one week, however, one or the other vehicle always remained at the repair shop and the owner stayed there, looking intently at the booth.

Finally, his wait ended. Qurban Mian spat his paan – a betel leaf chewed in South Asia with or without tobacco – into a handheld spittoon and took his guest to his small cabin. After shutting the door, he shouted at his visitor, "I told you not to come here and meet me tomorrow at Pragati Maidan instead."

"But Bhai, it was urgent," the visitor protested.

"Okay, okay. I suspect that something is going on here. Anyway, what is the matter?"

"There is a peculiar problem, Bhai. The dog handler says that the belt is heavier than expected and with this belt the dog cannot remain tasked for more than an hour."

"So, how does it pose a problem?"

"It can pose a problem if the minister comes late ..."

"Shut up. He is the examiner, not a minister," the Mian chided.

"Sorry Bhai."

"The examiner normally comes in time to every function. If he doesn't this time, call it off."

"So we go ahead with the exam at Navodaya School, Gole Market at the appointed time on Thursday."

"Yes."

On Wednesday morning, Qurban Mian was very tense. On Monday evening, he had personally visited the place where his men waited, along with the dog and dog handler. Everything was going as per plan. The minister would arrive at the school at 12 noon on Thursday to inaugurate an I.T. programme for the schoolchildren. The dog handler had already ensured that he would garland the minister. The garland would be sprinkled with a perfume, which the dog had already been trained to pick from a crowd. The dog would be signalled to run to the minister at an appropriate time. Nobody would find it odd even though the dog wore an all too visible strap around his neck. The strap would carefully conceal a belt filled with plastic explosives, undetectable by the usual security paraphernalia.

In any case, the minister, though an influential one, did not have as elaborate a security cover as the Prime Minister. The minute the dog reached the minister, another member of the hit squad, standing straight across near the school main gate some 200 meters from the dais, would press the button of a remote control. The explosion would kill the dog and the minister. Qurban Mian always loved doing things with flourish and innovation. He was not one to follow the beaten track. However, since this morning he had been pacing up and down in the little space his phone booth afforded him.

To add to his worries, the activities at the auto repair shop had increased. Just as he was brooding about the auto repair shop, his booth's main door was kicked open and in seconds, his neck was against the cold barrel of a gun. Several more guns were pointed at him. Two men entered the already crowded phone booth and walked up to him. One of them pulled a stool and sat barely a foot away from him. The man coolly lit his cigar, looked straight into the eyes of Qurban Ali and asked him sternly, "Where are the bazookas?" Qurban Ali knew in a flash that it was all over.

"There is no need for you to feign ignorance. All your men are in our custody, including the dog, the dog handler and, of course, the remote," the man with the cigar said.

"Where are the bazookas which you have smuggled from Kupwara?"

Qurban Mian's face had turned pale, like a jaundice patient.

The man with the cigar continued, enjoying every moment of his prey's discomfiture. "We had entered your booth and your cabin with duplicate keys last week and bugged the entire place," he said as he took two steps towards the cash counter and pulled out a bugging device. "A similar bugging device is planted in your cabin too. So, where are the bazookas or Baz in your parlance?"

"And what did you plan to do with the bazookas?" asked another officer who accompanied the man with the cigar.

"That I will tell you, Diwakar," Diwakar's senior said, puffing from his cigar. "These people wanted to take the level of militancy in Jammu and Kashmir to a new high by using bazookas, the incendiary weapon whose shells can have an effective range of at least 200 meters. When their shells hit the target, they explode into a fireball. The Afghan Mujahideen had used it against the Russians with deadly results during the Afghan war. So where are the bazookas?"

"I will tell you," Qurban Mian heard himself saying.

"You will also have to tell us where Ghazni Baba is?" said Diwakar.

"No need Diwakar," his senior said as he got up. Stubbing the cigar under his shoe, he signalled.

"He himself is Ghazni Baba," said Inspector General Dashamlav as he walked out. A stunned Diwakar understood the signal. Ghazni Baba was to be taken to Red Fort immediately.

It is not snowing. Not yet. Nevertheless, the sub-zero temperature is being felt by everyone present in the small colony of makeshift tents amidst high mountains in Kashmir. A strong wind is blowing, almost uprooting the tents, and lashing the inmates like daggers. A masked commander is authoritatively addressing an assembly of twenty odd young men.

"So, this is all I had to say to you folks. Get going now. I am with you. Our government is with you, Allah is with you. Go and teach these Hindu kafirs a lesson of their lives. Khuda Hafiz."

The commander had always appeared before the cadres in a black mask wearing black glasses. He lunged towards the exit, but quickly retraced his steps after suddenly remembering something important and said, "Last, but not the least, I forgot to assign one important duty. Fardeen, after your comrades are through with their respective jobs, I want you to tell this friend of mine, Mister Decimal, what an ostentatious fool he is. Khuda Hafiz."

The commander left immediately thereafter. No questions were asked about the strange name "Decimal".

Everyone present knew that the commander found the name "Dashamlav" quite a tongue twister and referred to the man bearing this name by its literal English translation. The cadres once again noticed that this time also, as on previous two occasions, the commander's voice was peculiarly modulated.

Less than a week later, Dashamlav received a message on his mobile phone. He read the message several times over and the dozen odd officials who were in his room were in no doubt that the SMS was important. The brighter ones among those who were present in the Inspector General's room for his daily Ops meeting could see that the message had unsettled the boss.

Diwakar was very keen to know what the message was, but he checked his curiosity. He reminded himself of the elementary rule of intelligence craft, which barred him from scouting information, and that too from his senior, unless it was spelled out. Dashamlav dialed an internal phone number and whispered something. The IB Inspector General carried on with the meeting for the next twenty minutes.

Diwakar knew that his boss was going through the motions, his mind set elsewhere. Then Dashamlav signalled an end to the conference with his characteristic concluding statement, "That's all, gentlemen. Any questions?"

There were none and everybody began to disperse. As Diwakar neared the door to leave, Dashamlav said, "Mister Diwakar, can you stay back?"

When everybody, except Diwakar, left the room, Dashamlav fixed his gaze on Diwakar, gestured him to sit down and said, "I have a bad news."

"I could sense it. It has something to do with that SMS you received during the meeting."

"Well, it's about Ghazni Baba."

"I could sense that too. Has he escaped from custody?"

"He doesn't have to."

"Why? Is he dead?"

"No. He is very much alive. But he doesn't have to escape for the simple reason that the man we picked up the other day from Jama Masjid area is not Ghazni Baba."

"But how can you say that?"

"Read this yourself and you would understand," Dashamlav said, handing his mobile phone to Diwakar.

The message on the mobile phone screen said: "Inspector General Dashamlav, if u think u have got Ghazni Baba, then u r a fool. We have thousands of the likes of the one u have got. Ghazni Baba is special. If u dare 2 catch me, come to Srinagar on New Year's Eve. If u don't, don't call urself a man again...Ghazni Baba."

"But sir, how do you know that this message is genuine?"

"Because the killings in J&K have neither stopped nor subsided. On the contrary, there is a spurt. For past three days in a row, we have had high-profile terrorist attacks. These are signature killings, the typical Ghazni Baba acts. Think of it Diwakar. If we get to the spider, the spider's web becomes meaningless. The spider is very much alive and kicking and we have got stuck in the spider's web; and, I suspect, at the periphery."

Diwakar's mind was racing as he was hearing from his boss a candid confession of the team's failure, his own failure. Three days after "Ghazni Baba's" arrest, dozen-odd terrorists, armed to the teeth, had stormed into a school in the valley. The terrorists' siege could only be broken after a 12-hour-long gun battle in which at least 50 children had been killed. It was no solace for the security forces that all terrorists had been neutralized, though the government in New Delhi as well as Srinagar claimed its success.

Hours after the school siege, terrorists drove an explosives-laden car right into the compound of the Chief Minister's residence. The car bomb blew up everything except the Chief Minister, who was in the back lawns admiring his rose garden. Only the distance from the blast venue to the rose garden saved the Chief Minister. Then the apocalypse nearly happened. The next day, terrorists fired a Stinger missile at the aircraft of a VVIP who was flying into the valley from New Delhi for visiting the victims of the school carnage. The missile had missed the target, not because the terrorists were inept but because the VVIP's plane was equipped with a special device, which emitted heat flares to bamboozle heatseeking missiles, such as Stingers.

The incident triggered off a major political quake in New Delhi and the Prime Minister of India spoke to his Pakistani counterpart. Telephones buzzed in New Delhi as well as Islamabad and the P5 from Washington, London, Paris, Moscow and Beijing urged for restraint. The signal was clear. The militancy in the valley had reached dangerous proportions and could get out of hand any moment.

Diwakar disengaged himself from the events of the past three days and returned to the present. "But sir, what about the mobile phone from which the SMS was sent to you?"

"Come on, Diwakar," Dashamlav said in a chiding tone. "Do you really think that these people would be so foolish as to send an SMS from a phone that can be tracked? Take it from me, the caller would have used a prepaid SIM card and destroyed it after using it just the once. But still, I have ordered an inquiry."

Just then, Dashamlav's internal phone rang. He spoke in monosyllables and then replaced the receiver. "There you are. True to the script which I gave you. The relevant mobile number is switched off. Rendered dysfunctional."

"So where are we now? The chap we have is not Ghazni Baba. At best he is one of Ghazni Baba's numerous satellites, he is actually unaware of who or where the real Ghazni Baba is, and we have to look for the real one? The spider."

"Yes."

Dashamlav ordered black coffee and instructed his PA that he would not take any calls for the next half hour. By the time he lit up a new cigar, his coffee had arrived. He asked the peon to leave the coffee on the small table at the far end of the room near a plush sofa where he used to have informal meetings. His mind was racing.

He was barely into his 35th year and had already become an Inspector General. It was a rarity. He was aware that he had become an IG at least one full decade before that status was normally attained. He was also aware of his enormous influence. It was only last year that the Prime Minister had himself penned a note in his personal file, nominating him to a Shaurya Chakra, a military honour. The Prime Minister had been so pleased with Dashamlav's daredevil espionage operation in a neighbouring hostile country that he had said in the note: "I elevate Mister Dashamlav to the rank of Inspector General with immediate effect and decide to award him the Shaurya Chakra. He will be the first non-military officer of the Union to receive this honour. I also make it clear that this is only a one-time exception and cannot be cited as a precedent in future."

Dashamlav had a pleasing personality. He possessed the toughness of a commando, was well versed with the strategic scenario in the country, in the region and in the world. What's more, he had often displayed that rare quality of thinking like a man of action and acting like a man of thought. To top it all, he was a master of disguises and had a countenance that could easily pass him off as a Kashmiri or a Gujarati, a rustic or a suave man.

There was one more facet of his personality, which not even the Prime Minister was aware of. In fact, very few people close to him knew this aspect of his personality. He was an accomplished writer, too, and had published several works of fiction under a pseudonym.

He had begun writing fiction when he worked as an undercover agent in a foreign country. His very first novel topped the list of bestsellers. Fame as a writer, though it was under an assumed name, did not matter to him; nor did it tempt him to give up his government job. For him, excelling in his official work was supreme and he stuck to it.

Dashamlav had always been an operations man. He always liked challenges. This time, he found himself face-to-face with a challenge from a man called Ghazni Baba. He knew that Srinagar beckoned him.

Mili was in a strange mood that evening. Later in the night, she was to catch a flight to New Delhi and next morning she would be flying to Srinagar for a fortnight-long packed schedule of shooting. She was furious that the producer was adamant on shooting in Srinagar. She was nervous at the thought of entering a Red Zone, infested with trigger-happy terrorists. Yet, there was a lingering sense of achievement that she would be shooting with the great Milind Kumar whom she was yet to meet in the flesh.

She had enquired from Satish Bhimani whether Milind Kumar would be joining the film unit in Mumbai or New Delhi. She became acutely aware of the meaning of superstardom, and secretly congratulated herself for not foolishly walking out of Bhimani's project, when the producer told her, "Milind will be reaching Srinagar in a private plane."

2

The Petals Unfold

A week later, Diwakar received an interesting phone call late in the evening.

"Sir, there is an overseas telephone call for you. The caller has refused to give his identity. He wants to speak only to you. He has an American accent. Shall I transfer the call?" his PA asked.

"Do it."

"Hello is that Mister Diwakar?" the caller asked with a distinct American accent.

"Yes. Diwakar here."

"My name is Jack Boucher from the CIA. I look after field operations in South Asia. I am calling from Langley."

"Yes, Mister Boucher. What can I do for you?"

"I wanted to get in touch with Inspector General Dashamlav urgently. I am told that he is not available."

"That's right. You can tell me what this is about."

"Well, it's about the Ghazni Baba case. But I can't tell you more because I have instructions to discuss this matter with Inspector General Dashamlav only."

"It's like this Mister Boucher. Mister Dashamlav is on Ghazni Baba's trail. It is an operational duty. We do not know where he is, nor are we authorized to find out. He can contact us anytime but we can't reach him until he wants us to."

"Do you have an idea where he might be?"

"Well, my guess will be like a philosopher's effort, trying to find a black cat in a dark room knowing there isn't one," Diwakar said, enjoying his impromptu wit.

"Okay, can you hold on for a minute?"

"Certainly."

As Yanni's music started streaming in, Diwakar knew that Boucher was consulting his superiors. The music stopped about a minute later.

"Sorry to keep you holding, Mister Diwakar. We have a classified information suggesting movement of some of the world's most wanted terrorists in your region. Kashmir, to be specific. According to our information, Ghazni Baba himself is a tiny tot in comparison to the kind of terrorists who are seen moving around in Pakistan administered Kashmir."

"You are talking about The Green Jihad leadership in Pakistan occupied Kashmir, not very far from the Line of Control?"

"You people are already aware of this?" Boucher could not hide his surprise.

"That's the only way India can survive. Otherwise, with the kind of efforts certain powers are making to bleed India white, we would have disintegrated years ago."

"That's good. Now let me come to the operational details. I have instructions to disclose to you that we have already diverted a specialized unit of commandos, already in Pakistan, to the Pakistan administered Kashmir. As you know, we are very keen on catching the entire leadership of The Green Jihad, dead or alive. These people are responsible for 9/11. Now please listen to me very carefully. Soon after this conversation, I will be sending you a fax through our secure network, giving the name and contact number of the team leader. Please pass it on to Mister Dashamlav as soon as he contacts you. We want the Indian Government to be on board with us on this operation. We also want Inspector General Dashamlav to be involved, because no one else knows that area better than he does. So good luck."

"Wait a minute Mister Boucher," Diwakar cut him short. "I can see my fax activating."

"But I haven't sent the fax to you yet!"

"The number is unlisted, Mister Boucher. This is a dedicated fax for Inspector General Dashamlav only. Perhaps his message may be of some interest to you."

Diwakar had already peered over the paper fast emerging from the fax machine.

"Yes, the message is indeed of interest to you. Now I read the message. 'CIA specialised unit arrived in that part of

Kashmir, about fifty kilometres from the LoC, six hours ago. Team looking for The Green Jihad leadership, seen moving in the region two days ago. Established contact with the Team leader Tim Gordon an hour ago. Will get back to you when required.' "

Diwakar knew the telephone receiver must have nearly slipped from the hands of Boucher.

"Fantastic. That man is a genius."

"So, would you still be sending the fax?" Diwakar needled.

"Operationally, there is no need. However, for official purposes, I reckon I will bloody well have to send the fax. Thanks a lot, Mister Diwakar. It has indeed been a pleasure talking to you," Boucher said and hung up.

Diwakar noticed that this time Boucher did not wish him "good luck" – two empty words which, he thought, betrayed a patronizing attitude. Now he read the entire fax again and again and again. He was foxed by the last three sentences, which he did not read out to Boucher.

"You might see an interesting development in Kashmir in the next 72 hours. I am in control. Thus far."

It was not morning yet, but the Chief Medical Officer's room in a military hospital in Muzzaffarabad, capital of Pakistan-held Kashmir, was bustling with activity. Seated in the CMO's chair was a Brigadier of the Inter Services Intelligence. Around him were six bearded men. Despite their heavy winter clothing, bulges at strategic places betrayed the fact that they were heavily armed.

"Brothers, I have called you here at this unearthly hour to apprise you of the dangers ahead. The Americans are in the area, already. Needless to say, the Americans do not move anywhere without purpose and without ultra modern gadgetry. They are looking for the Supreme Leader."

"That much we already know," a menacing looking young man snapped. "Tell us whether you are with us or with them?"

"I can see your love for the Americans. You have started using their language also!"

The Brigadier's taunt did not fall on deaf ears. The recipient's face muscles twitched. Sensing that the meeting was leading to a pointless exercise of accusations and counter accusations, a sober looking man, in his mid-forties, tried to rein in his young comrade in arms. "Relax Aziz Bhai. Let us see what Brigadier Sahib has to say. Please, go ahead."

"Thank you, Mohammed Bhai." Then turning towards Aziz, the Brigadier said, "As for your question, you already know the answer. You know very well that the government cannot be visibly with you. I hope that I don't have to over-emphasize the word "visibly". No government in the world today can dare to incur the wrath of the Americans. General Sahib is also doing the same. At the same time, we are sensitive to your feelings. That is why I am here."

The Brigadier could see a palpable improvement in the atmosphere now.

"So, I have a few suggestions for you people. Remember these are not instructions. These are suggestions only. For your own good. All Mujahideen are to be shifted to Leepa Valley in Kashmir with immediate effect. They are to lie low. This arrangement will be in place for a few weeks or months, depending upon the length of stay of the Americans in this area and other factors."

"What about our jihad in Kashmir?" Asghar Mian demanded to know. "Well, that will continue, Inshallah. We are going to raise BATs "Border Action Teams" for launching Mujahideen to the other side. And this time, the launches will be quiet, not accompanied by covering fire from the Army."

"That's all?"

"Last, but not least, we are going to upgrade your communication infrastructure. You will no longer function with the type of wireless sets you have. From today itself, you will be provided with Thuraya satellite phones or very powerful long-range wireless sets. Our Signals men are already here to train you people for using the new communications sets. Any question?"

"Why Thuraya Sat phones?"

"Because they uplink directly from ground to satellite without any intermediary stations and are less vulnerable to Direction Finder Antennae. This will make your communication network more secure and interception-proof."

"But what about the Americans who are here?"

"That you leave for us to handle. After all, we have been handling them for years, haven't we? All I ask from you is your cooperation. Do I get it?"

"Yes. Long live jihad. Pakistan paindabad," everyone in the room shouted.

The Brigadier noticed that Aziz Bhai's shout was almost a war cry.

A few hours after Diwakar's conversation with Boucher, several bulletproof jeeps of Border Security Force, an Indian paramilitary outfit, had already parked near the entrance of a narrow street in downtown Srinagar. More were on the way. Daybreak was two hours away. The jeeps' engines and headlights were turned off. There were no wailing sirens. No security vehicle used flashing revolving red lights. The security men tiptoed their way towards a dilapidated single-storied house.

An Inspector, who was leading the team, surveyed the house where terrorists were believed to be hiding. A senior IB official had briefed him about the impending operation and given him intelligence inputs. Knowing the reputation of the officer, the Inspector understood the importance of the operation he was going to undertake. The intelligence about the presence of terrorists in that house came from unimpeachable sources.

The Inspector noticed that the militants' safe house had a tiled roof. He divided his personnel into two assault teams. One stormed in from the main entrance by blasting it open. The second broke through the roof and jumped in simultaneously.

There were five men inside. Four were sleeping while one was keeping vigil. Even the one keeping vigil was taken completely unawares. He fired a few shots from his AK series rifle, but was overpowered. Just when all five suspected militants had been tied tightly with a rope and dumped in a corner and the Inspector radioed the "Mission completed" message, all five bit into their lockets. By the time the Inspector could realize what was happening, four heads lolled aside, lifeless.

In a flash, the Inspector understood that the terrorists had consumed cyanide. He was not prepared for this contingency because thus far militancy in Kashmir had not witnessed the LTTE-type cyanide culture. Obviously, he did not have any anti-cyanide drugs.

The Inspector spotted a funnel and a can of kerosene in the room. Kerosene is a commonly stored commodity in every Kashmiri household during winters. He ordered his boys to start the "funnel treatment" on the fifth militant who was perhaps late in biting into his locket and was still breathing. A funnel was forced into the militant's mouth and kerosene was poured in. Within minutes, the militant vomited out the deadly poison before it could get absorbed in the blood. He ordered his men to quickly take out the five militants on stretchers into ambulances, which had been arranged as part of the preparations for the operation. He told his smartest officer to rush the injured militant to hospital.

Then he radioed another message, this time to a more important official. His gut feeling was that the operation was far more important than he originally thought. Use of cyanide capsules was a firm indicator. The five men knew too much. There was a fair chance that one of them might survive to spill the beans. It was still dark. The small crowd that had gathered outside saw five dead bodies being put into ambulances.

A Thuraya set in Muzzaffarabad crackled about half an hour after the Srinagar incident.

"Yes Shakir. What news?"

"Sir, all the five boys have been martyred," a trembling voice spoke.

"Which five boys damn it? I have hundreds of them over there."

"Those who had done the recce for Operation Hasina."

"Had they done their job before getting killed?"

"They had done their job before they consumed cyanide."

"Had they given their report about their task before getting martyred?"

"Yes sir. I personally received their report. I have the necessary details. Then, as per your instructions, I came to my own place. I regret my decision, though."

"Why?"

"Because one of them was my younger brother. He would have turned 19 tomorrow."

"I am sorry to hear that. Shakir, you must understand that you are useful for the cause of jihad only when you are alive, not when you are dead. As for your brother and four others who consumed cyanide, you know very well that they will go straight to Jannat. But how do you know that all five were martyred?"

"Because sir, one of our men was an eyewitness to the five dead bodies being taken away in body bags."

"Okay. You will be met by one of my confidantes shortly. He is an important person of our group. You give him the report of the reconnaissance your boys had conducted."

"Can Operation Hasina still be on?"

"That is to be decided by someone higher up in the hierarchy. Since your own brother has laid down his life in this operation, I should tell you that I don't think we will go ahead with the Operation. But you give the report."

After the line went dead, the man dialed a number from his Thuraya set.

"Hello Rashid. It's me. Operation Hasina is on."

Around noon, the BSF organized a mass burial for the five militants killed before daybreak. An Inspector General of BSF had obtained a special permission for the burial from New Delhi. He himself supervised the burial ceremony. Ten elders from locality in which the operation took place were invited for the burial ceremony. The elders had laid one precondition for attending the funeral: that they would bring their own Maulvi for the burial ceremony. The BSF readily agreed.

The burial ceremony over, the BSF IG was driven straight to a private house where he was told a senior IB officer from Delhi had been camping for past one week. He was surprised that the "senior officer" who was equivalent to his rank, was very young.

"Thank you so much IG sahib for your help."

"You don't want to know how I procured a dead body for this burial ceremony? Luckily for us, one unclaimed body had been lying in the mortuary for weeks, the BSF IG said. "What is the condition of your man? Is he out of the woods?"

"Yes. He is fully conscious. And he has revealed all."

3

Operation Hasina

For the last few days, Mili had been shooting for Bhimani's film. Her happiness knew no bounds. She had never been to Kashmir before. She had only read about it or seen it in films. As a child she always wanted to visit Kashmir, "the Paradise on earth" as all newspapers and magazines described the place. Her affluent businessman father had hardly had any time to take his only child for a vacation in Kashmir. By the time, she grew up, Kashmir was no longer what it used to be. It had become the Death Valley, a place where guns outnumbered roses, where tourists were kidnapped and killed, where there was death and destruction all around.

These days, however, Mili was happy not because she was in Kashmir but because she was shooting with Bollywood's all-time great hero, Milind Kumar. It did not matter to her that he was not a good conversationalist or even an articulate speaker. After all, you do not require anything else when you have good looks, a charismatic screen presence and a mammoth fan following, she reminded herself.

Then there was another reason for Mili's happiness. All these days the unit had stayed in a hotel in Srinagar. Now for the last few scenes to be shot in Kashmir, she and Milind Kumar were being shifted to a houseboat on the outskirts of Srinagar. The rest of the unit members were to continue to stay at the hotel because the houseboat was far more expensive. Bhimani had told her that the newly built houseboat they were going to stay in was virtually a floating palace on the Nagin Lake and had become a major tourist attraction in the area. The owner, whose various businesses bloomed despite militancy, had announced high-priced tickets for tourists wanting a guided tour. Milind Kumar and Mili were going to become the first occupants of the houseboat.

As the Mercedes carrying Bhimani and the film's lead pair stopped near the bank of the lake, Mili looked at the houseboat with awe. It was aptly called "Jannat" (paradise). Like a child, she ran towards the floating beauty and booed Milind Kumar and Bhimani for lagging behind. The houseboat owner was himself present to welcome the two mega stars of Bollywood.

The owner, a dignified looking middle-aged man, held out an autograph book to the out-of-breath heroine but she ignored him. He persisted, "Madam, autograph please. My young kids have ordered me to get your autographs. I did not allow them to come here because you and Mister Milind would get disturbed. They agreed with a condition that I get autographs from both of you."

"Autograph can wait. First show me my room," Mili said, shooing off the houseboat owner with such a violent jerk of the hand that the autograph book fell down. She walked on, without caring to look back. As the houseboat caretaker moved back to pick up the autograph book, the owner signaled him to show Mili the Queen's Suite Mumtaz.

By the time the owner himself picked up the autograph book, Milind Kumar and Bhimani had arrived. He forced a smile on his face to welcome the guests, but hid the autograph book behind his back. "Mister Ashraf, what are you hiding in your left hand?" Milind Kumar asked.

"Nothing sir, it is an autograph book of my children."

"Oh, that will be a pleasure. Give it to me. What are the names of your children and what do they do?"

The hero listened to Ashraf's details intently and then signed the book, wishing Anwar and Saloni a bright future.

The next evening, Mili was in a foul mood. She and Milind had just come back from shooting. Milind had headed straight to his Emperor's suite saying, "I am too tired. I will sleep now. Don't wait for me over dinner."

She was stung to be cold-shouldered like this. It had never happened to her. And what did he say! "Don't wait for me over dinner." As if I am his wife. Who cares? she muttered.

Bhimani had told her to keep her baggage ready by morning as they could leave Kashmir the following day, depending on Milind Kumar's shooting schedule for another film. The inference was clear to hurt the pride of a star.

There was a knock on the door.

"Come in. It's open," Mili yelled.

"What will you have for dinner, Madam?" asked a well-dressed waiter, pushing the door half open.

"A tandoori Milind Kumar."

"Beg your pardon, Madam!"

"You don't have that dish?"

"No, Madam," said the perplexed waiter.

"Then get lost."

The waiter disappeared, without disturbing the half-open door.

Two minutes later, there was another knock. This time it was the security guard.

"Madam, your door is not closed. Shall I shut it? Sir has said it's not safe for you to keep your door open."

The actress was packing her last piece of lingerie in her suitcase when the unwanted intruder came.

"Who is this sir? Milind Kumar?"

"No, it is Ashraf sahib."

"Who the hell in this world is Ashraf sahib?"

"The owner of this houseboat, Madam."

"Then tell your sir to mind his own business. And you mind yours."

The security guard went away, leaving the door as it was.

This place is full of jokers. I am going to tell Mister Bhimani to take the first available flight out of this damned place tomorrow, she muttered to herself.

Barely had she shut her suitcase and, with some effort, dragged the heavy contraption to the floor, when the doorbell buzzed.

She had just taken her nightdress out. She had no plans to have dinner or to go the deck to admire the picture postcard lakescape of Nagin at night.

"Who is it now?"

"It's me, Madam. Qadir."

"Oh! Qadir. You are the Chief Minister of this state?"

"No, Madam. I am the caretaker of this houseboat."

"Then why did you give your name? Did I ask your name? Is your name so well known that everybody would know it?"

"I don't understand, madam." Qadir did not know whether he was angry or perplexed by this unexpected outburst; or whether he was angrier than perplexed or more perplexed than angry. This guest had got on his nerves from day one.

"Don't make any effort to understand if your brains are in your knuckles. What's your business here?"

"Madam, I just got a telephone call from Mister Bhimani to advise you not to pack your baggage because the weather office has forecast heavy snow storm tomorrow. So, all flights taking off from Srinagar may be cancelled."

"Why couldn't Bhimani call me up on my cell to give me this information? Why should he choose jokers as messengers?" Mili growled.

Though her last sentence was subdued by a massive thundering of clouds, the twitching of facial muscles of the caretaker said it all. He mustered every effort to remain calm and said, "Madam, you may talk to Mister Bhimani for that information please. Good night."

The caretaker left in visible disgust. The door was still half-open.

The actress looked at the packed suitcase lying on the floor and then thought of changing into her nightdress, which one of her heroes had bought her during a shoot in Paris. Her mind wandered to those heroes she had teamed up with so far. All of them had confessed to her, at one point or the other, that they had been smitten by her sensuous figure and beautiful face. Most of such confessions had come during outdoor shoots, within or outside India.

One hero had begged for her love, down on his knees, when they were shooting in Switzerland. Another had taken an overdose of sleeping pills during a shoot in Goa when she refused to go out to the beach with him late in the night because he was dead drunk.

Her photographs inundated not only film magazines but also national dailies. Several politicians had approached her to join their party and accept a nomination to the Rajya Sabha, the Upper House of Indian Parliament. She rejected all such invitations with impunity and did not consider even the demand for campaigning for political parties.

Here was Milind Kumar who treated her just like any ordinary woman in the world!

She was wearing a chiffon saree which glued to her voluptuous body like a serpent coils around a sandal tree. She was half lying on the bed. Her well-endowed bosom was threatening to erupt out of her tiny blouse. Partly because it was too tight. Partly because her anger made her breathe faster.

The security guard looked at the unexpected visitor. He surveyed him from top to toe as though he had just escaped from a zoo. The man was in his mid thirties and reasonably well dressed. His hair had become unkempt because of strong winds.

"What do you want?" the security guard asked curtly.

"I have an appointment with Mister Milind Kumar," the stranger said.

"But we don't have any information about it."

"Then you ask him."

"Saab is not well. He has instructed us not to disturb him. You come tomorrow."

"But he himself has called me. Why don't you...?"

"What is going on here?" It was the voice of the caretaker. He had just finished his day's work and was about to leave when he saw the visitor arguing with the guard.

"Qadir Mian. He has come to meet Mister Milind Kumar. He says he has an appointment with him."

"Do you know Mister Milind Kumar?"

"Yes, very well. I am his childhood friend."

"Okay sir. Please go straight. The last room is his. It'll be half-open."

As the visitor thanked the caretaker and left, the guard's mouth was half-open with surprise. "But that is the room ..."

"I know. Let Milind Kumar's childhood friend also taste this bitter pill."

The visitor barged into Mili's room and banged it closed. He saw a young woman looking her seductive best with her bare bust.

"Who the hell are you? What are you doing here? Don't you have any manners? How dare you enter my room like this? I will have you sacked first thing in the morning."

The visitor froze and stood where he was. For a moment, he thought that Milind Kumar might be in the washroom while this doll waited in the bed for him. But Milind Kumar had no such reputation.

Further angered by the dumbness of the visitor, Mili jumped from the bed and held him by the scruff of his neck. He was dumbstruck by the woman's aggression and his speech again failed him.

Mili pushed him towards the door but he quickly disengaged himself and turned 180 degrees. Now Mili was near the door and the visitor close to the bed. She again surged forward, got hold of his tie and gave him a violent push. The young man caught hold of her attacking hand but could not withstand the shove and collapsed on the bed. Mili fell upon him in an awkward position. Vatsayan, the ancient Indian sex guru, would have had no difficulty in pronouncing it as Position 69.

Just then, the door was flung open and several men in military uniform trooped in. Both the heroine and the visitor felt the cold metallic barrel of rifles in their necks and within seconds had their faces covered with black hoods.

There was some strange odour emanating from the black hoods that made its forced wearers lose consciousness rapidly but not before the young man heard the crackling of a wireless set, followed by three words:

"Operation Hasina completed."

It was almost twelve hours later that Dhruv stirred. By sheer habit, he extended his hand to fetch a glass of water, which he always kept on his bedside table. Realizing that he had located neither a tumbler nor the table, he gradually opened his eyes. He found himself in a strange room. He was lying on a cot with a thick quilt covering him. As he stretched himself up, he realized that his shoes were still on and though his coat had been removed, his tie too very much in place. He found it rather strange because he was used to coming home late, quite often after attending cocktail parties but he never got himself so drunk that he would sleep with his shoes and tie on.

His head was aching, which was nothing abnormal after a cocktail session. Then he realized that this was not his apartment, he was not lying on his bed, and there was one more cot lying on the other side of the room where somebody was sleeping. He jumped out of the bed with a start.

Two things struck him first. The other cot was occupied by a sleeping beauty. The high-ceiling room had no windows, only two small apertures that could be better described as light and air hoses rather than ventilators. He walked up to the young lady's cot and had a closer look at her. Last night's dramatic events suddenly came back to him.

Dhruv noticed that the young woman was breathing rather heavily, making her well shaped breasts all the more spectacular to watch. He first got concerned about her condition and wanted to stir her into consciousness but he quickly banished the thought from his mind when he remembered the lady's tongue-lashing and physical aggression.

He roamed around the room, which was at least twenty feet long and 15 feet wide. There was no carpet and the mud floor was very much visible. The ceiling had wooden planks, a boon at this time of harsh winter. The walls were absolutely naked and ugly. Obviously, it was not a living room but was used as a godown or a safe house.

Dhruv again looked at the young lady. Though he knew the woman was a celebrity, he did not know whether she was a heroine or a model or something else. Nor did he know her name. That was partly because he had been studying in UK for past one decade and hardly kept himself abreast of movers and shakers of Bollywood. Mili's most popular blockbusters were released at a time when he was studying the fine contours of the art of screenplay writing. The heroine was still in a deep slumber.

He went towards the entrance and nudged it, suspecting that the iron door would not budge from its position. The door creaked open and an alert security guard ran up to him, with an AK series rifle slung across his shoulder. The expression on the guard's face was not that of worry or threat. A genuine question was writ large on his face: "What do you want?"

"Where am I? Why have I been brought here along with this lady? Who are you people and what do you want?"

The guard turned back and slowly started moving towards the end of the courtyard where he had been deployed. Dhruv quickly changed tack as he realized that even if the security guard had answers to all his questions he could not be expected to answer even one.

"Can you get me toothpaste and a toothbrush please and show me the way to a place called toilet?" Dhruv heard himself asking.

Ten minutes later, Dhruv returned to the high-ceiling room and started a closer inspection. He was not startled to spot a couple of metallic buttons studded on the wooden planks, which were of the same colour. He moved his cot towards the heroine's bed and sat still, waiting for the woman to come back to her senses rather than jostling her into consciousness.

As he put his hands into his trousers' pockets, he knew two of his prized possessions were missing: his smartphone and his state-of-the-art goldplated, diamond-studded exclusive wrist watch.

His attention was diverted to thumping noises made by several pair of military shoes, which were headed in his direction. Two young men entered. One man set a tray in a corner of the room, turned back in a typical military movement and stood outside the room to wait on his senior, who was still inside.

"This is some breakfast for you and the Mohtarma. Hope you would find it okay," the man, who looked like an owner or boss of the place, said to Dhruv.

"Who are you people? Why have you brought us here?" Dhruv asked, ignoring the breakfast.

The man continued to walk, went out of the room, turned half a step back and put a counter question: "You really think that you are going to get an answer to that question?"

Dhruv knew he was not. Not from these clowns at least.

The slight movement in the room had had an impact on the sleeping lady. She turned and tossed, turned and tossed several times in the bed, the last time so violently that Dhruv had to physically grab her arms to preventing her from falling off the cot.

The young lady jumped from the bed like a wounded tigress, looked at Dhruv, the dilapidated room, the murky weather and, most importantly, Dhruv's hands which were still holding her tightly by the arms. She disengaged herself from Dhruv's grip, gave him a resounding slap and started shouting and shrieking. All the men who had just gone out came back running. They saw a comic scene, which was nothing but pain, tragedy and humiliation to poor Dhruv.

The woman was sitting astride on the hapless man as though he were a motorcycle and she a biker. She was holding him by the scruff of his neck and giving him violent pushes. There was no deja vu on the part of the beholders because the last night's operation had been performed by another set of people.

"Keep off me, you swine. Why are you glued to me like a leech? I will give you a bloody nose if you were to mess with me again."

After administering the last mental blow to the young man's confidence, the woman got up, looked menacingly at the bemused spectators and shouted: "Who the hell are you? Call this bloody Arif Bhai. Right away! This man has to be sacked. You should all thank your stars that I don't have a gun, otherwise ..."

Her words stuck in her throat, as she quickly perceived the enormity of the situation. This was not Jannat, the houseboat. It was a prisoners' cell and the men she was threatening to shoot were actually carrying Kalashnikov rifles. She also quickly realized that she was wearing the green chiffon saree, which she wore last evening for a dinner meeting with Milind Kumar and it was far too inadequate to beat the growing chill.

Small apertures on the ceiling gave a clear impression that it was a murky day and a snow storm seemed to be developing fast.

4

The Half Introduction

Mili and Dhruv had been sharing the prisoners' cell for two days. She was terribly upset about the turn of events. Her gut feeling of not agreeing to shoot in Kashmir eventually proved to be dead right. She was still full of rancour towards Dhruv, who, she was convinced, belonged to the tribe of men who chased everything from a frock to a skirt to a maxi or a mini.

That is why she had not spoken even 48 syllables to Dhruv in the past 48 hours. More galling, from her point of view, was the fact that the man also appeared unconcerned about her celebrity status; that too in a country like India, which is driven by three C's –Celebrities, Crime and Cricket. She was sure that he did not belong to any of the three C's.

She noticed that Dhruv remained calm, composed and quiet, as though preparing for an extreme test of patience, perseverance and stamina. He did not even cast a stray look at her and whenever she asked him any question, he replied dryly in monosyllables. The young man kept his rigorous schedule of physical exercises, jogging, bending and stretching in the room itself. At first, she dismissed his routine as a crude attempt to impress a Bollywood heroine. But, she was not so stupid that she could not see his body was chiseled, something which could not be achieved overnight.

She kept sulking, holding him the source of all her woes. She was quite convinced that his unwanted foray into her room had brought this misery in her life.

The captives had been given "suitable" clothes, a term used by a man called Javed, who appeared to be in charge of the place. Whatever was given, or not given, to the prisoners was approved by Javed. Mili was given two sets of dark coloured salwar kameez, a popular dress in the Indian subcontinent worn by girls and women of all age groups and religions. Dhruv had been given two sets of kurta pyjamas, which he kept but asked for a pair of jeans as well.

Mili was rather amused. Even in confinement, the man wanted to drape himself according to his whims and fancies. She was also dismayed to find that Javed, whom she found obnoxiously oblivious to her, listened rather attentively whenever Dhruv had something to say to him.

Only yesterday, Dhruv had confronted him with some questions, which had an accusatorial tone.

"Where have you kept my smart phone and my watch?" Dhruv had asked Javed.

Mili smiled when she saw Javed whizzing out of the room without bothering to look at Dhruv, and without answering his question. Javed returned quickly and dangled a small bag before Dhruv. He took the bag and took out its contents – his mobile phone and the watch. Then without saying a word, Javed looked straight into the eyes of Dhruv, snatched the two things from Dhruv's hands and before exiting gave him one long hard look, as though saying, "We are kidnappers, not pickpockets."

Mili could not cease to marvel at Dhruv's highly expensive wristwatch and the state-of-the-art mobile phone. Definitely, the man had taste.

She noticed that Dhruv's conversations with the security guards were pithy and searching and she was at her attentive best whenever such occasions arose, though such occasions were a few and far in between.

"What is your ransom demand? Have you already conveyed it? If so, to whom?"

The guard gave a hard look at Dhruv over his spate of questions, feeling no need to answer any one of them.

"You are continuing to increase the number of quilts and blankets. Are we being moved out of here or is it because of the weather?"

"This is one question that can be answered. In fact, I don't have to answer it myself. Just go outside and have a look at the sky."

She noticed that Dhruv was going deeper and deeper into his shell; and she could ill afford it.

"Why can't we have some variety in our breakfast instead of the daily dose of cold boiled eggs and kehwa? She asked Dhruv, managing to plaster the plastic smile on her face that had broken a thousand hearts.

"That's because you are in captivity. You are not on a picnic here."

"And who do you think has kidnapped us? The Indian Army or the Pakistani Army, who bickered on the question of jurisdiction where our houseboat was located?"

"Neither."

"Neither?"

"Neither."

"But how can you say that? Because they are surreptitious?"

"Partly because they are surreptitious. But mainly because they are not behaving like professional army soldiers."

"And pray, how do professional army soldiers behave?"

"It is easier observed than explained. There can be various reasons. Their boots are different. An army man is known from his boots and that too in this part of the cold desert. The way they have slung their rifles across their shoulders is unlike a professional army man."

"So, Mister Know-it-all, who are they and what do they want from us?"

"They are terrorists. They probably want the Government of India to release some of their most important colleagues in exchange for our release."

"And you think that our government would release them?"

"I don't know. I can't travel into the government's mind. I hope that they handle the negotiations well because they are dealing with the most important Islamic jihad outfit called Lashkar-e-Toiba."

"How do you know that we have been kidnapped by a terrorist outfit and that group's name is Lashkar-e-Toiba?"

"That is because these are the signature kidnappings for the Lashkar-e-Toiba."

"And what according to you, Mister Soothsayer, is our fate?" Mili was at her vitriolic best.

"One of the two: either we will be beheaded or released safely."

"What's your name?"

"Dhruv. And yours?"

"If an elephant sits down, even then he is bigger and higher than a dog."

"Is that the meaning of your name?"

"Shut up. I thought one could have a conversation with you. But you are a conceited pig. That is precisely what you are."

"But what have I done to earn this roll of honour from you?"

"Why are you playacting that you don't know my name?"

"There is only one explanation: because I really don't know."

"Aren't you an Indian? Don't you watch movies? Or were you born on Mars and brought up on Venus?"

"No, I don't watch movies. Are you a movie star?"

Mili's pride had been crushed to smithereens. She felt too disgusted to answer any further queries or even to continue with the conversation.

Some time later, there was the familiar sound of thick boots approaching their cell. The man put two trays on the ground and turned back. He ignored the now familiar pleas of Mili and the reticence of Dhruv – the former urging the captors to improve the menu, lodge them in a better room, give them newspapers, magazines and install a cable television.

The invisible wall of thick ice continued to remain firmly in place between Mili and Dhruv and the former continued to treat the latter with an air of casualness, if not downright disdain. However, their captors were beginning to think otherwise.

"Tell me, Mister Soothsayer, if you know anything about this situation of militancy in Jammu and Kashmir which has threatened to take away the state from Indian control."

"I don't know what you know, what you don't know and what exactly you would like to know."

"I am serious. I want to know how this situation started and how this wound was allowed to fester by the governments in J&K and New Delhi in the first place."

For the first time, Dhruv had seen a streak of genuine curiosity from the glamorous doll. He cleared his throat and started.

"Since mid-1989, hardly a day passed without a terrorist act in the valley. Initially, the bomb blasts were minor ones and the perception in the rest of the country was that secular, peace-loving Kashmiris were the last kind of people to embrace terrorism. This changed fast. Corrupt governments and self-seeking politicians in Srinagar and New Delhi made Kashmir a new hot spot of international terrorism. Ferocious terrorist acts became an order of the day. Early nineties saw an unprecedented threat of Kashmir slipping out of the Indian Union.

"Terrorists became more powerful than top cops, bureaucrats, ministers – all symbols of the might of the State. The secular fabric of the Jammu and Kashmir state was shredded to pieces. Virtually the entire Hindu population migrated out of the valley, abandoning ancestral properties and booming businesses. The spurt in militancy in Kashmir coincided, and was spurred by, a chain of fastchanging strategic scenarios in India's extended neighbourhood."

"What were they?" Mili asked, looking intently at Dhruv, whom she suddenly found rather scholarly. She was wondering whether such scholars could make a mark in the Hindi film industry, which essentially thrives on popular sentiments.

"There were several. This was the time when the Soviets had been driven out of Afghanistan by foreign-funded

Mujahideen. The Afghanistan fiasco hastened the collapse of the mighty Soviet Union in December 1991. The Mujahideen were suddenly rendered jobless, and more importantly, without an enemy. India's enemies decided to replicate the Afghan experiment in Kashmir. As part of these designs, foreign money, arms and ammunition and logistical support poured in for terrorists.

"Pushed to the wall, the Indian government deployed hundreds of thousands of security personnel all over the troubled state. The common man routinely got caught in crossfires between security forces and militants. The liberation of Kashmir, which seemed around the corner in 1993-94, the golden period of militancy in Kashmir, became more and more difficult with every passing year.

"As a result, terrorists became indisciplined and terrorism got institutionalised as an industry. Foreign militants came to Kashmir in big numbers not for jihad, but for women. Rapes became commonplace. Abortion clinics sprung up like barber shops in the state outside the valley in places like Jammu and Rajouri."

There was a silence of a few minutes in the room. Mili was reflecting on something. Probably she was framing her next question.

"Tell me, is there a single instance in modern world where terrorists have overthrown a government and seized control of the entire country?"

"Yes and no."

"What does that mean?"

"If your question is whether terrorists have overrun a whole country all by themselves without any covert or overt support from any country's sympathizing armed forces, then the answer is 'no'. Yet, it has happened. Afghanistan is one such example where lumpen elements seized control of a country with the benign help from a neighbouring country. Another example is that of Sri Lanka where the LTTE has been ruling vast chunks of the northern and eastern parts of the island country for close to two decades.

"As recently as 2005, terrorists managed to change the electoral mandate of such a developed country as Spain after deadly serial blasts in trains, which rocked the nation days before general elections. The ruling party, which was tipped to win by a landslide majority in most opinion polls, lost the elections. Countries like Sudan and Somalia almost fell to terrorists. Iraq today is another interesting example of this dogfight between state and non-state actors. But to answer your question in one line, no there has not been a single instance yet in the modern world history where terrorists have seized control of a nation state all by themselves."

"Is it possible?"

"Why not? The Taliban story is a good example. It shows how the greed of a nation state and political and law-and-order compulsions of a bunch of men of another nation state can be coalesced and a Frankenstein monster can be brought to life."

"What is the Taliban story?"

"It started off in 1995 when a band of 50 devout Muslims formed a group called Taliban. By the next year it had started ruling Afghanistan with active help from Pakistan's state machinery like the ISI and the Army."

"I have heard the name of Taliban which was probably a private army."

"Taliban is plural of the Pashto word, talib which is used for talib-e-ilm or seekers of knowledge in Afghanistan and Pashto-speaking areas of Pakistan. How the Taliban was born is an interesting story in itself."

Here Dhruv stopped. He spread himself on his cot and looked vacantly at the ceiling. Mili too kept quiet. She was convinced that Dhruv was acting coy and would not continue unless requested. In any case, she had nothing better to do. So why not buttress the bloated ego of this idiot, she argued within.

"So what is that interesting story?"

"Have you heard of the name Mulla Omar?"

"No."

"He was the founder chief of Taliban. It was literally a dream come true for Mulla Omar, a veteran Pushtun Mujahideen commander who fought against the Soviets in Afghanistan, and who turned deeply religious after the Soviet pullout from Afghanistan. Taliban cadres narrate a legend: how Prophet Mohammed manifested himself to Omar in a dream in 1994, and instructed him to put an end to the reign of terror unleashed by his own tribesman, who was appointed as a local commander of the ISI."

"Local commander of what?" Mili enquired.

"I am sorry. I should have told you first about the geo-political imperatives and strategic benefits of Afghanistan for the state of Pakistan as the Pakistani leadership perceived."

"You are confusing me now. You use very heavy words."

"If you want to know something then you have to have patience. Remember every long journey begins with the first step."

"And you are with me in this journey?"

"I have no choice."

"You know you are very dry. Had there been a warmer person in your place, he would have said something more interesting, more meaningful under such peculiar circumstances."

"Such as?"

"I mean, he would have been far more romantic than you."

"Look here madam. I am not here with you by choice. It is not a situation, which I have contrived myself. I am a victim rather than a plotter. I don't even know who you are, what you do, what your name is. Nor am I interested to know unless you yourself would like to volunteer these details. So where is the question of being romantic with you? Just because you are good-looking and I am alone with you in a cell for the past two days and nights, I should cajole you, woo you and be amorous with you? This is not romanticism. This is expediency. Right now, to me you are not even a woman, let alone a beautiful woman; you are just a cell mate."

Mili did not know what hit her. She had never been subjected to such plain speaking. It was extremely galling. To her own surprise, she did not do what she would have definitely done under such circumstances: launch a stronger attack.

Dhruv's harsh words seemed to be like a bikini to her, which concealed more than it revealed. She was no longer interested in the story of Taliban. Her new-found focus was the man sitting in front. The man is, after all, worth noticing, she told herself.

"I see your point. I also do agree now that you genuinely don't know my name, identity or profession. My name is Mili. I am a cine star. In Bollywood, I am regarded as the hottest and most talented heroine ever produced. Producers give me millions in advance to cast me in their films. I have millions of fans. I have employed a staff of ten people only to handle my fan mail. It is dizzying to have such fanatic fans. I read about at least two such fans who committed suicide after they read an imaginary interview of mine in which I was quoted as saying that I would be marrying a business tycoon a few weeks later. Many of my fans in southern India have built temples for me where they actually worship me. I hope, now you understand my anger at your ignorance about my identity?"

"I do. Now I also understand the real reason behind this kidnapping."

"What's that?"

"Obviously they have carried out the entire operation only because of you. You are the pivot of their plot. I am just the fifth wheel."

Had Dhruv uttered these words some minutes before, Mili would have been very pleased and taken them as unadulterated flattery. Now, Dhruv's words sounded ominous.

"Are you suggesting that I face a greater threat than you because I am a high-profile target?"

"Our threat perception is equal even though you are a target of much higher value than me."

"So, you do not see a scenario in which you are released and I am expended?"

"I really can't say. But frankly, I don't see such a scenario."

"Are you saying that to keep me in high spirits?"

"I am merely saying what is coming to my mind."

"Do you ever go 15 inches down?"

"What does that mean? Is that a line from some film dialogue?"

"I mean you always talk about your mind. What about your heart, which is 15 inches below that? You never use that?"

Dhruv kept quiet.

"Suppose such a scenario comes up. They execute me if the government does not agree to their demands and decide to release you for the simple reason that they would not like to stain their hands with your blood unnecessarily. How would you react then?"

"They are not going to do that. They can't afford to do that. I will be a security risk. That's not how terrorists operate. For them it does not make a difference whether they kill one or ten."

"But if this were to happen, then what will be your response. I am sure you will be happy to be released."

"It is one thing to be happy momentarily; quite another to lead an entire life with visions of guilt, real or imaginary."

"You can make a good politician. You never answer a question straight. The question is simple. Will you be happy if you alone were to be released?"

For the first time, Mili saw Dhruv stumped for an answer. She enjoyed the sight. Dhruv was brooding, struggling hard. His face was the perfect conveyor belt of the conflict that was raging inside him. He knew that Mili expected an answer, an answer he did not have. How he hated to be groping for answers!

Mili could see the discomfiture of Dhruv. She no longer revelled in it after some minutes. Then there was an unexpected one-liner response from Dhruv.

"I would not like to be released alone."

It was a cathartic experience. For both.

5

The Storm

The prisoners' third day in captivity started with a surprise. Javed came in with two of his hangers-on. The fact that the trio's entry into the room was preceded by a knock on the door was not lost on Mili and Dhruv.

"What would you like to have for breakfast and lunch today?" he asked matter-of-factly.

Mili grabbed the opportunity to score a point over Javed. "Is it Eid today?"

"No"

"Surely it is not Bakrid today? Then why are you asking us the menu for breakfast and lunch? Fattening the goat before slaughter, eh? Why no enquiry about the dinner? Does the slaughter take place before dinner time?"

"Madam, I have instructions to ask you what I have asked."

"Instructions from whom?"

"That is none of your business," Javed said curtly, indicating the limits of his patience.

Dhruv intervened. "Okay, you give us whatever you can. Only thing we request is if it can be different from cold boiled eggs, toasts, egg curry, and Nan, which we have been eating for the past two days. We will be grateful if the food is hot."

"From now on the food will be hot because so far we were getting the food from outside."

"So now you have opened a pantry for us here?" Mili took another potshot.

Javed ignored the jibe. He turned to Dhruv and said, "Anything else?"

Dhruv had a good mind to ask for the reasons of their abduction – whether any negotiations were on with the Indian authorities and what were their demands. However, he restrained himself from asking such questions, which he knew, could not be answered by this man at this time.

"If you are so benign, how about allowing us to go out for about half an hour? We have been in this dungeon for over two days."

Javed spoke in Kashmiri to the two young men whom he had brought with him. The two shook their heads in disapproval.

Dhruv decided to make a final effort. "See the weather seems to be better today. And we cannot escape even if we want to."

"That is not the point. The improved weather you are talking about is actually deceptive. It is a lull before the storm.

Our local experts have warned of fierce snow storms and blizzards. They predict extremely bad weather in the next few days. Here the locals are warning of the worst snow storm of the century. We can't expose you to such extreme conditions. It is a matter of few hours only when the sky starts packing clouds. That is why we had to make arrangements for preparing the food here in this complex only."

"You mean you are making arrangements for making food here exclusively for us? So we are in for a long haul here?" Dhruv asked.

"You ask too many questions. These arrangements are not for you people exclusively. We are expecting a VVIP movement shortly."

"Who is coming? A Minister or a General?"

"We have nothing to do with them. They don't mean anything for us," Javed said and turned abruptly towards the door, not sure, whether he had done the right thing in disclosing information they could have done without. Before leaving, he told the captives that they could go out for ten minutes after breakfast.

Mili and Dhruv realized that Javed was right. By the time they finished with their breakfast of steaming hot omlette, toast and coffee, the sky had become overcast. They came out of their cell but voluntarily decided not to utilize their full ten-minute parole because of bone-chilling winds.

The storm had begun.

Breakfast over; the captives braced themselves for another round of conversation. Mili took the initiative.

"Your story remained unfinished yesterday. You might as well complete it now."

"Which story?"

"The story of Taliban. You were saying how the Taliban was born literally in a dream of Mulla Omar. You were also going to tell me about the strategic significance of Afghanistan for Pakistan, whatever such heavy words mean."

"You really are interested in all this?" Dhruv asked with genuine surprise.

"You think I am a dumb doll. Uneducated. Only beauty, no brains. Let me tell you that I am a first class graduate in political science. My father wanted me to take up academics for a career but I had other ideas. So start your story. I am all ears."

"Alright. Point conceded. Over the past couple of decades, Afghanistan has emerged as an area of high strategic importance, which few other landlocked nations can rival. It connects South Asia to Central Asia and eventually to Europe. This region has attracted another great energy rush after the Middle East. Pakistan's Afghanistan policy is driven by its desire to participate in the latest great game for oil and gas in Central Asia, which cannot be done without a strong presence in Afghanistan. This game is making strange bedfellows. Iran, Armenia, Russia, Tajikistan, Kazakhstan, Uzbekistan and Kyrgystan, apart from the US, China and India, have emerged as key players in this game. China is being viewed as a rival by Western companies, both as an investor and as a market. Then there is Turkey, which though historically suspicious of Russia and currently not having the best of relations with Iran, is increasingly being driven to this regional quest for control of potential oil and gas reserves."

To Dhruv's surprise, Mili was listening intently. "You speak like Dr Raichura."

"Who is Dr Raichura?"

"He was my favourite teacher in college. Anyway, please continue. Where is the Taliban angle to all this?"

"I am coming to that now. Pakistan's quest for control of Afghanistan's road system became a major obsession and focal point of ISI's major covert operations by the early nineties, second only to Islamabad's fixation with Kashmir. In 1991, the ISI embarked upon a grand plan to control the highly strategic Kushka-Herat-Kandahar-Quetta highway."

"How is this highway important?"

"This highway stretches from former Soviet Central Asia through western and southern Afghanistan, feeds into the road system of southern Pakistan and goes up to Karachi, Pakistan's main port. According to Pakistani strategic thinking, this is the only arterial road network which is in good condition after years of turmoil and could be rebuilt or repaired to carry long convoys. Building this highway would provide immense profits by cutting hugely on time and costs of travel. Moreover, a network of pipelines along this highway to transfer oil and gas from Central Asia and northern Afghanistan holds the key to Pakistan's future economic development."

"So with this objective in mind Pakistan must have undertaken massive repairs of this highway inside Afghanistan. What next?"

"That's right. This highway continues to be Afghanistan's sole gateway to Western goods. It is another matter that after 9/11 and the ousting of the Taliban regime from Afghanistan, powers other than Pakistan are reaping these benefits. To go back to the mid-nineties, the ISI hired local Afghan leaders and chieftains to protect the convoys through the Afghan highway. The ISI lured them with money, weapons and outlets for their illicit narcotics they grew in Helmand valley in southwestern Afghanistan."

"Now the role of the drug cartel," Mili butted in like an enlightened student, a talib.

"That's right. This move of the ISI created chaos. Local Afghan chieftains got involved in bloody battles over the allurements offered by the ISI for ensuring safe passage of the convoys. By 1994, Pakistan found itself confronting a situation wherein most of the ISI-propped chieftains were killed. A new generation of aspiring warlords mushroomed quickly, waiting for the ISI patronage. They got it. However, this move, too, backfired. Within months, these greedy guards started raiding the convoys they were paid to protect."

"This is indeed interesting. You seem to have done a Ph.D on Afghanistan, Pakistan and Central Asia," Mili said jovially.

"Far from it! I know very little. What I am telling you is based on whatever books, journals and newspapers I have read. I am not an academic."

"Then what happened?"

"This development set the ISI bosses thinking. Some way had to be found to achieve total control of the Kushka-Herat-Kandahar-Quetta highway. Plan B was conceived: creation of a new force for securing the highway. I had already told you about Mulla Omar's dream in 1994 and how, as legend has it, Prophet Mohammed instructed him to put an end to the reign of terror of an Afghan warlord who was ISI's local commander. Mulla Omar quickly organized an armed force of fifty former Mujahideen who had served under him in guerrilla war against the Soviets in Afghanistan in the eighties. The erring warlord was killed by Mulla Omar's force and his property and weapons were seized."

"So Taliban was born with just fifty men as a sort of a movement?" Mili asked.

Dhruv was noticing an actress metamorphosing into a scholar student who was trying to fathom arenas beyond the arc lights. He continued.

"Mulla Omar laid down strict rules of conduct. His first task was to distribute the killed warlord's vast riches and properties among the needy of his native place, Kandahar.

With this act, Mulla Omar acquired a Robin Hood image and his outfit, the Taliban, endeared himself to the masses. This was the modest beginning of the success story of Mulla Omar and the Taliban. Kandahar was the epicentre of the Taliban movement and the city was the first military conquest of the Taliban in November 1994.

"The ISI bosses were quick to seize upon this windfall of opportunity. By December 1994, the ISI-Mulla Omar nexus had been forged. This did not go down well with Gulbuddin Hekmatyar."

"Now who is this character Hekmatyar?" Mili asked, bringing her cot closer to Dhruv's, as the fury of harsh weather outside made it impossible to hear from her distance across the room.

"Hekmatyar had long served as a strategic weapon for the ISI and commanded a large militant force by the name of Hizb-e-Islami. He kept complaining to Islamabad for shifting its loyalties from himself to Mulla Omar."

"The ISI obviously would have denied having any truck with Mulla Omar," said Mili, imbibing every bit of this story of political maćhinations involving Pakistan and Afghanistan.

"Precisely," Dhruv continued. "The ISI was playing the familiar double game the intelligence agencies world over are well known to play. While arming and supporting the Taliban not so secretly, the ISI kept the Hekmatyar faction in good humour. You know it is the age-old time-tested strategy of intelligence agencies to not to keep all their eggs in one basket."

Suddenly, Mili clasped Dhruv's hands and asked in a conspiratorial tone, "Are you an intelligence man?" By now, she was sitting on Dhruv's cot. Both were oblivious to the strange bonding taking shape between them.

"No. I am not." Then disengaging his hands, he went on. "By February 1995, the Taliban had become a virtual army, its strength having swelled to a fearsome 25,000 members. It essentially remained a predominantly Pushtun force, though one thousand-odd Uzbeks and Tajiks were also on its roll."

"Then what happened to Hekmatyar. Was he liquidated by the Taliban?"

"No, but conditions were no longer conducive to operations of Hekmatyar and his men. Soon, the Taliban was knocking at the gates of the Afghan capital, Kabul. The Taliban reached up to Maidan Shahr, some 30 kilometres south of Kabul and marched menacingly to ChaharSiyab, forcing ISI's discarded love, Hekmatyar, to flee ChaharSiyab. While fleeing, Hekmatyar's men left huge quantities of arms and ammunition which were put to good use by the Taliban in their forthcoming battles against Hekmatyar."

"That's how the Taliban came to rule Afghanistan until the Americans dislodged them after the 9/11 incident," Mili said, sensing an end to the amazing story of Taliban.

"Yes. By the middle of 1995, the Pakistani dream corridor between the Indian Ocean and Central Asia had come under total and undisputed control of the Taliban. As the year 1995 rang out, it was clear who was in control of Afghanistan and with whose support. Islamabad had pulled off a neat strategic coup of conquering Afghanistan by proxy and increasing its strategic depth."

"This was also the time when Kashmir was burning the most. So, Pakistan's strategic moves made things more difficult for the Indian government in Kashmir." Mili was already speaking a language much different from the show world's lingo. This was the language of Dhruv, which she had innately adopted.

"But this was not without a series of adverse diplomatic fallouts for Pakistan. Islamabad's relations with Iran and the neighbouring Central Asian states like Uzbekistan, Tajikistan and Kyrgyzstan, apart from Russia and Turkey, took a nosedive. A major flashpoint came in mid1998 when the Taliban overran Mazar-e-Sharif, the nerve centre of northern Afghanistan, which is just 60 kilometres south of the Uzbek town of Termez. Russian and Tajik troops were put on high alert along the Tajik border and Moscow warned Islamabad that its continued assistance to the Taliban was a threat to international peace and security. The fall of Mazar-e-Sharif had caught Iran by surprise. By the first week of September 1998, Iran had made a massive buildup along the Afghanistan border as part of its Ashura 3 exercise."

"So, in a way, Pakistan's forays into Afghanistan shifted its focus from Kashmir which enabled the Indian forces to regain lost ground in the Kashmir valley."

"I think that would be a fair assessment."

"Does it mean that Pakistan could not keep firing on both the cylinders , Kashmir as well as Afghanistan, simultaneously? What did the Pakistanis get out of it?"

"The Pakistanis had set their sights on bigger strategic victories. In their wisdom, they thought of first tightening their control over whole of Afghanistan to make it their fifth province. They were not even bothered that their nexus with the Taliban had already started sowing a bitter harvest of diplomatic ill will all around. They were convinced that once they were well entrenched in Afghanistan; it would boost their chances of replicating the same proxy war pattern in Kashmir with even better results. After all, their reasoning was that Kashmir was their backyard and the Kashmir phase of the operation could wait."

"Coming back to my earlier question, what did Pakistan get out of Afghanistan?"

"My view is that Islamabad's only visible and concrete gains in this whole game were the plans of a pipeline from Turkmenistan to Pakistan via Afghanistan."

"Finally they had to content with the pipeline, is it?"

"Even that did not happen eventually. Just when the Taliban was poised to take over the whole of Afghanistan, UNOCAL, the giant American company that was leading the international consortium constructing that pipeline, announced the suspension of its plans to construct the much-trumpeted pipeline. Thus, the geo-strategic victory Pakistan was in pursuit of in Afghanistan, finally remained elusive. Pakistan also forgot an important history lesson."

"What was that?"

"Islamabad forgot that Afghans are fiercely independent people who have never been subjugated by any foreign power for long. They have successfully taught a lesson to three major superpowers of the day in past three centuries – the British, the Soviets and now the Americans. In fact, it would not be a wrong conclusion to make that the collapse of the Soviet empire was hastened by Moscow's military misadventure in Afghanistan."

By now, Mili was full of admiration for Dhruv. Being a spontaneous woman, she did not attempt to hide it.

"Shall I tell you some thing? You are brilliant. You should come to the film industry and write screenplays. I will help you in that. The way you have narrated this complex story of political intrigues in such a simple, easy-to-understand manner, you will go a long way in life."

"Provided I get to live. Correction, provided we get to live."

The two laughed boisterously, both holding each other's hands. This time, Dhruv did not attempt to disengage his hands from Mili's.

Outside, the storm was raging with even more ferocity.

6

No Guns, Only Roses

The storm worsened the next day, the fourth day of captivity of Mili and Dhruv. The snowfall had not stopped even for a minute in 24 hours. The captives could make out hectic activities going on outside despite the inclement weather. The kidnappers seemed to be engaged in snow clearing operations on a war footing. Several men were atop their cell with picks and shovels to clear the snow or else the dilapidated roof of the cell could collapse by the sheer weight of the fast accumulating snow.

Dhruv went to the door, opened it slightly to have an outside view and frantically signalled Mili to see what he was seeing. Two snowskis were parked in the compound under a tin shed. The shed had been constructed just about an hour before. The snowskis were locked and chained to a metallic hook.

"What are those things for?" Mili asked Dhruv in utter disbelief.

"Those are snowmobiles. The guys are well-equipped indeed," Dhruv said in a tone of admiration. "It gives them a lot of operational leverage."

"You mean they can evacuate us with the help of those snowmobiles if such a need arises?"

"These are not meant for us, you moron."

Mili was amused by Dhruv's epithet for her but she did not mind. On the contrary, she appreciated the fact that the ice between the two was melting in the midst of a snow storm.

Dhruv smiled at her and did not feel the need for saying sorry for using a derogatory word for Bollywood's top heroine, which would not have gone unpunished or unchallenged under normal circumstances.

"Those gadgets are probably meant for certain VVIPs who are either here already or expected any moment," he explained. The two returned to their respective cots.

Just then, Javed breezed into the cell, virtually breathless. He had not knocked before coming in, which he had been doing without fail for the past 24 hours.

"You have ten seconds. We are leaving this place immediately. No questions."

Dhruv and Mili stared at each other and then hurried to their respective cots where their clothes were lying.

"No need for picking up those dirty clothes. You will get new ones. Just pick up a blanket each, cover yourselves from head to toe and follow me."

The two followed the instructions. Two men came forward, covered the captives' faces with black hoods, and took them out of the cell. This time the hoods were not chloroformed. They did not protest. They heard some sounds. Apparently, the snowskis were being unchained and unlocked. Each one was made to sit on a snowski, sandwiched between the driver and an armed escort.

They were driven for about twenty minutes. The ride was slow and bumpy. They had no idea of direction. The only thing they were experiencing was that the snow had drenched their blankets and icy winds were piercing to the bone.

Their ordeal ended when the snowmobiles stopped and they were taken inside a building. Their heads were still masked but the warmth of the place was a clear indication that they were not under the sky, which was still disgorging snowflakes at an ever-increasing rate.

After their hoods were removed, the two looked around and then stared at each other. The amazement in their eyes said it all. They were standing in a big hall, which looked like a lobby of a small hotel or a drawing room of a big bungalow. The roof had chandeliers. The flooring was carpeted. The walls were tastefully decorated with tapestries, paintings and wall hangings. A giant bukhari at the centre of the room kept the place warm.

There was a huge dining table at the far end, with a service window opening onto the kitchen. Some ten feet away from the dining table were two teakwood doors that led presumably to washrooms. The particular section of the hall where they were standing was meant to be a living room. There were no sofas or chairs. Instead, four huge mattresses were placed to form a square. The four mattresses were at some distance from one another. At the centre was a big, sturdy stool where a smaller bukhari was placed. The room was brightly lit and a pleasant perfume filled the air. Towards the far end of this section was a huge teakwood door.

"Where are we? Is it the Circuit House of J&K government?" Mili asked.

Javed chose to ignore the question and told the two to follow his men to a room for changing their wet attires.

"Are we going to that room," Mili asked pointing to the door, which had a metallic plate with an Urdu inscription.

"No, not that room. My colleagues will take you to your rooms."

"Rooms? Are you going to lodge us separately," Mili asked.

"You need separate rooms for changing, isn't it?" Javed's brief responses were now getting on Mili's nerves.

"Whose room is that? What is written on its door?"

"That room is the Tiger's Den and is reserved for the VVIP."

Dhruv signalled to Mili to keep quiet and follow the instructions. They were taken out of the room through the main door. The blast of cold air unsettled both Mili and Dhruv. While passing through a corridor, they saw it was a plush bungalow with thick, tall trees all around. At the end of the corridor were two rooms. They were shown their respective rooms and were told to change into a new set of clothes, which had already been provided inside. Javed's final instruction to them was to return to the drawing room for some hot kehwa.

Each of the two rooms had modest but comfortable furniture: two single beds, a settee and a table. Mili jumped with joy when she sighted a television set. A neatly ironed salwar kameez was placed on the bed. Dhruv's room had almost the same furniture with two changes. There was no television set but there were two English newspapers. There were no telephones.

Ten minutes later, there was a gentle knock on the door of Dhruv's room. It was Javed. He instructed him to hurry up and come to the drawing room immediately. He also told him to bring Mili along with him. Dhruv had already changed into a nice fitting pair of jeans, shirt and a thick pullover. He had also had a look at the newspapers, both Pakistani and three days old. Both the newspapers had banner headlines about the kidnapping of Bollywood's superstars Mili and Milind Kumar. A prominent box item in the lead story carried a two-paragraph report from a wire service whose office in Srinagar had received a call from a spokesman of the Lashkar-e-Toiba, claiming responsibility for the abductions. The spokesman said the kidnappings had been carried out by The Green Jihad in association with the Lashkar-e-Toiba on instructions from the Supreme Leader.

Dhruv picked up the newspapers and went to Mili's door, which was half-open. The television was on and Mili was watching a news channel. He entered the room, and then suddenly came out, remembering the weird happenings in the houseboat Jannat, minutes before their abduction. He knocked at the door.

"Come in Dhruv. The door is open," Mili said without looking at the door.

She was glued to the television set, watching an Indian news channel which was airing a panel discussion of experts on the kidnappings. On the bottom of the television screen was red-lettered "BREAKING NEWS" which said, "No contact yet between kidnappers of famous film actress Mili and the government."

Mili gestured him to sit down and kept watching the television. A news bar scrolled at the bottom of the screen. Almost all the one-liner news headlines pertained to the abduction of Mili and Dhruv: "Whereabouts of the captives still unknown", "No demand yet from superstar's kidnappers", "Abductees believed to be safe" Etc.

Dhruv looked at Mili who had apparently had a shower and was looking resplendent in a bright salwar kameez, which fitted her so well, that it was hard to say that the clothes did not belong to her. He showed her the two Pakistani newspapers. The owning of responsibility for the kidnappings by the Lashkar-e-Toiba did not go unnoticed by Mili. She smiled and then surfed all the Indian news channels. The kidnappings were the lead stories on every channel.

Dhruv told Mili about Javed's instructions and the two trooped out of her room. The drawing room was the hub of activity. One man was busy in dusting operations. Another was laying crockery at the dining table for lunch. A third man had just set a tray of teapots, teacups and biscuits on a small table situated at the centre of the four mattresses.

Javed invited them to sit down on the mattresses. "You can enjoy some hot kehwa before lunch is served."

"Why have we been moved to this palatial place? Whose house is it? Who are you people? Why this sudden change in your treatment towards us? What is going on here?" Dhruv fired a battery of questions.

"Probably you won't have to wait long before getting answers to all these questions and more. Have a little bit more patience," Javed replied politely.

Dhruv knew there was no point in arguing with the man who obviously had instructions to clam up. He turned his attention to hot kehwa and biscuits.

Mili's cheerful mood had vanished. She clearly had some questions.

"Are we going to remain in separate rooms?"

"You want to remain in the same room?" Javed asked, turning to Dhruv.

"I have no hassles. Whatever you decide."

"But I have hassles. I don't want to live alone. Either I go to Dhruv's room for the night or he comes to mine." Her face was trembling with fear.

"That is for you two to decide. We have no problems."

"Okay then I will be in your room. We can watch television together,"she told Dhruv.

"But my room does not have a television."

"Then you shift to my room which has a television and two beds," she ordered Dhruv. He smiled and acquiesced.

As Javed took them to the dining table ten minutes later, Mili had another question for Javed.

"Can you please answer a straightforward, uncomplicated question?"

"Shoot."

"Why are we being given this VIP treatment?"

"Because I have instructions."

"Instructions from whom?"

"You will get to know that later tonight."

Half an hour later, the captives were in Mili's room. As Dhruv sat on the edge of his bed, Mili directed, "Relax Dhruv. Take it easy; this too shall pass."

Dhruv was emboldened by Mili's optimism. He removed his shoes and sprawled himself on the comfortable bed which was very different from the small cot in the dark and cold cell.

As he lay down on the bed and watched the wood-panelled ceiling, he did not fail to notice two button-sized cameras. He distinctly remembered that similar devices were located on the ceiling of their earlier venue of captivity. He was dead tired. A warm three-course lunch had made him sleepy. Mili, too, was yawning. The two dozed off on their respective beds.

A couple of hours later, the door opened and several men entered. Dhruv got up and sat upright on the bed. This time, Javed was playing a secondary role to a burly, bearded man in his forties who first measured up Dhruv and then set his sights on the fast asleep Mili. The middle-aged man looked brutal and authoritative.

"Dinner is going to be late because we are expecting an important visitor. We have made arrangements for some high tea for you here in the room itself," the burly man said with a grin.

"And the important visitor is your Supreme Leader?"

"That's right."

The conversation woke up Mili. She looked at the new face, which she did not like one bit.

"Has our government met your demands? Are we going to be released?"

"That is for the Leader to decide, Mohtarma. But we have not placed any demands on your government," the new man said. Then turning to Javed, he growled: "Javed, make sure that they are comfortable here. Put a bukhari in the room and some extra blankets. The storm is getting fiercer and fiercer by the minute."

"Your wish is my command, sir," Javed said obediently and the small group exited.

Mili was tense. "What's happening, Dhruv? I don't understand a damn thing. Who is coming here tonight?"

"I myself don't understand anything. I don't know whether we have been shifted to these five star comforts because our earlier cell was not safe or because their Supreme Leader wanted us to be here."

"Who is their Supreme Leader?"

"I think it is none other than Amaso himself."

"Amaso? The most sought after terrorist the world has ever seen."

"I can't say for sure. This may well be the case. My gut feeling says that Amaso is expected to be here later tonight."

"If that were so, what does it mean for us? Is it going to be good or bad?"

"One thing I can tell you for sure. We are not going to be summarily executed now. In fact, if Amaso were to come in here tonight, it can only be good because our condition cannot be worse than this."

The promised high tea was sent in less than half an hour. Mili helped herself to some pakoras and washed them down with two cups of tea. But Dhruv was eating as though it were his last meal. He had already had kababs and was now devouring pakoras.

As he prepared to pour himself a third cup of tea and fill his plate with chicken tikkas, Mili lost her cool.

"Will you talk or keep on eating like a famished dog? Do

you eat to live or live to eat? Don't you want to get out of here?"

Instead of responding to Mili, Dhruv continued with his feast and signalled her to wait. After he had consumed the last ounce of snacks and the last drop of tea, he let out a sigh of satisfaction.

"First thing first. I want to get out of here. However, there is no way we can do it. Assuming even for a minute that these Johnnies are not here to keep a vigil on our movements and we were to escape from here, there is no escaping from the nature's fury. We won't be able to walk even for one kilometre and our bodies would not be found."

"Why do you think Amaso is coming here to tell them how to kill us? Why should they kidnap us in the first place? Don't ministers and their sons and daughters make much better targets? Worth their efforts? Value for money, as they say."

"Ministers and their kin are thoroughly discredited and a common Indian would not care two hoots if a Minister lives or dies. Kidnapping of a politician serves a purpose for a terrorist outfit only when he commands a massive fan following and possesses virtues of a do-gooder statesman. You know a politician has a limited vision. He can't think beyond the next election, whereas a statesman thinks of the next generation. They are an endangered species. In many countries, this species has already become extinct. In our country, too, there are not very many statesman-like political figures. Their numbers are steadily on the decline and, in any case, such personalities are heavily protected."

"I have heard of cases where popular film stars have been kidnapped for ransom," Mili butted in. "Even famous sportspersons, industry tycoons and celebrities get threatening calls. In most cases, these people move around with a massive personal security cover. Michael Jackson, for instance. Most of these non-political people face threats from criminals and mercenaries, not from terrorist outfits. Palestinian terrorists have killed Israeli sportspersons during the Olympics. But at least I am not aware if such people have ever been kidnapped by any terrorist group."

"Well, there is always a first time. You may perhaps be the first glamorous guinea pig for a kidnapping experiment by terrorists."

Glamorous guinea pig! Mili was amused by the term.

7

Enter Amaso

It was 10 pm. The captives had just been ushered into the drawing room. Javed signalled them to sit down. New silken sheets had been put on the mattresses. The chandeliers' lights had been dimmed. The dining section was unlit.

Javed once again was in command. The burly, bearded man who had visited Mili and Dhruv in their room was not to be seen.

"You people need anything? Kehwa, coffee or me?" Javed asked. For a change, his query was accompanied by a smile and was addressed to Mili.

"The last one the least," Mili said with a straight face.

Javed did not seem to mind the joke at his expense.

"Thank you. We don't need anything," Dhruv said.

Javed kept standing for a minute and then said, "No questions?"

"None whatsoever. We are trying to master the art of waiting and watching," Dhruv said.

Javed departed. Dhruv sprawled on the mattress while Mili reclined against a *masnad,* a voluminous pillow. Dhruv looked around for spy cameras but could not locate one. There was none else in the hall. Everybody seemed to be outside. For five minutes, there was complete silence.

Mili kept looking intently at the face of a pensive Dhruv, his eyes wide open.

"What are you brooding about?"

"I am thinking about the plague in Somalia, starving children in Uganda, the moons of Jupiter and the Tse Tse flies of Africa."

Mili understood the taunt but was not offended. The man had a refined sense of humour. Some animated conversation was going on outside but nothing was audible. More people seemed to have collected outside. Loud instructions were being given in a language Mili and Dhruv did not understand. Inside the hall, there was complete tranquillity.

Dhruv was lying still and did not seem to be in a mood to talk. Mili knew that they were waiting. Even the people outside were waiting. Almost half an hour passed like this. Nothing changed inside or outside the hall.

Bored with this long bout of silence, Mili tried to strike up another conversation with Dhruv.

"You never told me what do you do for a living?"

"That's because you never asked me that question."

"Why are you so secretive?".

"Secretive is a wrong word. I work on a need-to-know and need-to-talk basis."

"That's being snooty."

"Another wrong usage of a word."

"You talk as if you were a wordsmith!"

"Sort of."

"Okay, Mister Wordsmith, will you please tell me now what do you do for a living?"

Suddenly all hell broke lose outside. A vehicle screeched to a halt in the driveway. Then another, and another and yet another. At least half a dozen vehicles had entered the complex. The vehicles' doors opened and banged closed in quick succession. People with heavy boots could be heard running all over. Mili and Dhruv immediately sat in an upright position and looked intently at the main door.

They jumped up in utter disbelief as a fair complexioned, tall, slender man in white flowing robes walked in. He must have been at least six feet two inches. His eyes were greenish. His face was long and radiant. There was an unusual softness about his face, a feature normally associated with sages rather than terrorists. His white flowing beard enhanced this feature further.

The man who followed him was a stark contrast. The same man had briefly visited Mili and Dhruv in their room earlier in the evening. His demeanour strongly suggested that he was the second-in-command.

"Amaso?" Dhruv exclaimed.

"Yes, my name is Amaso. And yours?"

"She is Mili, the famous Indian film star..."

"We know who she is. But who are you?" Amaso asked rather sternly.

The brief exchange had evaporated the shortlived bonhomie that had prevailed between the captives and the captors ever since the two had been shifted to the bungalow. Everybody was standing. Mili began to perspire and beads of sweat were already visible on her forehead.

"My name is Dhruv."

"That also we already know. Dhruv what? What do you do? Are you associated with the Indian film industry in any manner?"

"I am Dhruv Vyas. My father is a retired General of the Indian Army. My mother is a diplomat, presently posted as Indian Ambassador in Thailand. I am a professional writer and I make quite a decent living from my writings. I am not associated with Bollywood. At least not formally, as yet."

"Was your father a spy?"

"No. His forte was preparing long-term war strategies, collection and analysis of intelligence and use of latest scientific gadgetry like spy satellites, thermal sensors, unmanned aerial vehicles etc. His last posting was as Chief of Military Intelligence of the Indian Army."

"What does he do now?" Amaso shot another pointed question. He had not cast a look at Mili so far. His gaze was fixed at Dhruv's face. Everybody was still standing.

"He is leading a retired life. He built a large farmhouse on the Delhi-Jaipur highway and pursues his hobbies like farming, gardening and reading."

"Is he not associated with the Government of India in any way?"

"The government keeps consulting him every now and then on issues of his expertise which I just enumerated to you."

"Are you yourself associated with the Government of India in any way?"

"No."

"None whatsoever?"

"None whatsoever."

"Are you not a spy, or an Indian intelligence man, or an agent?"

"That's the most outrageous allegation, and one which I firmly deny." Dhruv said it in a blatant and deliberately defiant tone, looking straight into the eyes of Amaso.

The room's already electric atmosphere was further charged. The bukharis were no longer required to keep the room warm.

Mili was trembling with fear. Javed was trying to hide himself in a corner, as far away from Amaso as possible. Dhruv remained calm and composed.

"Okay, relax everybody. Let's sit down. You first, Mohtarma," Amaso said, for the first time looking at Mili.

"You are indeed as pretty as a heartthrob of millions should be. I hope both of you have been treated well?"

There was thunder and lightning outside. The storm had become fiercer, but the atmosphere inside had eased dramatically.

Amaso did not occupy his special mattress until Mili had sat down. Then everybody followed suit. Amaso called out for Mehmood Mian. The burly, bearded man lunged forward and said respectfully, "I am here Sheikh Sahib."

"Please tell your people to get some kehwa or tea. Soup can follow half an hour later."

Javed had already retreated to the kitchen even before Mehmood Mian turned to him.

Amaso was still looking at Dhruv. It was clear that he was still not convinced that Dhruv was not an Indian spy. Mili was stunned. Her lips had gone dry. Her tongue remained tied in her mouth. She was amazed at the confidence and conviction of Dhruv with which he tackled Amaso's barrage of questions. Mehmood Mian also looked impressed with Dhruv.

There were five people present in the room, but there were only two protagonists.

Amaso was seated alone on the biggest and the cosiest mattress. Mili and Dhruv were seated opposite Amaso, and Mehmood Mian and Javed sat on the third one while the fourth one was unoccupied. Two Kalashnikov-armed guards in army fatigues were deployed at the main door. The guards were expressionless. Perhaps they were trained like that, or perhaps they did not understand the conversation that had been going on in English. They had Uzbek features.

A man brought kehwa and small eats and served the five people seated on the mattresses. Amaso signalled to Mili to start drinking her kehwa. She took it as a commandment and had a long sip, slightly burning her lips in the process. Amaso smiled benignly. Everybody smiled and started sipping from their respective cups. The bonhomie was back in the room.

Dhruv looked up from his kehwa. "Do I have the right to ask questions?"

"Wrong usage of the word, my dear. Remember those are your own words which you uttered to the Mohtarma some hours ago."

For the first time since Amaso's entry into the room, Dhruv was nonplussed. His jaw fell. He had an inkling that he and Mili had been under 24-hour surveillance for the past four days but he could not imagine even in the wildest of his dreams that Amaso had been kept updated about every bit of their conversation.

"I beg your pardon?"

"Okay, first thing first, one of your favourite expressions. A prisoner has no right to ask any questions. Since you seem to be special, I grant you the right to ask as many questions from me as you want. It will be up to me to answer them or not."

"Thank you Sheikh Sahib."

Amaso smiled again, this time in appreciation for Dhruv's agility in latching on to the title Mehmood Mian had used for him a little while ago.

"You can start your questions but don't ask me for any operational details."

"Why have you staged this kidnapping? What leverage do you expect out of it particularly when I understand you people have not made any demand from the Government of India for our safe release?"

"The answer is exactly what you gave to Ms Mili earlier in the day. Besides, I can add one thing. We are in the business of jihad, which you people, or the so-called civilised world, describe as terrorism. We have a vision how the world should be run. Don't believe self-styled security experts and terrorism analysts who say that we want the whole world to be a caliphate. We are against social injustice and inequalities and the policy of might is right so blatantly practiced by the US and the UK. We are not against nonMuslims. Both of you are Hindus. Have we harmed you or ill-treated you? You have been kidnapped because we are constantly evolving, mutating and experimenting. We have to be trend-blazers, not trend-followers. We are always a step ahead of the security forces because of only one reason: the element of surprise. Quite often, this element is lost because of traitors among us. Therefore, we have to constantly come up with newer and newer ideas, technologies, plans and experiments. This is our R&D. We want to see how masses and governments react when celebrities, who do not hold any public office but rule the hearts of millions, are kidnapped. We want to se how they react when the kidnapped celebrities are killed or released unharmed."

"What is our fate? Are you going to kill us?"

"I warned you not to ask any operations-related question."

"Sorry about that. You talked about your experimentation in kidnapping of celebrities. I am not a celebrity. So why am I here?"

"That's our goof-up at the local commander level," Amaso said, turning his face to Javed.

Javed's face turned white with fear.

"Our original plan was to kidnap the hero and the heroine. You came in the frame at the last minute."

"But even a blind man can see the difference between me, a non-entity and Milind Kumar, Bollywood's greatest-ever star."

"Given the parentage you claim, you ought to know such goof-ups do occur when an operation has to be completed in seconds, not minutes. Moreover, you are also quite young and by no means bad looking. The situation was further complicated by the kind of intimate posture you were locked in with Mohtarma," Amaso said with a twinkle in his eyes.

It was now Mili's turn to hang her head. Javed's face, on the other hand, lit up with the Supreme Commander's solid argument.

"One minute please. You used the phrase 'Given the parentage you claim'. Are you doubting whatever I have told you about myself?"

Amaso was about to respond to this when he stopped on seeing two men carrying soup trays. After the soup was served and Mili was the first one to get it, the Sheikh started speaking again.

"Of course I have not believed every word of yours. I will not believe it until we get all the facts cross-checked and corroborated. The kinds of credentials you have given for yourself are easily verifiable, but we have to be extra watchful. We are in the business of perennial doubts because we live in a shadowy world. Remember, even a white bird has a black shadow. That is the difference between reality and virtual reality."

"So you don't trust anybody?"

"Trust is another name for suicide in the business we are in. We take extreme precautions to make sure that we don't leave any trails. That is why in this 21st century when my own cadres are heavily dependent on things like computers, internet, email, satellite phones, mobile phones, walkie-talkies and wireless sets, I don't use any of these. Why? Because I am the leader. I have to lead by example, and there is no greater example than sacrifice. It is not unlike a King who lives like a hermit and sleeps on a bed of nails."

Mehmood Mian and Javed were listening to Amaso's words with rapt attention. The former, who was Amaso's constant companion, had never found his leader speaking so much. That, too, to kafirs!

"Okay now you have asked your quota of questions. I need to find out several things from you."

"One last question, if you will allow please," Dhruv pleaded.

"Shoot."

"Why have you chosen to meet us? Do you meet all your captives or is it because this kidnapping is an important experiment for your R&D laboratory?"

"You should have been a journalist. You ask pointed and pithy questions and this one is the best of all. I never meet my captives; whatever may be the profile of the captive and whatever experimentation may be involved in the operation. There are several reasons for this. Security considerations are the first and foremost. Then there are operational factors. We have a huge kidnapping network spread all over the world – Chechnya, Iraq, Afghanistan, Turkey, Saudi Arabia, Egypt, Yemen, Spain, Philippines, Pakistan, Israel and Kashmir, just to name a few. Kidnappings are a money churning industry for us. We also use kidnappings with a premeditated intent of killing the victim or victims, irrespective of the fact whether any ransom is paid or not. This is to strike terror in the hearts of our enemies and potential fence sitters among us."

Amaso could see his last words had indeed struck terror in the hearts of his captives. Milis face mirrored it, while Dhruv maintained a stiff upper lip. The Sheikh, meanwhile, had ordered that dinner be laid in the next five minutes.

"Now, to come back to your original question: why meet you people and break an unwritten law. There are two reasons for it. She may not know, but we know that you have all along been aware, or at least suspicious, of the fact that you people are under round-the-clock surveillance. All your conversations were tapped by powerful bugging devices placed inside your cots and your movements were videotaped round the clock. That is our normal practice but generally, we don't mount such close surveillance unless the target is either a traitor or a high-profile military or political official.

"Javed, who was in charge of your earlier prison complex, was initially baffled by the unusual coldness between you two, which is highly unnatural between two co-stars. Our propaganda machinery had already informed the press that Bollywood's leading hero-heroine pair had been kidnapped from the outskirts of Srinagar. Javed thought it was a put on show and after consultation with Mehmood Mian, he continued to snoop on you. That is why you were not lodged separately.

"By the next day, it was confirmed that instead of Milind Kumar, Javed's men had picked up you along with the heroine. Mehmood Mian, who is an Afghan war veteran, directed Javed to continue with the surveillance and report to him twice a day. Your observations, analyses and comments bore the signatures of a military or an intelligence man. Mehmood Mian suspected that you could be an Indian intelligence mole whose appearance on the houseboat

Jannat minutes before the operation was to be carried out was choreographed.

"At that stage, Mehmood Mian consulted me as I happened to be in the neighbourhood for certain operations. I called for all the audio tapes of your conversations with Ms Mili. I tended to agree with Mehmood Mian's assessment and eventual treatment of the situation. The turning point came when you narrated the story of the Taliban to the heroine. The story was completely factual and only a few people could be expected to know such minute details. Now Javed started reporting to Mehmood Mian four times a day. I myself was briefed extensively about your conversations. My curiosity increased with each passing day.

"The second reason was the weather. Local veterans warned us of an impending snow storm that could well be the worst in living memory. So all our movements were put on hold till the weather improved."

"So my blabbing has landed me in this soup?"

"I don't know whether it landed you in this soup, but it has definitely landed you at a dinner table with me. Let me divulge a little secret here. You two are the first, and probably the last captives, with whom I am going to have meal."

Amaso got up. Dhruv noticed, for the first time, that he was carrying an old AK47 rifle, which thus far had remained hidden under the shawl in which he had wrapped himself. Everybody else got up. Amaso waited for Mili to lead the way to the dinner table.

After ensconcing himself at the head of the table, Amaso said, "There may be a third reason for extending this honour to you."

"What's that?"

"Your real identity."

"But that you would not know for sure till you crosscheck my personal details."

"I think there may not be a need for that. I have a feeling that I am aware of your identity."

Mili could not believe her ears. Mehmood Mian and Javed also looked clueless. Dhruv's face was inscrutable.

"Now it's my turn to ask you questions. Needless to say, one lie may be your last one in life," Amaso said while picking up a roasted chicken leg.

"I am waiting for your questions," Dhruv said, his plate still empty.

"You said you are a professional writer and that's how you make a living."

"That's absolutely correct."

"You also gave your complete name as Dhruv Vyas?"

"Right."

"What do you write? Fiction or non-fiction? In which language?"

"Fiction. In English. My works have been translated into dozens of other languages as well."

"What do you write? Novels, short stories, drama or poetry?"

"Mainly novels and short stories."

"How many of your books have been published?"

"Twelve so far. Ten novels and two short story collections."

"What are these about? Romance, social subjects or thrillers."

"Thrillers. Romance has no place in my life."

Everybody else at the dining table, except Dhruv, noticed Mili shuffle in her seat.

"Which of your novels is your most favourite?"

"Moonstruck."

"How about 'Shipwrecked In Antarctica'?"

"But that is not a novel."

"That is a short story collection."

"Yes, but how do you know? That came out just last year."

"Because I have read it."

Mili dropped her spoon. Mehmood Mian nearly fed his nose biryani. Javed froze in his seat. Dhruv scratched his face.

"But you told a lie. Or perhaps a half lie."

"How?"

"You don't write in the name of Dhruv Vyas."

"Right. I write in the name of Dhruv D Vyas."

"What does 'D' stand for?"

Without batting an eyelid, Dhruv replied, "D stands for Dinesh, my father's name."

"Then why did you furnish half information when I demanded to know your complete name?"

"One, because I never thought the letter D was so important. Two, I was not filling in a passport application form."

Amaso laughed heartily at Dhruv's repartee. Mili and the others were by then used to Dhruv's amazing confidence.

"Let me tell you Mr Dhruv D Vyas. The letter D is not just important for us; in many ways it is a thorn in our flesh."

"I don't understand Sheikh Sahib."

"Let's not venture into operational details. But I am inclined to give you a deal which no jihadi would ever have given to his quarry."

Everybody had finished dinner by now and the impeccably dressed waiters were busy clearing the table. The head waiter had announced that the dessert was about to be served.

After everybody had his or her pick of dessert, apple custard and hot chocolate ice cream, Mili, Mehmood Mian and Javed looked at the two protagonists. The conversation was getting curiouser and curiouser.

They wanted to know what deal Amaso was going to give to Dhruv D Vyas. Everybody looked expectantly at Amaso, but he did not seem to be in a hurry.

Amaso cleared his throat and said, "I have an idea but the thoughts are still to crystallize. Let me chew over it for a short time. We will discuss it tomorrow during lunch. Now you can retire."

Then he issued brief instructions to Mehmood Mian in a language which even Javed could not understand and signalled them all to leave. While going out, Mili and Dhruv noticed that the armed guards were still standing upright.

Mehmood Mian asked Javed to wait and took upon himself the duty of escorting the VIP prisoners to Mili's room.

Mehmood Mian closed the door after three of them had entered Mili's room. "Now, some necessary instructions. You know by now that both your rooms are bugged and fitted with surveillance cameras. Now I will tell you what you do not know. Both these rooms are special in many ways. The entire flooring is collapsible by the push of a button located somewhere outside. So don't try anything silly because we will not let any misadventure go unpunished when the Supreme Leader is around. Khuda hafiz."

Mili and Dhruv did not give a damn to Mehmood Mian's warnings. A misadventure did not figure in the wildest of their thoughts and dreams. Right now, they were only bothered about one thing: Amaso's deal.

8

The Deal

It was almost a week since Diwakar or anybody else in official circles in New Delhi had heard from Inspector General Dashamlav.

Diwakar had just reached his office. It was eight o'clock on a Sunday morning. He had to deal with some urgent files, which made the calendar and the clock irrelevant. He had barely settled in his chair when the RAX buzzed. IB Chief was on the line.

"Good morning sir."

"Morning. Can you see me?"

"When sir?"

"Right now?"

"At your residence, sir?"

"No. I am in my North Block office. Come right away."

Diwakar knew it had something to do with Kashmir's famous kidnappings that continued to dominate the print and electronic media. The Prime Minister, the Home

Minister, the National Security Advisor, chiefs of intelligence agencies and top bureaucrats like the Cabinet Secretary and the Union Home Secretary had nothing more urgent on their hands these days than the Kashmir kidnappings.

Seven minutes later, Diwakar was in the DIB's room. The Director of Intelligence Bureau was pacing up and down. As soon as Diwakar entered the room, the DIB picked up a thick file, superscribed "TOP SECRET", held Diwakar by his arm and ushered him out of the room. While locking his room with his personal key, the DIB said, "Come. There is no time to waste. We will talk in the car."

The driver knew where he had to go. Puzzled, Diwakar asked, "Sir, where are we going?"

"To the Prime Minister's residence. An emergency meeting of the CCS has been convened. Everybody, including the Home Minister, the Foreign Minister, the Defence Minister and the NSA has already reached the Prime Minister's residence. The meeting cannot begin without two of us."

"What's the agenda? The Kashmir kidnappings?"

"What else?"

The fact that the CCS, or the Cabinet Committee on Security, was seized with the issue indicated the importance the country's top political leadership attached to the kidnappings. CCS is the apex decision-making body of the Government of India on all security and strategic issues.

"The Maharashtra Chief Minister has insisted on his presence at the meeting, though you know very well Chief Ministers are not members of the CCS," the DIB continued. "He has already reached the Prime Minister's residence. In fact, he has been camping there for past half an hour. He says he is under tremendous pressure from the film industry. Moreover, he claims to have a vital piece of information which, he says, he will disclose only before the CCS members."

"What information he could have which we don't have?"

"Only God knows, but you know these are the problems of coalition politics. Has Dashamlav contacted you?"

"No sir. Not since the pre-dawn BSF operation at Lal Chowk, which was six days ago. I thought probably he was in touch with you directly."

"No. There has been no contact from his side."

When they entered the conference room at the Prime Minister's residence, they found everybody waiting for them. The Prime Minister himself was chairing the meeting of the Cabinet Committee on Security.

A glum-looking Home Minister started the proceedings. "What's the latest on Kashmir kidnappings," the minister demanded to know from the DIB.

"I'm afraid we don't have much to offer, sir."

"The reason?"

"Because our man in charge of this operation has been absolutely incommunicado for almost a week."

"You mean Inspector General Dashamlav?"

"Sir."

"He is an extremely capable officer. There must be some reason behind this silence."

"You said it, sir."

"What kind of intelligence machinery we are running in our country when we don't have even the most elementary information about such a sensational kidnapping?" The speaker was Anant Medhekar, the Chief Minister of Maharashtra, who was the President of a powerful regional party whose support was vital for the survival of the Central government.

The caustic remark had electrified the atmosphere. All eyes were fixed on the DIB.

Now the Prime Minister spoke. "I think we have gathered here to review the shocking incident and not to attack our intelligence machinery. Before I ask the DIB to give us the latest update on the case, I would request Mr Medhekar to speak first because I believe he has some hard inputs to provide."

"I will do that, Mr Prime Minister. That's why I am here. But before that I would like to know what the intelligence agencies know," the Maharashtra Chief Minister said. The Prime Minister signalled the DIB to start with his presentation.

"Sirs, the brief facts are as follows."

The DIB began at the beginning. He started with the Qurban Ali arrest and then talked about the foiling of a terrorist plot to assassinate a union minister at a school function and the spate of high-profile terror attacks in the valley. He made a special mention of the taunting SMS received by Dashamlav purportedly from Ghazni Baba in which he had thrown a challenge to the Inspector General, which the latter had accepted. The IB Chief concluded his presentation by telling the CCS members about Dashamlav's eventual trip to the Kashmir valley where he had been incommunicado for almost a week.

Then Diwakar gave his own presentation. Diwakar gave details of the telephone call he received from CIA official, Jack Boucher, the CIA's intelligence about movement of high-value targets in Pakistan-held Kashmir and the last fax received from Dashamlav wherein he had talked of establishing contact with leader of the CIA crack team on the trail of top terrorists in POK. He also talked about Dashamlav's warning that 'an interesting' terrorist operation was about to take place in the valley.

Now the DIB took over. "It is a queer case. Virtually a blind case in which there were no leads. I would urge you not to see the cause for panic because we have the best of the very best operational man in the valley. It is a difficult case because there is no trail. The matter has worsened because the kidnappers have not made any demands so far. This could have a dangerous inference: that the hostages may have already been harmed."

"That is precisely the information I have come here to give," the Maharashtra Chief Minister butted in. Of all the 28 Indian states and seven Union Territories, Maharashtra is the only state whose Chief Minister is in direct contact with the glamorous Bollywood. "I have reliable information that the hostages have not been harmed."

"How can you say that?" the Defence Minister asked.

"I have my own channels of information. It is not for nothing that I have been in Maharashtra politics for the last four decades," Medhekar boasted.

"Do we know where the hostages have been kept?" The Prime Minister asked gently.

"We do know for sure that the hostages have been taken to the other side of the LOC. Local shepherds have confirmed that piece of information. Their assessment is that the hostages may be within twenty kilometres inside the POK from the Line of Control," the IB Chief said.

"Can we launch a commando operation for rescuing the hostages?" Medhekar asked.

"No, not right now."

"Why?" Medhekar asked with irritation.

"Because the weather there is extremely bad. It has been snowing there heavily for the past four days. We have to wait till the weather clears up."

"We cannot and should not launch a military rescue mission," the Foreign Minister butted in. "Because for that our forces will have to cross the LOC and this would bring us international condemnation. I am sure Pakistan will paint it as an act of war and the Chinese, as usual, would either keep quiet or side with Islamabad." The Foreign Minister happened to be the brother-in-law of the Maharashtra CM. Medhekar's jaws dropped after the candid remark of his brother-in-law, which went contrary to his own opinion.

"So what is our best bet?" the Prime Minister asked.

"Inspector General Dashamlav," the DIB and Diwakar said in unison.

Shortly after the CCS meeting concluded and participants started dispersing, the National Security Advisor asked the DIB to meet him in his South Block office half an hour later. He also instructed the DIB to make sure that the chiefs of Research and Analysis Wing (RAW) and Military Intelligence (MI) were also present at the meeting. The NSA then asked the Army Chief to go straight to the War Room located at the South Block headquarters of the Ministry of Defence and call select senior officials for a brainstorming session.

The NSA took the Foreign Secretary to a corner out of the earshot of other officials. The consultations went on for about five minutes. The NSA went back to the Prime Minister's chamber for a one-on-one discussion. After five minutes, the Foreign Secretary was also called in. The Prime Minister's consultations with the NSA and the Foreign Secretary lasted about 25 minutes.

The NSA then rushed to his office where the chiefs of IB, RAW and MI were waiting for him. Having been in senior positions in the government for decades, the NSA knew that operational matters could not be discussed threadbare in the presence of politicians. Politicians were required only for giving or blocking executive clearance.

The NSA's meeting with the intelligence chiefs went off very well. The situation on the Kashmir kidnappings front was not as murky as the CCS deliberations had suggested, after all. He was given inputs about operational plans that were still in the germinating stage. As the NSA walked through the South Block corridors along with the intelligence chiefs to attend the War Room meeting, the consensus was that things had still not gotten out of hand and various options were still available.

The purpose for the War Rom meeting was two-fold: to get a cartographic visual presentation of the areas in Pakistan-held Kashmir where the captives were suspected to be kept, and to prepare a blueprint for a commando operation. The second one was more ticklish and eventually generated a heated debate among officials from the Ministries of Defence, Home and External Affairs who attended the War Room brainstorming.

The chiefs of Military Intelligence and Military Operations gave separate accounts and inputs, focusing on the 50 square kilometre swath on either side of the Line of Control in Jammu and Kashmir where the operation had to be carried out, subject to the political executive's necessary approval. Strategic locations on either side of the LOC were marked by red and green flags, indicating the two parts of Kashmir under control of Pakistan and India respectively.

They discussed the places where small but well-equipped teams of their best commandos could be deployed without attracting attention. Use of reconnaissance aircraft's fixed wings as well as choppers was ruled out, even if the weather were to improve because these machines were sure to act as flying advertisements to the adversary. The use of unmanned aerial vehicles (UAVs) was also ruled out for similar reasons. The focus was to be on 'humint' – intelligence parlance for human intelligence.

Now it was the turn of the Foreign Secretary to give his inputs. On the NSA's instructions, the technical staff and mid-level officials who had a role in cartographic presentations and computer simulated military operations were thanked for their help and asked to leave the room. Only the core group of officials remained in the War Rom.

The Foreign Secretary's brief presentation put the things in perspective. Most officials got to understand the enormity of the situation only after the Foreign Secretary's remarks. Those who were wondering why the entire machinery of the Government of India was being geared up for tackling the abduction of a Bollywood star and a nondescript person, got their answers when the Foreign Secretary spoke.

"Gentlemen, we have spent at least four hours in examining the issue from military, intelligence and operational points of view. Now can we turn our attention to the diplomatic aspect of the whole thing?"

"Are you asking us or telling us something," the DIB asked, thoroughly puzzled. The NSA was as alert as a tiger.

"I am going to tell you something. Are you gentlemen aware of the American angle to the entire episode?"

There was total silence in the room. Everybody waited with bated breath for the Foreign Secretary to resume.

"We have been approached by the Americans several times in past 24 hours for our help. They believe that the super terrorist, Amaso, is himself present in the area. They are unable to locate his exact position despite their most modern gadgetry and spy satellites that are focused on the region these days round the clock. Amaso may or may not be linked with the kidnappings of Mili and Dhruv. In any case, the Americans are not interested in the captives. They want Amaso, dead or alive. They know that they can't depend on Islamabad for getting Amaso. That's why they are not discussing the issue with the Pakistani government. The Americans have offered us a deal. The NSA is in direct negotiations with the Americans on this deal and he has been briefing and updating the Prime Minister about it, virtually on an hourly basis because the situation is fluid."

"What's the deal," the DIB asked.

"They are prevailing upon us to launch a limited military offensive across the LOC."

"For our hostages?"

"That they are not bothered about. They are interested in Amaso only. They say that if we are able to capture Amaso, dead or alive, they will shower India with such strategic advantages as they have done to no other country ever before. They are even ready to back us for the permanent membership of the United Nations Security Council with full veto powers."

"But what about the reactions of Pakistan and China, if we were to cross the LOC for a military operation?" the MI Chief asked.

"They are assuring us that there will be no military fallout between India and Pakistan if we were to carry out this operation. Pakistan will obviously make noises and launch a diplomatic offensive, but the buck would stop there. It will be all posturing. As far as China is concerned, even Beijing is concerned about Amaso's activities. You know very well the situation in Xingjian. Beijing has been flooding Xingjian with the majority Han Chinese to change the demographic structure of the province and to counter the local Uighurs whom it suspects to be Amaso's sympathizers. So the Chinese response too would be muted."

"Do the Americans want a joint operation or do they want us to do it on our own?" the RAW Chief asked.

"That is negotiable. They would be game in either situation. However, what I gather is that they would prefer it to be an out-and-out Indian operation. They see it as a game of billiards. You hit the red ball when you actually want to net the green ball. Our army commandos would be well within their right to launch a rescue mission for our two nationals who are being held captive in territory under Pakistani control. But the real target would be Amaso and his top lieutenants."

The Foreign Secretary stopped to drink water.

"What is your own view in this regard?" the DGMO asked.

"I see logic in that. The American soldiers' presence in the area can't go unnoticed. The news will spread like wild fire. Besides, given the compulsions of coalition government in our country, the American soldiers' presence in our country for a military operation, and that too in a politically sensitive region like Kashmir, would be suicidal for the government in New Delhi. You know the blatant anti-American attitude of several allies of the present government. In such a situation, the government allies would do what the Opposition has been itching to do for a long time – pull down the government."

"Now coming back to my original question," the DIB asked. "What's the deal from the Americans?"

"The deal is we give them Amaso, dead or alive, and they make India a superpower in the next five years – economically, militarily, politically."

"But what about our hostages?" the DIB persisted.

"They are expendable, as far as the Americans are concerned."

"And what is the Indian leadership's position? Does the Prime Minister also feel that our hostages are expendable?"

"I don't know."

Mili and Dhruv had spent a quiet night. They got up earlier than usual. It was Day Five of their captivity. When a man brought tea, Mili told him that she and Dhruv wanted to go for a stroll outside. The man said he would come back after seeking instructions.

After five minutes, Javed entered the room after knocking at the door twice. Dhruv repeated Mili's wish for a stroll outside.

"You must be joking," Javed said. "Our men have worked through the night in snow-clearing operations in the complex. The damned snowfall has not stopped for a minute in the past thirty six hours. Reports are that the conditions are going to worsen in the next forty eight hours. Even the Supreme Leader has not been able to stir out of this complex, despite urgent matters."

"What do you normally do in such times? Snow storms like these must be a regular feature," Mili asked politely.

"I am 30. I have never seen such a fierce snow storm thus far in my life. Our chief cook is 65 and he was just telling me that he does not remember such a long spell of heavy snowfall in his entire lifetime. We are faced with a situation like this for the first time in living memory."

"What is the Supreme Leader doing right now? Has he woken up?" Dhruv asked.

Dhruv actually did not expect his question to be answered, but Javed did reply. "The Supreme Leader is an early riser, no matter what time he goes to sleep. He is with Mehmood Mian for the last one hour. I have a feeling he is going to call for you people earlier than the lunch time."

Javed had brought two new sets of clothes for the captives. As Javed left, Mili poured tea into two cups and sat on Dhruv's bed.

"You are quite an unusual man. I must say I am impressed by you."

"Are you alright?"

"Is that a question or a taunt?"

"If it is both?"

"A question has to be answered. A taunt can be ignored. So you choose how you would like to categorise it," Mili said. Dhruv was rather surprised at the heroine's effervescence.

"Okay, treat it as a question," he said keeping his cup on the bedside table, expecting a long-winded reply.

Mili also put her teacup on the table, pounced on Dhruv and kissed him violently for a good thirty seconds. Dhruv was stunned. He did not return the kiss but made no efforts to push her away. Mili looked into Dhruv's eyes and hugged him tight. Dhruv found himself stroking her beautiful hair. She pulled a blanket over them and tightened the embrace. Within minutes, she was fast asleep. Dhruv's body was electrified, but he controlled his emotions.

Mili must have slept in Dhruv's arms for about an hour

when there was a knock on the door. She woke up but did not bother to release Dhruv from her embrace.

"Please get up. Someone is at the door."

"Let him wait for ever. Don't open the door," Mili said.

"Don't forget the room can't be locked from inside. So whoever it is will come in any second," he whispered.

"Let him come in. Who cares?"

There was another knock and the door was pushed open. The same man, who had brought tea an hour ago, came to collect the empty teacups. He saw Mili's bed empty and two cups of unconsumed tea. He looked at Dhruv who was half-reclining while Mili was cuddled inside the blanket with him.

"Shall I get you some more tea after Madam comes out of the washroom?"

"After half an hour please," Dhruv said.

"The Supreme Leader wants to see you both an hour after breakfast. Please get ready. I am getting you fresh tea after ten minutes."

Mili jumped out of the bed after the door was closed, stood for a while and then again threw herself over Dhruv. This time she was smooching Dhruv's entire face like a child. Dhruv planted a warm kiss on her cheek and said, "What is happening to you? Remember we are being watched. Please get up and get ready."

Mili got up like an obedient child but did not move out of Dhruv's bed.

"You are a strange woman indeed!"

"I am not a woman. I am a girl, and a virgin till date. You must be thinking that film heroines are like doormats or carpets, willing to be laid anywhere, anytime by anyone who pays a price."

"No, no. You got me wrong. Who am I to question your morality or your virgin status?"

"You can test it, if you want," Mili said naughtily.

"Now you are back to your film dialogues."

"These are no film dialogues, you idiot. For the first time in my 28 years, I am my own script writer."

"Thanks for your indulgence which I don't deserve."

"That is for me to decide. And I have decided."

"Decided what?"

"I will tell you that at an appropriate time."

"Right now there is time for only one thing."

"What?"

"Amaso's deal."

An hour later, Dhruv and Mili were sharing the dining table with Amaso and Mehmood Mian. Javed was conspicuous by his absence.

Strangely, Mehmood Mian initiated the conversation after formal exchange of pleasantries. "The weather is showing no signs of improvement even though the snowfall stopped about an hour ago. But the temperature is constantly dipping and more fierce snow storms are expected soon."

The two captives looked at each other. They suspected that the snow storms were long over, between two of them.

Dhruv looked at Amaso who did not seem to be in a hurry to come out with his promised deal. As omlette and toast was served, Dhruv decided to set the ball rolling.

"You were to offer us a deal, Sheikh Sahib. Have you crystallized your thoughts finally?"

"Have you read The Arabian Nights?"

"Who hasn't?"

"I haven't."

"You must have heard the stories of Aladdin and his Lamp, Alibaba and the Forty Thieves, Sinbad and his weird travels and the exploits of Harun alRashid."

"Who hasn't?"

"These stories form part of The Arabian Nights. Actually, the name of the original book is "The Thousand Nights and One Night."

"That is too short an introduction. If you are telling something, explain in details," Amaso protested.

"Well it is about a king who finds himself unhinged when he is betrayed by the wife he dotes on. He is forewarned about his wife by his brother who himself had been cuckolded by his wife. King Shahryar spies on the Queen, discovers her adultery and kills her instantaneously. From then on, he orders his wazir to get him a virgin whom he ravishes during the night and kills before daybreak. This bloodshed continues for three years until the capital runs out of virgins. The wazir, who himself has two young and beautiful daughters of marriageable age, returns home in a sullen mood. The daughters get to know the plight of their father and the elder one, Shahrazad, embarks upon a plan with her sister Dunyazad. As per the plan, the wazir takes his elder daughter before the King the next day. The King becomes very happy after seeing Shahrazad. He wants to take her but she starts crying. She stops only when the King assures her that her sister will be allowed inside the room after he was through with her. Now when the King is trying to doze off after taking the virginity of Shahrazad, her sister praises her skills of telling tales and beseeches her to narrate a story to pass time. Shahrazad agrees subject to the King's approval. The King was not feeling sleepy and had nothing better to do. Shahrazad starts her first tale. She so cleverly weaves tales within tales within tales and laces them with such fantastic incidents that the King is hooked to these tales. Days turn into weeks and months turn into years as the King keeps listening to these tales. It is a happy ending story as the King and his brother marry Shahrazad and Dunyazad respectively."

Dhruv was rather surprised by the unduly rapt attention he commanded from everybody.

Mili was the first one to come out with her enthusiastic response. "I had a fair idea about King Shahryar and the storyteller girl Shahrazad and I, like everybody else, had heard the famous stories of Aladdin, Alibaba and Sinbad. But I never knew that these stories were part of the Arabian Nights or the Thousand Nights and One Night."

Mehmood Mian said, "I never understood how anybody on this earth, and a King to boot, can have so much time and patience to listen to stories."

"But if you were to look at The Arabian Nights from another perspective, it is all about human enterprise, skill and willpower to survive the odds and eventually emerge the winner," Dhruv explained.

"Very well said. However, if you were to look at it from the King's point of view, it conveys how a perfectionist can be misunderstood as a murderer and a despot. It shows that the King was, after all, neither a fool nor a psychotic killer. Rather, he was looking for a perfect combination of beauty and brains, which he ultimately got. In the process, the minister's daughter's skills were put to the test."

"Now can we come to the brass tacks? You can call it an existential question. We are your prisoners and at your mercy. There are only three possible scenarios. It is up to you to keep us captives forever, or kill us or release us. I would like to know which of the three scenarios our fate is."

"Thank you for putting it succinctly. But remember, there are no free lunches."

"Meaning?"

"You can be freed but you have to earn your freedom."

"How?"

"You claim to be an accomplished writer. I have read your works also. But how do I know whether the Dhruv who is my captive and the Dhruv D Vyas are the same?"

"But how can I prove it?"

"I will tell you. Let's play a game. A mind game. You tell a story which you have not yet written. You claim to be a thriller writer. I have a passion for reading thrillers. You weave a thriller and narrate it to me. You stop before you bring the twist in the tale. I will guess your twist in the tale. If I guess it right, you lose. If I am unable to see through your twist, you win. Needless to say, the lives of you two will depend on your success or failure."

"But what do you get out of it? Where is the need for it? You yourself said yesterday that my credentials are such that they can be corroborated easily."

"There are two reasons for this. First, I am still not convinced about your identity. The letter 'D' in your pen name is a bit of bother for us. Even if you are the son of a Major General father and a diplomat mother, your amazing familiarity with security matters is a source of concern for us. The second reason is that nobody can move out from here for days because of the weather. One can fight an army but not the nature's fury. Since you and I have nothing better to do, why not play this game?"

"Okay, now I am beginning to understand. You must have read all my books, which appear without my photograph. You want me to conceive a new story so that you can establish my bona fides. At the same time, it gives you a chance to satisfy your intellectual and literary appetite – an impossible task for you under normal circumstances."

"That's right."

"There is a problem."

"What's that?"

"For you, it is only a mind game. But for us it is a matter of life and death."

"So be it. You are not in a position of pick and choose. At least I am giving you a chance to earn your freedom, by your sheer capability and intellect. I can assure you one thing as a devout Muslim. I will never violate my promise. If I am defeated, I will gracefully accept my defeat and will direct Mehmood Mian to personally escort you to your land safely. I am sure you are also a devout Hindu. I don't have to tell you the basic Hindu philosophy of 'karma'. A day of 'karma' with duty and conviction is better than a thousand year's prayers in a place of worship. So do your 'karma'."

Dhruv was floored. Mili could not believe that a terrorist could be so learned, so patient and so persuasive. For Mehmood Mian, his Supreme Leader's every word was a pearl of wisdom, whether he understood it or not.

"Think it over with a cool head. Discuss it with Mohtarma. She would definitely be a source of strength for you after all those passionate kisses she showered on you this morning."

Mili's face turned red. Dhruv flashed her "I-told-you-so" looks.

"Never mind. I am not a fanatic who would come in between two lovebirds. I am firmly of the view that you can win all mind games with the power of pure love because love transcends all. You go to your room. Discuss your strategies. Prepare your game plan. We meet again here in this room after two hours for setting the ground rules."

Amaso got up and waited for Mili to do the same. Before turning to his room, Amaso said, "Two more things. To ensure a level-playing field, I am ordering your room to be swept clean of all bugging and surveillance devices. It should instil confidence in you that whatever you are discussing between yourselves remains strictly between you two only. You can take it as a confidence building measure from my side. Secondly, the story Mehmood Mian told you last night about the collapsible flooring of your room was a falsehood by my instructions, with the sole purpose of psyching you out. I know this tactic is no longer required because the situation has changed."

Amaso retired to his room but not before leaving necessary instructions with Mehmood Mian. Two men were dispatched to sweep the room clean of all surveillance devices.

Ten minutes later, Mili and Dhruv hurried to the room; to test Amaso's profound words that one could win all mind games with the power of pure love. Because love transcends all.

9

Rules of the Game

It was early morning on a Muslim holiday. Despite that, the imposing Pakistani Foreign Office building in Islamabad was abuzz with activity. Several flag cars had already arrived and more were still coming. The Foreign Secretary had convened a review meeting on instructions from the President to discuss the latest developments in Kashmir.

Ten select officials from the Foreign Office, Interior Ministry, Defence Ministry, Army, Inter Services Intelligence and the Intelligence Bureau were seated in the Foreign Secretary's room. The Foreign Secretary, Aziz Haider was a suave and successful diplomat who had handled several sensitive assignments in his 32-year-long distinguished career. The President understood his methods very well and valued his advice. News from the grapevine in Islamabad was that Haider could well be the next Foreign Minister of Pakistan.

"What's the latest on the Kashmir front?" the Foreign Secretary asked the ISI Chief as soon as impeccably dressed waiters had served tea and snacks and left the room.

"I will focus my brief presentation on two issues: the sudden interest of the Americans in our Muzzaffarabad region and the kidnapping of two Indians, one of them a top Bollywood heroine. More than a week ago, a 16-member crack team of American commandos arrived in Muzzaffarabad after obtaining necessary clearance from your office. They made no bones about their real intent: the capture of Amaso, whom they believed to be in the region. I am happy to announce that the Americans left last evening after satisfying themselves that their information about Amaso's presence in the region was incorrect."

"Do you believe that the American pullout is not a tactical decision?", the Foreign Secretary asked.

"I think the question is extremely valid. It may well be a tactical pullout. They don't send their men anywhere just like that. Their ongoing relationship with the Indians is a matter of concern to us. But what is more alarming is that they have focused one of their numerous spy satellites on Muzzaffarabad region which is sending real time data and imagery straight to Washington round the clock."

"What steps you have taken to ensure that our country's image is not sullied by certain irresponsible acts on the part of Kashmir Mujahideen outfits in this delicate period?"

"Brigadier Arif, who is in charge of Muzzaffarabad region, held a meeting with the leaders of Mujahideen outfits. Brigadier, you may like to brief the Foreign Secretary on that."

"Sir, I sensitized the Mujahideen leaders about certain operational do's and don'ts. I also made sure that they disperse to other parts of Kashmir and keep a low profile. The ISI Chief was already sagacious enough to completely revamp their communication network with such modern gadgets that are hard to be intercepted. And finally, I held a pre-dawn meeting in the CMO's room of the Army Hospital in Muzzaffarabad to maintain utmost secrecy," Brigadier Arif concluded.

The Foreign Secretary smiled at the last input. These military guys are innovative, he thought.

"When was the last time when we handed over to the Americans certain jihadis wanted by them? And how many?" The Foreign Secretary's question was directed to the Interior Secretary.

"It was more than five months ago when we handed over five of their wanted men. But that included one real big fish."

"I think the American whale needs some more fish. Make some efforts. But don't do anything drastic without the personal permission from the President himself." The Interior Secretary nodded and looked at his Joint Secretary colleague, who took notes. The Foreign Secretary then turned to the ISI Chief and said, "Now the second part of your presentation, the Bollywood heroine's kidnapping?"

"This case is rather interesting. The episode remains a whodunit mystery even for us. I have checked up with every Mujahideen group we are supporting in the Kashmir valley. All have flatly denied their involvement in the kidnapping."

"But I read in newspapers that the Lashkar-e-Toiba claimed responsibility for the act and none other than their spokesman, based in Muzzaffarabad, rang up newspaper offices in Srinagar for this. How very irresponsible!"

"We have questioned the LET spokesman. He said he never made any such statement and did not call up any newspaper offices in Srinagar. We have checked up telephone records and find his contention to be correct."

"So what does it mean? Is the LET involved or not?"

"My assessment is that the kidnappings bear hallmark signatures of the LET. It was a meticulously planned operation; so much so, that even we are not aware where the captives have been kept, if at all they are in Azad Kashmir. Unusually bad weather conditions in the region are an impediment for us for launching our own investigations into the kidnappings and sending foot patrols. The spokesman is right in his denial. I think the game is being played at much higher levels."

"What's the problem? Talk to the LET Chief."

"This leads us to another problem. The LET Chief is incommunicado for the past several weeks. His men have not approached us for money or weapons in the last month. I suspect these guys are up to something."

"What's your suspicion?"

"I have a feeling that the LET is forging newer alliances to acquire a global character and presence. Amaso seems to be their best bet. We have established LET's cooperation with the Amaso group in at least four major cases of drug running and arms deals.

"That's probably their newest source of funding. But I don't understand one thing."

"What?"

"If the LET is indeed involved in the heroine's kidnapping, which I believe it is, then can the Amaso angle be far behind? What can Amaso's interest in the heroine be? He used to be a womaniser decades ago. But you know how puritanical he has turned over the past few years."

"A pretty face can launch a thousand ships. You know that. Amaso, after all, is a human being, irrespective of his stature of demigod among the jihadis of the world."

The ISI Chief did not appear convinced by the Foreign Secretary's colourful observation.

"Okay gentlemen, we conclude this meeting here. Thank you all," the Foreign Secretary said. Everybody except the ISI Chief, the IB Chief and the Interior Secretary got up and left the room. The three officers had already been told to stay back for another round of discussions.

Haider called for more tea and started. "Now we come to the core part of this meeting. Actually, the National Security Advisor was to chair this meeting. However, you know he had to leave for Washington last night for urgent discussions with the State Department. The Americans have offered us old wine in a new bottle. And I must say the new bottle is attractive."

"It pertains to Amaso?" the ISI Chief asked.

"Absolutely right. They have told us that the American President is very keen on getting Amaso, dead or alive. Earlier, they were offering us things like massive economic aid, F16s and the like, but their latest offer is almost irresistible. I have discussed the matter with the President early this morning and he is quite upbeat about the American deal."

"What's the new deal?"

"They say that they will offer a civilian nuclear energy cooperation deal to us, like they have signed with India, despite our dismal record in the nuclear proliferation arena. Moreover, they have promised a Foreign Direct Investment of a hundred billion dollars spread over five years in core infrastructure areas like power, dams, expressways, ports, airports and irrigation. A hundred billion dollars of FDI is a hell of a lot for a developing nation like us. It can transform us into a superpower within the foreseeable future."

"All this in exchange for Amaso?"

"Yes."

"So, what are the ground rules?" the Interior Secretary asked.

"The ground rules are, first and foremost, keep a close watch on Amaso's movements. Strike when the iron is hot.

Take instructions from none other than the President on the Amaso issue. Most importantly, sanitise your respective departments and rid them off officers having sympathies with Amaso's group. The President agrees that this is a tall order but not insurmountable. If you don't want Pakistan to become a failed state and if you want to see your nation emerging as a superpower, even ten Amasos are expendable. Any questions?"

"Just one," the IB Chief spoke. "How do you know that the Americans have not made a similar or more lucrative offer to the Indians in nabbing Amaso? The Indians have the capability to launch lightning commando strikes in our part of Kashmir if they have specific information. They have a perfect alibi too for launching such an operation – the heroine's kidnapping. You know very well the capabilities of Inspector General Dashamlav of the Indian IB. You know he remained in Pakistan incognito for years and substantially harmed our nuclear weapons programme. He is believed to be in Kashmir. What are the ground rules for that, if any?"

"You are right. We don't know if the Americans have made a similar or more lucrative offer to the Indians in the context of Amaso. Actually, the Indian heroine's abduction could not have come at a worse time. The sooner this drama is over the better it will be for the state of Pakistan. Now let me turn to your concern about a possible limited military strike by India in Azad Kashmir. The President is personally monitoring the situation. That is why he has cancelled his trip to Saudi Arabia. As for your last query, there is one ground rule which is the mother of all rules under the circumstances."

"What's that?" the IB Chief asked.

"Get Amaso before Indians get him."

Mili and Dhruv had animated discussions for a good two hours before their scheduled meeting with Amaso. While transiting through the long corridor, they saw that the heavy snowfall was continuing and at least six men were busy in snow-clearing operations. They could make out that the workers' focus was to keep the driveway, the snowmobile parking shed and the roof of the bungalow clear of snow round the clock. Despite the unabated snowfall for the past two days, the entire bungalow complex was unobstructed.

Once inside the hall, they were instructed to sit on the mattresses where they had sat when they first met Amaso. The Supreme Leader appeared after about 20 minutes, with Mehmood Mian in tow. There were only these four people in the room. The security guards were outside the room. Javed was once again absent.

Amaso looked tired and pensive. "So, what have you decided?" he asked.

"Beggars cannot be choosers," Dhruv said, managing a broad smile on his face.

"You are not a beggar. Not even once have you begged me to spare your lives. You have maintained an amazing control over your faculties despite the worst of circumstances. I am well aware of that. I like people with this attitude."

"So set your ground rules."

"I believe in a level-playing field. Therefore, ground rules will be from both the sides. You will be free to seek amendments in the rules I lay down."

"Thank you very much. I really appreciate your generosity."

"You have to thank the weather, not me. Weather is our only binding force and an ally."

"An ally for us alright. But how is it an ally for you?"

Mehmood Mian frowned at the question that he found unnecessary. "You are exceeding your limits in asking questions, Mr Dhruv D Vyas," he said in a menacing tone.

Amaso raised his hand gently. "Relax, Mehmood Mian. He is inquisitive. Let me answer this question. It is obvious in any case and by now, we know he is not a dumb fellow. Okay, Mr Dhruv. I think that you know that I don't stay in one place for more than 24 hours. These are security imperatives. I am the most wanted man on earth. Individuals and governments can and will go to any extent to catch me, dead or alive. Still I have kept my organisation and myself afloat for years, only because I have genuine symapthisers and admirers, wherever I go. If I am staying here for longer than 24 hours and have time and inclination to listen to your stories, it is only because even my betrayers and enemies cannot conquer nature. This fury of the nature is my ally.

"Now coming to the ground rules: you will tell me a story. I am sure a writer of your calibre can quickly spin a yarn. In fact, you already must have done so. The only condition is that you should tell a story that has a twist. Because I like twists in the tales. You stop whenever you think the twist is coming and I will guess the twist. The rest we have already discussed."

"How many stories?"

"That depends on the weather. Because I will leave as soon as the weather clears up."

"Are you fond of cricket?"

"No. Nevertheless, I am aware that this game is a rage in this part of the world. But why do you ask that?"

"When two countries play cricket, the normal practice is to play a best of three or best of five match series. One-off matches are rare because one-off match does not do justice with the real test of the two teams' capabilities. So, I will request you to agree to a three-match series."

"It depends on you. You will have to conceive three stories quickly."

"What is the minimum time your local people say will take for the weather to clear up," this time Dhruv's query was directed at Mehmood Mian. Amaso quietly appreciated Dhruv's confidence building tactic. It was not too long ago when Mehmood Mian had growled at Dhruv.

"Weather is not going to clear up for four to five days. However, snow storms may stop within the next 48 hours. And the Supreme Leader cannot remain here for a minute longer after snow storms stop."

"Two days are more than enough for me to tell you three tales."

"Alright. So we agree to a three-match series, as you put it," Amaso said.

"Any other ground rules?"

"Yes and an important one. Before you start narrating your story, you will write down the twist in your tale on a piece of paper. We will keep this paper in a sealed envelope and open it after I have made my guess and you complete the story."

"But why make it so complicated?"

"Quick thinking is an integral part of the art of deception. You have a razor sharp intellect. Suppose I make the right guess about the twist in the tale. Still you can change the story at the last minute and win the match by cheating. This will eliminate the possibility of cheating."

"I beg to differ," Dhruv stuck to his guns. Mehmood Mian's eyebrows were again raised. He was not used to the sight of the Supreme Leader being confronted and challenged so often. Amaso looked at Dhruv questioningly.

"Let me explain my objection and I am sure you will come round to my view after hearing me out. Let's not have this envelope business. One, it will break the flow of the story.

Two, it casts a poor reflection on us and conveys a sense that we cannot have elementary trust in one another. Three and most important, I will not cheat against you and I know that you won't do the same to me. Then I come to the most important argument. If I were to be in possession of such extraordinary skills that I could pull wool over the eyes of a man like you by some last-minute quick thinking, then why should you grudge my victory? Don't you think that a fair man like you could concede me my due?"

Mili was convinced by Amaso's benign smile that Dhruv had won the point and Amaso's heart as well.

"You have a point there. Agreed. No envelope business. All you have to do is to stop at a near climax point and I will try to guess the climax. While I would be looking for a twist in the tale you will have the operational advantage of going for the double twist or even triple twist, thereby making my guess either completely redundant or correct only 50 per cent or 33 per cent."

"Any more ground rules?" Dhruv asked.

"Now the primary ground rule for you. If you accept it, I am ready for the contest," Amaso said.

"Please spell it out."

"None of your stories will touch on subjects like intelligence, espionage and terrorism."

"But why? You said you like thrillers."

"That's right. But a story can still be a thriller even if it does not relate to jihadis and spies."

Mili could sense trouble now. Dhruv suddenly looked unsure of himself.

Mehmood Mian was elated at his Supreme Leader's masterstroke. "I think I can make a suggestion to you, subject to the kind approval of the Supreme Leader. You accept defeat and beg for mercy. I can see the Supreme Leader likes you. He may accept your mercy petition." Mehmood Mian looked at Amaso, expecting a prompt approval.

Dhruv was furious. He was still collecting his thoughts.

Amaso waved his hand at Dhruv and said, "Relax. Let me tell you why I called it the primary ground rule. I have already told you that I am still not convinced about your real identity. The letter D in your name is a matter of worry for us. We are making all possible efforts to check your antecedents. Javed himself is on the job. The parentage you claim has been established. That is not all for us. We want to make sure that you are not an intelligence man. Unfortunately, for you, your sharp intellect has become your own enemy. It is easy for an intelligence man to cook up a cloak-and-dagger mystery and introduce twists, double twists and triple twists at will. On the other hand, if you are actually a literary man, it will not be difficult for you to weave a yarn on topics other than those forbidden by me. I want to be hundred percent sure of your identity and this is your only chance. You can take your time to decide on this but remember your life is on a short fuse. Weather will not remain your ally for long."

Mili had instinctively held Dhruv's hands by now. She was

trembling with fear. "Can we go to our room and come back after five minutes," she pleaded, her eyes moistened.

"By all means, Mohtarma. Take as much time as you want."

Dhruv liberated his hand with a jerk.

"I am ready, Mr Amaso."

"How dare you call our Supreme Leader by his name!" Mehmood Mian flared up.

Mili had just gone through two shocks in the span of a few seconds. First, Dhruv's confident acceptance of the mother of all ground rules and then Mehmood Mian's outburst, full of sycophancy.

"Shut up, Mehmood. Enough. He is a writer and therefore an artist, until proven otherwise. He can call me by my first name. I give you this license, Mr Dhruv. So you agree to my last ground rule?"

"Yes."

Mili whispered something in his ear but he declined. Obviously, she wanted to go to the room for consultations in privacy.

"When do you want me to start?"

"Whenever you wish."

"I want to start right now."

Amaso smiled and appreciated the man's confidence.

Mili could no longer control herself. She got up, held Dhruv by his arm and said to Amaso, "Excuse me sir, I want to take him out for one minute only. Can I?" He readily consented.

"Are you crazy? We haven't even discussed what story you are going to narrate. You should discuss it with me first." She said as soon as the two had gotten out of the room. The security guards did not disturb them and looked away.

Dhruv noticed that a man dismounted from a mule, handed over a thin envelope to a gun wielding man deployed in the porch, got back on his mule and galloped out of the premises. Dhruv was thankful to Mili for dragging him out of the room at such an important time. The security guard reacted promptly and dashed to the Supreme Leader. The guard did not stand one second more than required, handed over the sealed envelope to Amaso and came out, taking care not to disturb the VIP captives.

Dhruv was standing at a vantage point from where he could see what was going on inside. Amaso immediately read the single-page message that the envelope contained. He got up without delay. Mehmood Mian was already a picture of alertness and sitting like a kho-kho player to sprint at the word 'go'. The two retired to The Tiger's Den.

Another guard emerged from inside the hall they had been sitting all these days. They had not seen him so far. Nor did Dhruv have an idea where he came from. The guard walked straight to Dhruv and told him that it was better to talk inside and not expose themselves to extreme cold conditions any longer.

The two obeyed immediately. Dhruv understood in a flash the importance of this little incident. This was the secret of Amaso's success in keeping the world's security agencies at bay. He did not believe in scientific gadgets because each one of them left a trail. A trusted lieutenant, riding a mule or a pony to boot, never leaves a trail.

He knew that Amaso must have been getting dozens or scores of envelopes like this every day. This is how he keeps himself afloat and runs his jihadi organization worldwide. Getting sealed envelopes through human couriers must be his usual practice that may partly explain Amaso's fascination for envelopes, he told himself.

Mili was continuing to present her emotional arguments. She was too engrossed in explaining things to Dhruv to notice the man on the mule. Dhruv knew that they should not take their captors for granted and told her that it was time for them to get back.

"Don't worry. I am well prepared."

"Sure you want to start right away?" she asked as the door of The Tiger's Den opened and Amaso and Mehmood Mian walked out.

"Absolutely sure. There is no time to lose. Let's be done with this life and death contest. Wish me all the best."

"I wish you all the best, honey. Love you."

Reassured that Dhruv had become his usual confident self, Mili sat attentively on the mattress, waiting for the proceedings to start. Tea and sandwiches had already arrived.

Amaso suggested everyone have tea before starting the first match. Dhruv readily agreed.

"What is the title of your story?"

"Is the title necessary? Is it a ground rule?"

"Not at all. But I have always had a fascination for titles because I believe that the title reflects the calibre of the writer."

"I totally agree there. The title is '64 Squares'."

"Good title," Amaso said approvingly. "I think your story revolves around a game of chess."

"How can you say that?" Mili asked spontaneously, a rare occasion when she had put a question directly to Amaso.

He readily obliged her with an answer, "Because there are 64 squares on a chess board."

Mili's jaw dropped. Mehmood Mian was awe and admiration personified for the Supreme Leader's intelligence.

Dhruv knew he was up against a formidable challenger. Mili was reciting Hanuman Chalisa (a Hindu prayer) as Dhruv began the first match.

10

64 Squares

As he entered the club's car parking lot, he nearly missed a step. Probably a heart beat too.

He saw the familiar silhouetted figure in the dimly-lit parking lot and as he walked closer to her, she smiled. He was flummoxed. This was the third consecutive night he had seen her. Every time almost the same place, the same time and, of course, the same inviting smile.

Venkat boasted of having a quick mind. None could dispute this. After all, he was the chess champion of his multinational company! Yet he was puzzled. Why this young beauty should greet him with a smile? Is she a call girl? He dismissed the idea as soon as it flashed in his mind. He was 42 and women were familiar turf to him. Agreed that call girls could be very young and could have drop-dead looks, like this girl, but they did not have such x-ray eyes, he reminded himself. Moreover, call girls solicit while she never went beyond a smile.

He made up his mind to talk to her as he reached within handshaking distance.

"Hi!" he said. He deliberately kept the greeting as short as possible. After all, he was an accomplished chess player. He would open out slowly, size up the opposition and wait for the counter move.

"Hi" was the measured response from the girl.

He immediately realized that he would have to open out quickly or else the game would be over even before it could begin.

"I am Venkat. I am the chief of the HRD Division of Zedong International." He thought his official status at a famous multinational software company would widen the eyes of any young, educated girl. He soon realized he was wrong.

"Hi," she merely repeated, this time with a more seductive smile.

"Er, what is your name?"

"Lucy."

"Lucy what?"

"Lucy Santiago."

Venkat found himself up against an iron wall. Unfazed, he decided to deploy his long strike chessmen. "I have been seeing you here for past couple of days. What do you do? Are you in college?"

"I finished college last year. I have been working as a copy writer in an advertisement company here for the past three months."

His guess was correct. She was an educated young girl in her early twenties, though she could easily pass as a teenager. Just as he was thinking of how to carry the conversation forward, Lucy herself paved the way.

"You play very well," she said.

"Thanks. But where have you seen me playing? Are you a member of this club? I have never seen you in the chess room!"

"One doesn't play cricket in chess room. Does one?" she teased.

"Oh, I see. You saw me playing cricket. That must be last Sunday at the club ground. I thought you were talking of chess. I am the chess champion of my office. And mind you, Zedong International has 1200 employees in the city," he bragged.

"Of course, I was talking about cricket only. I hate chess."

"Why do you hate chess? It is such a gripping game."

"I hate all that which I don't understand."

Venkat was surprised, not so much by her over generalisation but by her being definitive about certain things at such a young age. He looked at her more closely. Not very tall, maybe just about 5'1'' but toxic eyes, voluptuous lips, beautiful face, long silky hair and a stunning figure. He had decided. He wanted her in his bed.

"Care for a coffee?"

"No, I am waiting for someone."

He wanted to say "Your boyfriend" but checked himself before the words could leap from his mouth.

"Maybe tomorrow, if you are free." He heard her saying. His heart had started pounding faster. Had he heard her correctly?

"I am in a hurry but we can have coffee tomorrow if you have time," she said, looking straight into his eyes.

"Here only? What time?"

"No, not here. At Black Rose restaurant tomorrow at 3 pm. Bye."

Venkat kept looking at her swinging hips as she trotted out of the parking lot.

Venkat puffed from his expensive cigarette, still not believing his good fortune. Beads of sweat were hanging on his forehead, though it was a winter afternoon. He looked at her, lying beside him in his bed and once again kissed her naked back and shoulders, this time lightly. Her words were still ringing in his mind. "I am a virgin," she had whispered into his ear as he was preparing to make forays into her; and she was right. She was indeed a virgin.

WAS.

Lucy had gone into a deep slumber. Venkat did not want to disturb her. Not yet. He lit another cigarette. He liked revisiting his moves and the opposition's counter moves after every chess game he won. It had taken him one full month of torrid courtship with a girl exactly half his age before he could successfully take her to his bed. He first kissed her a week after the courtship began. From then until now, he had to make do with kissing and caressing only. He was happy with the limited liberty Lucy had allowed him. He was careful not to cross the line, too much too early, for fear of losing her. He was patience incarnate. He knew that getting physical proximity to women was like going on a fishing expedition. You don't disturb the waters and just bide your time.

His time had come today. The fish had swallowed the bait, hook, line and sinker.

Venkat was single. He had never married. It was a conscious decision. He did not see the need for being tethered to one woman alone for his entire life when he could have new ones every week.

Lucy was different, but, unlike other girls, nay women, she never asked him for any favours. She was happy with her job and had declined his repeated offers for a job in Zedong International with a 300 percent hike.

As weeks flew by, Venkat was faced with the worst mid-life crisis. Lucy dominated his psyche as none had done before. He had had sex with her six or seven times thus far but, from his point of view, the relationship had gone far beyond carnal desires.

He noticed another departure that he unwittingly made from his usual style when he bedded Lucy three days ago. He wanted to use protection for the sake of Lucy. He was genuinely concerned that she might get pregnant, but Lucy declined.

He insisted, arguing that it was for her only he had suggested this. Her one-line reply shook him. She said, "It will rob me of my pleasure."

She was so clear in her thinking, he wondered. She could make a brilliant chess player. In fact, he floated the idea to her several times and offered his services as a coach. However, her position was unswerving from what she had told him at their first meeting in the club parking lot: that she hated chess.

The more Venkat saw of Lucy the more he was intoxicated by her. He was not unmindful of some seriously disturbing lacunae, which his chess games had always taught him to be wary of. Why is it that the opposition has made a move that means sure sacrifice of the pawn with no tactical benefit in sight? Why a bishop, a knight, or a rook has been sacrificed when it does not give advantage to the opposition one bit and the queen, the most potent weapon in chess, has still not been moved from its house?

A stage comes in a man's life when winning or the habit of winning does not make him happy anymore. Sometimes, he wants to take a break, sit back and analyse the things to understand not so much what moves he made, but what moves the opposition made or did not make, what moves the opposition was in with a chance to make but eventually did not make.

Therefore, after having sex with Lucy six or seven times, Venkat was in such a mind frame.

He did not have answers to many questions. Why Lucy fell for him? Was she in love with him? Why was she so mysterious? Why had she never told him about herself? What did he know about her except her mobile number, and the contours and curls and curves of her body that were carved on his psyche? Why had she never asked him about his own personal life? Why did she keep disappearing from his life suddenly for a day or two and remain incommunicado with her mobile phone switched off?

Probably the only thing she had ever enquired from him was about the photograph of a girl Lucy had found in Venkat's personal album. He dismissed it as an obvious female rivalry, where one beautiful woman cannot tolerate another beautiful woman in her midst. He simply told her that the girl in the photograph was Gita, with whom he had had no relations, except that she had come to seek his help as her coach in chess. Lucy had not put any questions to him after this.

Venkat was going through a painful churning process. He did not have any answers. He realised that he had only one question to ask her.

"Will you marry me?" Venkat asked Lucy that summer evening. He had taken her out to a quiet open air restaurant, which was never crowded as it was too expensive.

"Why do you want to marry me?" Lucy asked in a matter-of-fact tone, her eyes betraying no emotion.

"What do you mean why?" Venkat said irritatingly, his male ego hurt.

"I mean, why do you want to marry me when you are getting everything from me even otherwise?"

"Look, don't be stupid." Venkat purposely went on the offensive. "Sex is not everything. Is it? I want to give you status in the society as my legally wedded wife."

"Which means that you are thinking of poor me and you want to do me a favour?"

"Listen Lucy, I don't know what kind of mood you are in. Probably you are not well. You actually are looking sick. I have never seen these black rings under your eyes. And what is this bandage I have been seeing on your right hand ring finger for the last two days?"

She ignored his other remarks and focused on the last point of the question.

"I cut my finger while slicing tomatoes."

"Then what did you do? Did you see a doctor? Did you call me? You just wrapped your wound with a silly bandage," Venkat demanded to know as devoted husbands do.

"My wounds do not heal fast," was the terse reply he got from her.

Forty minutes after an intensive discussion, miles long questions from Venkat and inches long answers from Lucy, the issue was clinched. Venkat and Lucy were to get married on the following Monday, in court.

It was only Thursday. Venkat was in the seventh heaven. His friends told him he had never looked so happy before. He told them it was only because of one girl: Lucy. None had seen her or heard of her.

As for Venkat, he hardly had time for such niceties. He did not even have the photograph of Lucy to show to his colleagues because he had never photographed her. In any case, where was the time for all this? So much had to be done. The witnesses had to be arranged. The relevant documents had to be prepared.

It was getting impossible for Venkat to wait until Monday. The hands of the clock had suddenly become lead-coated. On Friday, Lucy said to him, WWML. This was a bilateral code conceived by Venkat. He would ask her WHEN WE MAKE LOVE, whenever he wanted sex.

First, Venkat was aghast. Here is a to-be-bride who is asking for sex two days before marriage. Then he realized that she was too young to be faulted.

Lucy, however, was not the one who would waste her breath for nothing. She repeated the code and Venkat politely refused.

"Not today darling, there are still so many loose strings to be tied."

Lucy murmured her acquiescence.

The next day, she again asked the codified question, WWML. A flabbergasted Venkat thought it wise to go ahead with it rather than avoiding it or else it gives wrong signals. That day, Lucy was at her vigorous best.

The next evening, she again put the same question and Venkat thought the best thing he could do was to say yes. He did not even remind her that their marriage was less than 24 hours away. Much to his surprise, she wanted an encore each time after the act, in which she had not participated physically or emotionally.

Venkat had to go through the motions thrice on Sunday evening.

On Monday morning, the day of the wedding, Venkat called Lucy on her mobile.

"Hi darling, hope everything is fine?"

"Yes, everything is fine. You have had me 24 times so far."

Venkat felt somebody had poured molten lead into his ear that was attached to the mobile. He paused and then heaved a sigh of relief when he did not get any more volleys from her. By now, he had adjusted to her black humour. He hung up after getting an assurance from her that she would reach his house at 9 o'clock sharp so that they can be at the court by ten o'clock.

It was already 9.10 on Monday morning. Still there was no sign of Lucy. He thought it prudent to wait, but there was no sign of her even at 9.30.

Venkat called her mobile. Just after the first ring, the call was rejected. "Network trouble, hell!" he muttered and re-dialled. She again rejected the call, after the very first ring.

He was very confused. Before he dialled her yet again, his mobile beeped. A message had come. He immediately opened the message, which said, "C my mail".

"Now, why the hell does she want me to check her mail at this time?" he thundered and chose not to reply.

Lucy had asked him twice before to check her email, saying that there were some problem in accessing the internet from her place.

He called her again. She rejected the call again. The same message flashed again on his mobile's screen: "C mail". Then another message came: "blackrosexyz1234@yahoo.com"

Then there was another message alert. "My password is 64 squares".

Venkat opened Lucy's mail but found no new message. He was again going to dial her number when he checked himself and chose to SMS her. "No new mail in ur inbox", he wrote.

"C DRAFT of blackrosexyz1234.yahoo.com" the reply came.

By now Venkat knew, it was something serious and not a prank. He cast aside his coat and tie, his briefcase and focused his mind on the computer screen. He typed the email id he was given and then wondered that she had never given this email id to him.

Like a robot, Venkat immediately typed the password "64 squares" and clicked on Draft. Lucy's text filled the computer screen.

"Venkat," the email began. The absence of words like "Dear" or "Darling" or even "Mr" was noticeable.

"You remember Gita..."

Venkat thought Lucy was referring to Bhagavad Gita, the Hindu scripture.

"I am talking about Gita, the beautiful girl, you mauled five years ago."

Venkat's brain was suddenly exploding with activity, making calculations like a super computer. The name Gita immediately registered. How could he forget such delicious feminine body he savoured so many times? Why is Lucy talking of Gita? Where is Gita?

"Gita was my elder sister. She was elder than me by five years. We were the only two children of our parents. I lost my father and mother before I was ten. Gita reared me as sister, mother and father. I can never forget that when I was 13 I was down with a mysterious disease. As part of the treatment, I had to be given blood. I became okay after the blood transfusion but since then I developed problems that started complicating by the day. .."

Venkat stopped reading. His mind was wandering. He was unable to focus. After a while, he resumed reading.

"My sister reached your city five years ago in search of a job. She was a very good chess player and was told that she could kill two birds with one stone if she could crack the code called Venkat of Zedong International. She was told that her search would finish at Venkat not only because he could get her a job in Zedong International but also because he was the most eligible bachelor in town.

"Gita was of course too simple to understand you or your chess moves. You asked her what she wanted to become and she told you that all that she wanted to do in life was two things. One, to win National Chess Championship and secondly to save her younger sister who was suffering from a dangerous disease.

"Within days, you were all over her. You were not satisfied by having her. Soon you had other ideas about her. You got her a job in your Zedong International saying that it was only for one year as it was against a temporary leave vacancy of an executive who had proceeded on maternity leave.

"You thought she did the job because it gave her a fat salary. She needed the money not for herself but for her ailing sister. You used her like a call girl. You used her not only to satisfy the lust of your own bosses but also the Minister. She did your bidding for about two years because she only believed that she was selling her body only to take care of her soul – me!

"The last straw on the camel's back came when you sent her to the Minister. She was your love. This is what you had professed to her thousands of times. Everybody, except Gita, knew that the Minister was debauch, a psychopath. But still you chose to serve her to him on a platter."

Now Venkat could have a sense of what was coming. His marriage with Lucy was just not going to take place. He could also sense that Lucy was up to something, but what exactly he had no idea. He also realized that Lucy had left no evidence of whatever she had done to him. He had no photograph of her. Even her name was most certainly not her real one because Gita's sister cannot be Lucy, a Christian name.

Then this weird way of conveying through email was not lost on him. This was not her usual email ID. Probably this was the first and last time she had used this email ID. Moreover, no mail was sent because he was reading a message from the Draft section. To top it all, his personal computer had been used for the entire operation. End result: no legally tenable evidence for the cyber police, in case he were to choose to go to them.

What was she up to? What had she done to him? He read on.

"The inevitable happened when Gita went to the Minister. He brutally cut her nipples, burned her breasts with cigarettes and bit her lips and cheeks as though he were sinking his teeth into an apple. He had her four times that night and the last time he shoved a wooden bar up her arse. The sadist ignored my sister's shrieks for help, which were silenced by the loud music emanating from his suite.

"Gita was shaken when she was released from the Minister's clutches. Not because her clothes were bloodstained, but because she had been mauled. Not just physically, but psychologically and spiritually too.

"The next two days were crucial for Gita. She pulled herself together and wrote everything, every slightest detail, in her diary. She put her diary in a packet, wrote my address and mailed it to me. Shortly afterwards, she jumped from the 22nd floor of the Zedong International building.

"I got the packet several days after Gita's death by which time she had already been cremated incognito. However, one most remarkable thing I noticed in Gita's diary was her admission that she had been used and sexually exploited by 64 men. She gave details of all the men who did her this outrage. Her diary also talked about her passion for chess and her love for me. I decided to destroy both.

"By my 20th birthday, I was told by my doctor that I had assumed the properties which I had been eagerly looking for."

Dhruv stopped here. Amaso had been listening to the tale intently. Mehmood Mian seemed to enjoy the story as well, particularly the minister's performance. Mili was confident that Dhruv was on the right track. She herself was clueless what the twist in the tale could be.

"So you are close to the twist part?" Amaso said.

"Yes. What is your guess?"

"It is clear that the girl is not going to marry Venkat. She is after Venkat for revenge. She is an AIDS victim and she is using the deadly disease as a weapon."

Dhruv was taken aback. Mili was worried.

"How could you figure it out? Did I drop too many hints about Lucy's disease?"

"I was alert. But you can definitely do better than this," Amaso spoke like his publisher-editor. Dhruv continued.

"Let me tell you I had contracted AIDS because of blood transfusion during my childhood. My sister tried to keep me afloat by expensive treatment, but could not.

"When I met you, or rather snared you in the club parking lot, I was already a full-blown AIDS case. When I disappeared from you during our courtship, I was busy chasing those bastards who were responsible for defiling my sister. It was not difficult because you men are easy conquests. And I am proud to announce to you that I have infected each of those 64 men, including the Minister, who defiled my sister."

Venkat nearly fell from his chair. It was check and mate.

Six months passed. Venkat's life had been devastated. His close friends, who were aware of the storm in his life, told him he had been through hell and it was time for him to come out of it. He corrected them with a one-liner: "No, I don't call it hell; I call it purgatory."

Venkat had become a transformed man. For the first two months, he was so scared that he went for HIV tests twice a week. Then he ceased to bother. He had become deeply religious, given up smoking, drinking and womanising. He had smashed his favourite bone china chess board which he had bought from London for 1500 pounds. He had literally used a hammer for destroying the chessboard and made sure that he turned the damned thing into 64 pieces.

One thing that did not change, and in fact grew in intensity with every passing day, was his love for Lucy. What an irony it was! He did not even know her real name. He took three months' leave from his office. During this period, he roamed around the city from early morning to late night, visited parks, markets, restaurants, hotels, bars, cinema halls and parking lots, looking for Lucy. However, she was not to be found.

Venkat had an innate feeling that Lucy was still alive. She was a daring girl and such girls don't commit suicide. He rejoined office and worked even more efficiently, though quietly. He decided to have force multipliers for searching Lucy. He engaged a private detective firm whose CEO was his friend. He paid a hefty amount in advance, despite the CEO's offer of free services. The brief he gave to his friend was simple: look for the girl in every private and government hospital in and around the city, keep surveillance on all diagnostic labs and chemist shops that sell medicines for AIDS patients.

The detective, Ravi, formed a team of ten of his best men and fanned them out all over the city. Blood banks and AIDS-related NGOs were also being regularly tapped. Months passed away and there was no trace of Lucy.

Six months after Lucy walked out on him, Venkat made an important decision. He set up a charitable trust called Gita Memorial Charitable Trust for Welfare of AIDS Victims. He mobilised his corporate network and his contacts in the government and made sure that the Trust was launched with a corpus fund of Rs 100 million. Of this, he had contributed Rs one crore from his personal account after selling a flat in Mumbai. The launch of the Trust was a mega media event and was covered extensively by every newspaper and television channel.

Venkat's profile had gone up by zillion miles. He acquired the image of a social activist, but he did not quit his job with Zedong International because he needed a source of sustained income for searching Lucy.

Almost eight months after he had engaged the services of the private detective firm, the breakthrough came. Ravi called up to say that his detectives had just learnt about a young girl patient with full-blown AIDS symptoms had been thrown out of a private hospital for non-payment of bills and a well-meaning senior citizen had got her admitted to a government hospital.

Within minutes, Venkat was seated in the office of the Medical Superintendent who welcomed him like a VVIP. The MS confirmed that a young woman had just been moved into an isolation chamber meant for last stage AIDS patients.

He said the woman was unconscious but he could see her from outside the glass chamber.

Venkat's heart came in his mouth when he saw Lucy lying still on the bed, gasping for breath. She looked like an apparition. If the Lucy of eight months ago was a sex siren, the Lucy lying on the hospital bed in front of him was like a rabies-struck dog.

Lucy was immediately shifted to a luxury room of a super-speciality hospital. For next one month, Venkat lived life with a single point agenda: Lucy had to be saved. He also made sure that Lucy does not come to know that she had been discovered by him and was being looked after by him at his expense. She had been shifted to special suite of the hospital. Ravi's wife Rekha, a well-educated housewife, had been roped in for this covert operation.

Rekha posed as a volunteer worker for an AIDS victims' NGO called Sacred Hearts and convinced her that the cash rich American NGO had taken her up as a test case for injecting hope among millions of AIDS patients worldwide. Venkat had even organized media coverage to that effect and a thick file of press clippings was given to Lucy by Rekha. The two women had become close friends.

As Lucy's condition improved with sustained quality treatment after a month, he embarked upon another project. He established contact with the Minister who had defiled Gita years ago. In his capacity as Urban Development Minister, he had good contacts with the builders' lobby.

Venkat obliged the Minister in so many ways that he was itching to do a big favour to Venkat. He told the Minister that he would take his help when the right time came.

It was three months now since Venkat had discovered Lucy. She was nearly back to her old self, though she still felt very weak and felt giddy after her now customary evening walks in the hospital garden. Ten days later would be their first wedding anniversary if Lucy had married Venkat on the promised date. It was now time to reveal him upon her.

That very night, Lucy was leafing through a magazine when the door opened. She was aghast at the sight of Venkat. He looked very different. As he came closer, she noticed the difference. The swagger and the flamboyance that used to ooze out of his persona had gone. He looked very calm and dignified. Rekha and Ravi followed. The last entrant was the biggest VIP of the hospital, R R Mirchandani, the owner of the Rs 1000-crore hospital.

"How are you feeling now, Lucy?" Venkat asked softly. She turned her face away. He placed a bouquet of choicest roses on her lap. She instantly threw it out of the window.

"Mr Mirchandani, please ask this man to leave my room immediately or else I will call the police." This was the second time she was seeing Mirchandani. She was surprised when the hospital owner had called on her about two months ago to inquire about her health. The hospital owner's courtesy call on her led Lucy to believe in Rekha's story.

"I am leaving but please hear me for 60 seconds."

"Okay your time starts now."

"I have only one thing to say. I know that I do not deserve your love. Hate me as much as you can. It will not deter me from continuing to love you. Just do one favour to me. Please forgive me. Take care."

Lucy was surprised that Venkat actually took less than 60 seconds and went away quietly. Rekha spent that night with Lucy and the two talked through the night. Rekha revealed her identity and narrated the entire story of Venkat's transformation in past one year.

"I can't believe it. A zebra can change his stripes but men like Venkat can never change."

"Then why do you think he has done all that for you if it is not for love?"

"There can be only one motive: revenge."

"Listen Lucy. You are at least ten years younger to me. Let me give you a free advice. No emotion in this world is stronger or nobler than love. A self-negating, motiveless love is like a divine fire that can instantaneously burn a million sins. By doubting Venkat's intentions and integrity, you are committing a crime against yourself and a sin against Venkat," Rekha said with fire in her eyes.

"Okay if you choose to be the Devil's advocate, please also explain the crime and sin part of the whole thing."

"It is a crime to be ever suspicious even when circumstantial evidences are glaringly pointing otherwise; it is a sin to deny some one the cathartic process that is his due.

I am leaving now and will not come back to see you unless you yourself want it. Nevertheless, don't worry about your treatment. Venkat will look after you until his last breath. He will do it not out of revenge but out of love. Goodbye."

"Rekha?"

"What's it?" She demanded to know from the door without bothering to look back.

"Can I see Venkat?"

"What?!"

Lucy repeated her question.

"When?"

"Right now. But you don't go please."

"Okay, you will have Venkat here in less than 60 seconds."

"How? Was it planned like that?" Lucy was again getting suspicious.

"Nothing is planned in life, baby. I am saying that because of my gut feeling. I am sure that Venkat and Ravi would not have left the hospital premises even for a minute. The man is in turmoil. Because of him, my husband too is in turmoil. Let me check."

She took out her mobile phone and dialled her husband's number. "Ravi, are you around? Can you come? Ya immediately. Of course with him."

Rekha was right. Lucy was looking at her wristwatch. Ravi entered the room on the 55th second and Venkat on the 57th. Venkat was looking miserable.

The husband-wife team stepped aside as Venkat walked slowly towards Lucy. She stretched out her hand, her eyes moistened. He grabbed the quivering hand and kissed it again and again. Ravi and Rekha were sobbing with joy.

"You did not sleep the whole night?" Lucy asked.

"I have not slept for the past 355 nights."

"What's this number 355?"

"You left me 355 days ago, you idiot."

Lucy embraced Venkat. Ravi and Rekha quietly stepped out.

Dhruv stopped again. Mili was visibly moved and increasingly appreciative of Dhruv's skills.

"Finished finally?" Amaso asked.

"No, I have stopped for you to guess the climax."

Now it was the turn of Amaso and Mehmood Mian to be shocked while Mili was rapturous.

"You mean a second twist or what you people call a double twist story?"

"Yes."

For the first time, Dhruv and Mili saw Amaso running his fingers through his flowing beard, a clear sign of puzzlement.

"I really can't guess the second twist, though I have rightly guessed the first one."

"In case you choose not to guess the second twist and if your first one was guessed right, we split points fifty fifty. So, if one story has ten points, we will end the first round with equal honours."

"I guess that should be so."

"But you still have an option to guess. What do you lose in guessing wrong? After all, there are two more stories to follow."

"I hate to walk on a shaky ground and you have put me there. The way you have changed gears and lifted the story from revenge theme to love theme is truly remarkable. That in itself is thrilling. I would much rather accept my defeat in being unable to guess your second twist instead of firing aimlessly. Go ahead. I am keen to know the climax."

"As you say Mr Connoisseur," Dhruv resumed after gulping down another glass of water.

Venkat and Lucy talked for hours. Rekha and Ravi had left with a promise of coming back with home cooked lunch for the four of them.

"When are you taking me home?" Lucy asked.

"Nine days later."

"I am not going to die before marrying you, unless you have changed your mind now."

Venkat gave her a gentle slap. "Who is allowing you to die?"

"Are you taking over the powers of the God?"

"I dare not. But the final script of this drama is yet to be written," he said with a grave face.

"What happened? Is everything all right? What about you? Are you all right? You also must have contracted AIDS virus by now?" Lucy's voice began trembling.

"Don't worry. Everything is all right. Everything will be okay. Gods can't be so cruel to me."

"You are hiding something from me."

"No, I am not. I owe you a debt. And the repayment time is approaching."

Days flew by. Lucy surprised medical experts with her stupendous recovery. She had started looking nearly as normal as she was a year before. She was alone in her room hardly for a minute. Scores of new visitors, all friends and well-wishers of Venkat, came to see her and brought flowers. Her hospital room resembled a garden.

Rekha was doting like an elder sister. She had replaced Gita as far as Lucy was concerned. She had started spending the night in Lucy's room despite her remonstrations. Lucy pleaded with her not to ignore her own family for her sake but Rekha rejected the protests saying that Lucy was her family. Lucy was overwhelmed. What more one could wish in life! She was waiting for Venkat's Day number 365 when he had promised to take her home. That day was still 72 hours away.

As she started counting hours, Venkat's appearances in the hospital became briefer. She was concerned about Venkat's schedule that had suddenly become busy. However, she was no longer suspicious.

On Day 364, Venkat came with a team of lawyers and a briefcase full of legal documents.

"What's all this?"

Wagle, the leader of the lawyers' team, explained: "Madam, these are some property transfer papers. You are required to put your signatures."

"What property papers. I don't own any property."

"You may not own any property as of this minute. But you are going to be the sole owner of properties worth Rs 100 million which Mr Venkat owns and is now transferring them in your name."

Lucy was stunned. "But I don't want to. Why are you doing all this Venkat?"

"Listen, you are wasting precious time. I told you I have no time for the next 24 hours. After that, every second in my life is yours. There are many more documents after the property papers. So be a doll and please hurry up," Venkat chided.

Lucy kept on signing for the next ten minutes as lawyers turned pages after pages.

Then Wagle took out another set of document.

"What's that?"

"You have been nominated the Executive Chairperson of the Gita Memorial Trust for Welfare of Aids Victims. Its corpus started with Rs 100 million. Now it has swelled to Rs 500 million. You will be the sole power to sanction all money withdrawals."

"And who has nominated me to this post?"

"The Board of Trustees headed by Mr Venkat."

Lucy was busy for the next five minutes.

Finally, Wagle pulled out another set of documents.

"Now what is this for?"

"This one says that you accept Mr Venkat as your legally wedded husband one month from now."

"I refuse to sign this document."

Venkat went pale. He was struck by deja vu.

"You don't want to marry me?"

"I want to marry you tomorrow as you had promised, not one month later," Lucy said giving Venkat a tight hug.

"You made me faint nearly. Of course, we are getting married tomorrow. It will be a proper Hindu marriage. But this document is for registration of the marriage for which a month's notice has to be given in advance to the court."

Lucy took seconds to sign this document.

Venkat thanked Wagle and his team and asked them to wait for him outside. He kissed her passionately and said, "I won't be able to see you till tomorrow morning. But do have a look at tomorrow's newspapers."

Lucy did not know whether she was puzzled or apprehensive.

As he stepped out of the hospital and took leave from Wagle and his team, Venkat dialled a number from his mobile. The man on the other side received the call warmly. "Ya Presidential suite, Hotel Meridian. Top Floor. At 7 pm sharp. The suite will be open. Just enter and enjoy. I will join you around 9 after finishing my work. Leave a message for me at the reception after you are through."

Around 9.30 pm, Venkat walked up to the Reception of Hotel Meridian. "Is the honourable Urban Development Minister staying in this hotel?"

"Yes sir, he is in the Presidential Suite?"

"Er, would you know whether he is alone or busy with some meetings?"

The reception clerk managed to suppress a smile. "I am afraid, he is not alone."

"Okay then, I will come in the morning. He must be busy in some official meetings."

"Wait for a moment, sir. I think there is some message from the Minister for one Mr Venkat."

"I am Venkat."

"The Minister is waiting for you. In fact he has inquired twice about you in past ten minutes."

"Thanks. Can you send a waiter with me because the Minister may not like to wait for placing an order?"

"Sure sir."

The waiter took Venkat towards the elevator. "Let's take the stairs. The Presidential Suite must be on the first floor."

The waiter smiled at Venkat's ignorance and politely said, "No sir, it is on top floor."

Venkat pressed the Presidential Suite buzzer. As per the script, a half-naked young girl swung the door open. She was drunk. The waiter's eyes nearly popped out when he saw two bare-breasted beautiful girls lying in bed with the Minister.

The Minister was too drunk to notice the waiter who quickly ran out of the room. Venkat signaled to the girls. They quickly picked up their clothes and went to the adjoining room of the suite.

"I hope the girls looked after you well."

"Very well. Where do you get such gems from?"

"I think I must thank them."

"Ya, ya. You must.You must." The Minister could barely speak.

"But your glass is empty. Let me fix you a drink first."

"Oh thank you very much. You are so nice."

After handing him his drink, Venkat went to the girls' room.

"How many pegs you have given him?"

"Lost count sir. He drinks like fish. Must have consumed one full bottle by now," said a 25-year-old girl who was the eldest among the three.

"But sir, he is very cruel. See this, "the 20-something girl showed her cut and bruised breasts. The third one bared her bottom, which the Minister had torched with cigarette butts.

Venkat pulled out three wads of thousand rupee notes. This is Rs one lakh each for you.

"Thank you sir. But we would not come back again to this beast even if you were to pay us double the amount."

"Don't worry. That will not happen. But do remember your final part of the script after which each of you will be given the rest of Rs two lakh each."

"Two lakh more for each of us? That you did not tell us. We will be willing to come back again whenever you want, even for this animal. For you yourself, we will not charge you anything."

"That won't be required. But remember your final roles."

"We will, sir."

"Now you can go home. Rememeber you have to attract as much public attention as possible while you are passing through the corridors, the lift and the lobby."

"In any case we will chat loudly after drinking so much."

"So you also had a shot?" the Minister asked fiendishly.

Venkat displayed a synthetic smile.

"So what proposal you have brought?"

Venkat poured en extra large drink for the Minister and said, "I have an NRI builder friend. He wants to invest in real estate markets here. He is interested in making things like chains of shopping malls, multiplexes, luxury residential apartments and office complexes at prime locations. For that, he needs your help. He is willing to pay a good price but he wants that you attach wheels to the files."

"How much money he wants to invest?"

"One billion dollars in the next 12 months," Venkat saw the minister's eyes widening. "Your share will be Rs 1000 million, whether you take it cash in Dubai or get it credited to your Swiss account. But the files must move fast."

Venkat poured another stiff one for the Minister.

"For this much amount, I will make the files fly. He will get the necessary approvals within a week."

"No, he wants it faster."

"He seems to be a man in hurry. How much faster?"

"He wants all necessary approvals in 48 hours flat. And he is ready to pay you double the amount."

"You mean Rs 2000 million?"

"Ya," Venkat said and this time poured a double extra large.

The Minister gulped it down in one go. Venkat could see the Minister's head was spinning. He grabed the opportunity.

"I think it is getting stuffy in the room. Let's go out and walk in the corridor. You will feel better."

"You are right. Let's go."

Venkat took him by the hand and started talking loudly. Waiters and housekeeping staff members covered their noses as they passed by the drunken Minister. Venkat took him to the far end of the corridor where a lot of construction activity had been taking place for past one week from morning to evening. The engineers were putting up two more lifts. While one was installed, the other was expected to be installed in the next three or four days. The shaft had already been dug out and the entrance was blocked by wooden bars.

"What is the name of this friend of yours?"

"That would not register to you. I will tell you the name which should ring a bell."

"What name?" The minister could barely walk now. He had already come close to the dug up lift shaft that somehow had been left open tonight.

"He is the brother of Gita."

"Who is Gita?"

"You don't remember that young girl whom you enjoyed the whole night?"

"The same girl who had committed suicide?"

"Ya, the same girl."

The Minister got a jolt. "But why do you put me to the brother of such a girl?"

"How does that matter to you? You be bothered about your money."

"Who will give the money? You or someone else?"

"Someone else."

"Who? Where?"

"Gita, who is up there," Venkat signaled his finger skyward. "But for going up there, you have to first go downstairs." He shoved the Minister into the shaft. The drunken man fell like a stone and landed 26 stories below with a loud thud.

Venkat quietly took the stairs down and took a lift to the lobby from two floors below.

Lucy could not have missed the news. All newspapers published the news of how the Urban Development Minister had fallen to his death in a highly inebriated condition. All the papers carried photographs of the fiend who had defiled Gita. TV news channels were going live in their morning news editions, giving juicy details of the Minister's revelries. Three call girls, in fact, went to the extent of giving bytes (with their faces blacked out, of course) to TV reporters what a degraded beast the Minister was and had consumed more than a bottle of scotch. Then there were formal interviews with a hotel waiter who saw the Minister in compromising situation with naked girls in the Presidential suite, a housekeeping staff who saw the Minister going to the lift area in an inebriated condition.

The government was hugely embarrassed by the scandal. The Opposition had already started gunning for the government on the issue. The Home Minister personally instructed the Police Chief to hush up the matter quickly and close the case file as an accident.

"Let's go home," Venkat said as he entered Lucy's room alone with a bunch of flowers.

"So that was the debt you owed to me?"

"Yes. Will you marry me? Now."

Lucy hugged him. Her tears drenched his shirt.

"So what is the score?" Mili asked Amaso, as Dhruv ended.

"I think Mister Dhruv was right. We split honours equally. If one story has ten points, we end the first round 5-5. You people go and have some rest. We meet at dinner time again, story or no story."

11

A Game of Chess

Mili wasted no time in cozying up to Dhruv the moment they reached their room.

"It was an absorbing story indeed."

"I don't make much of it. You would have liked it because it had all the usual themes – love, sex, revenge, murder."

"On the contrary, I liked it because, as Amaso said, you successfully managed to change the tone and tenor of the story from a revenge drama to a romance. This man Amaso is too sharp. How could he figure out that the heroine was suffering from AIDS?"

"That's why he is the Supreme Leader of the world's jihadis. As a Hindi proverb goes, he can count the feathers of a flying bird."

"What's your next story?"

"I have a rough picture in my mind but it is yet to be worked upon."

"Give me the broad outline. I may help you there."

"I don't think it is not going to work that way. Fiction is essentially an individualistic work. Just as two human fingerprints cannot be alike, two human brains also cannot be on the same creative wavelength."

"Why are you so secretive? Hope you have nothing to do with intelligence agencies?"

Dhruv gave her a sharp look, got up from the bed and sat on a chair. Mili followed him.

"Don't be upset with my question. I just asked it."

"Your stupid questions like this can have our throats slit. Can't you see how concerned he is about the possibility of my being an intelligence agent? First, I am not an intelligence agent. Even if I were, you are committing a grave mistake by putting me that question because it indicates that you can take an enemy's bait hook, line and sinker. It shows that you faithfully believe what Amaso told us that he is getting our room debugged."

Mili's eyes widened. "You mean we continue to be under surveillance despite Amaso's assurance to the contrary?"

"I don't mean anything. The rule of thumb is that one should never lower one's guard, least of all in a situation like this."

"I see your point. I am sorry." Mili sat on the floor and put her head in Dhruv's lap. It was by sheer reflex action that Dhruv's fingers were stroking her hair.

Luckily, for them, the storm still showed no signs of subsiding.

"Tell me something I never asked you so far. Why did you come to the Jannat on that day?" Mili asked, continuing to be half on the floor and half in Dhruv's lap.

"I had come to see Milind Kumar."

"Milind Kumar? What for?"

"We are old school friends and studied together from class five till we finished college."

"But you look older than him."

"That's because he is in show business. I am not. Otherwise, we are same age – 35."

"And what do you discuss when you two meet?" Girls? Money? Cricket? Or films?"

"None. That day he had called me specifically for rewriting the screenplay for the movie which you two were shooting in Kashmir."

"But how can he decide on rewriting the screenplay? That is Bhimani's decision."

"Then you don't know Milind Kumar. He is a perfectionist. If he gets involved in a film project, he gives two hundred per cent. He is conscious of the fact that the higher the climb, the harder the fall. He immerses himself completely in the film he is doing. That is why you see him doing barely one film per year. But there has hardly been a Milind Kumar film which does not do well in the box office."

"Now you will be rewriting the screenplay for this film?"

"I don't know. Milind Kumar is keen that I make my debut in the film industry. I am not averse either but it is a new field for me. I will be glad to do film screenplays provided my literary creativity is not compromised."

There was a knock on the door. It was opened by a man who asked, without entering the room, "The Supreme Leader wants to know whether you would be ready for the dinner meeting half an hour later?"

The two looked at each other and said in unison, "Yes."

Amaso was looking much more relieved and cheerful than he had been in the past two days. There was another change. Javed had returned to share the mattress with Mehmood Mian. The fourth mattress was still vacant.

Dhruv wondered whether there was any purpose behind having the fourth mattress in the room apart from the appearance of symmetry.

It was a confident Javed who initiated the evening's discussion. "So you have managed to draw level with the Supreme Leader so far! Are you ready with the second story?"

"I am afraid not. I will have to think through the night. I should have a story tomorrow morning. What is the news on the weather front?"

"Luckily for you, no respite expected in the next 48 hours."

"Do you play chess?" This was Amaso's voice.

"I used to play once upon a time, but no longer. Hardly any time for it. It is a very time consuming game."

"I like the game very much. It reminds me so much of life itself. How about a game of chess?"

"Now?"

"Right now."

"They don't know how to play chess?" Dhruv asked puzzled, pointing towards Mehmood Mian and Javed.

"They do, but I would like to play with you. I am sure you must be a good chess player."

"How can you say that?"

"Because you have a head on your shoulders, because you use your brains. Anybody who is brainy is potentially a good player of chess."

"You are right. I used to be champion of my college club. But I have not played for years."

"Neither have I. Aren't we, both of us, doing weird things perhaps for the first and last time in our respective lives? So why not do another weird thing," Amaso prodded.

"With stakes?"

"I leave that to you."

"Okay let's play only one game of chess without stakes."

Within minutes, the two adversaries were poring over a marble chessboard between them.

Dhruv wanted to play it safe and resorted to Sicilian defence. Amaso, on the other hand, was aggressive and deployed his pieces quickly and strategically. When Amaso castled, Dhruv noticed how quickly and close the enemy had come, barely five minutes into the game.

"This castling which you did just now is a new idea added to chess about four hundred years ago. It is aimed at consolidating the King's position. Do you know that once upon a time, the king could be captured in the game of chess as it was played then?"

"Really?" Amaso said, quickly removing Dhruv's rook.

Unfazed, Dhruv deployed his Queen and threatened Amaso's rook and knight.

"This is one piece which has the most interesting history," Dhruv said. "Over the ages, it has been variously called as ˜minister" or ˜general". Do you know that nowadays when you play chess and lose your Queen, you feel that you have lost your most important weapon? But till about 500 years ago, the queen moved only one square diagonally and thus was the weakest piece."

"I did not know that. But do you know that you have just lost your most important piece?" Amaso said, moving his knight and placed it such that it threatened both the King and the Queen.

Dhruv was speechless. Mili thanked their stars that Dhruv had not linked the game of chess to their freedom.

Two moves later, Amaso said, "Now let me tell you something I know about this five thousand year old game on earth. It is common knowledge that the name "chess" is derived from the Persian word "shah" that means "king". Do you know that the expression "checkmate" is derived from the Persian 'shah mat', meaning 'the king is dead'. Check and mate.

Dhruv was stunned. He had lost the game in 18 minutes flat. He did not recall if he ever fell to such nadir during his college days.

Amaso did not gloat over his facile victory. He ordered removal of the chessboard. He did not discuss the game of chess after that. Dhruv was sure that there was a greater design behind Amaso's move.

The head cook announced that the dinner had been set and the five people shifted to the dining table. The dinner proved to be stormy.

Dhruv set the ball rolling when he surprised Amaso with a frank question.

"Why do you have double standards vis a vis America? Love your money but hate your culture – that kind of a thing?"

Mehmood Mian was visibly furious with this impertinence. However, he was restrained after Amaso had chastised him last time. Javed and Mili were equally tense, though for different reasons.

Amaso was unruffled. So was Dhruv. The two protagonists were already enjoying a very unusual chemistry. What is more, the two were innately aware of it. Dhruv knew he could get away with asking tough questions. Amaso took it as one long and extended interview the like of which he had given to many western journalists. He suspected Dhruv to be an intelligence mole but he had a feeling that apart from that, Dhruv had as much finesse in espionage, strategic affairs, diplomacy and the art of articulation: all the qualities found in a good journalist. Perhaps, somewhere in Amaso's heart of his hearts there was an irrational conviction that not a word of what he was saying to Dhruv was going to go waste. He also felt that Dhruv might well be a flagbearer among all his publicists across the world.

"Quite an angry question for a start, eh?" was how Amaso reacted.

Dhruv was mature enough not to repeat his more dangerous questions. He treated such questions like a game of roulette – luck or no luck. His patience brought rewards in this context. Dhruv's piercing question prodded Amaso and brought out his best, not unlike a cornered tiger.

"I will give you an example of these Americans. A real incident took place in Abu Ghraib prison in Iraq in 2005. Which means two years after the US invaded and occupied Iraq," Amaso's voice dragged in pain as he spoke the last words.

Dinner had become a by-product. This conversation, this Q & A session, was keeping the three onlookers on the edge of their seats.

"A junior American official had hung an Iraqi citizen upside down in one of the many soundproof cells of Abu Ghraib prison. The young hapless man did not have a shred of cloth on his body. He had been among the six Iraqi taxi drivers picked by the Americans on suspicion of being a Saddam Hussein loyalist.

"The pro-democracy American, born and brought up in a free society, could not tolerate the sight of a man who dared to look straight into his eyes while answering his most stupid questions. That is why this treatment for the Iraqi. The American officer beat him black and blue with every ounce of physical brutality at his command.

"He was interrogating the upside down hung man for more investigation leads. He beat him up for more than half an hour. He had been turned into a punching bag at least ten minutes ago but the American thought that the smart Iraqi was playacting. So he continued with his job. He would have continued for another one hour had his mobile phone not buzzed.

"It was his immediate boss on the line who wanted him at another prison for performing a similar yeoman's service to the great American nation. The officer administered a final kick to the human punching bag, locked the cell with his personal key and went to address the call of duty in another city in Iraq.

"Three days later, while still away from Baghdad, the officer remembered that he had a detainee in his personal cell. He ran to his car and drove like mad to Baghdad. Not because he was worried, that something might have happened to the man. His only point of worry was whether somebody had a duplicate key of that cell.

"Fortunately for the American officer, nobody had a duplicate key. His movements were suddenly relaxed when he saw the cell still locked. He turned in the key and entered. It was a great human gesture on his part to remember to restore the young prisoner to his correct position. Though he checked the pulse, there was no need for that. Only one in a million could survive extreme tortures of this kind and the young lad was not in that rare category.

"The American officer spread out the body on the floor, lit a cigarette, and called a girl friend from his mobile. Just when he was about to stub out his cigarette, a car screeched to a halt outside the cell and a sexy kitten rushed in. The well endowed woman kissed the officer passionately for several minutes before asking him: "What is the problem? You seemed quite worried. Can I help?"

""Can we have sex?"

""Okay."

"The girl had so far not even bothered to look at the body lying feet away from her. Here she was. Her legs apart, close to a body whose legs had been pushed apart in circumstances which in no way gave pleasure."

Dhruv and Mili had long before stopped eating dinner. Their fists were clenched. The reactions of Mehmood Mian and Javed, who must have been aware of the Abu Ghraib torture story, were well understandable.

"And mind you, this is no fiction. This is the story as reported by the American media itself. The man and his woman were proceeded against. A nineteen year old man is hung upside down, beaten mercilessly with sticks, hands, and kicks, and made to die a dog's death three days later just because the American god forgot about his victim. You can check the veracity of this story from the annals of the Iraq War II dossier. There may be some discrepancies because stories like these graduate into myth in no time. One such myth creates a thousand jihadis.

"This is what is happening in Iraq and Afghanistan today. This is what is going to happen in many theaters of jihad across the world, including in Europe and the Americas. That young man never killed even a flea and, therefore, was useless for the cause of jihad when he was alive. After his death, he became a pivot of jihad in Iraq. More than a hundred Americans were killed after this incident.

"Now to come back to your question. We never initially hated Americans; they made us hate them. It's Newton's Third Law of Motion which gets invoked in this 'Us And Them' relationship – for each and every action, there is an equal and opposite reaction."

Dhruv came up with another bizarre question. "Why don't you divide territories and have a sort of a no-war pact instead of being at each other's throat all the time?"

"I see nothing like that happening. Not in this new age of jihad."

"It is workable. When you realize that you can neither completely wipe out each other nor convert each other to your respective philosophy, the best option is to co-habit and co-exist."

"We want to co-habit and co-exist. But America will not allow that to happen."

"Why do you blame America after you razed their World Trade Towers to the ground?"

"They reaped what they sowed."

"What they sowed?"

"You don't know?"

"I would like to know from you what the Americans sowed against themselves."

"Three things. First, since 1991, the US has been occupying the lands of Islam in the holiest of places: the Arabian Peninsula. They have turned its bases in the Peninsula into a spearhead through which they fight the neighbouring Muslim people. Second, there is their naked aggression against Iraq, the strongest Arab state, and one which has the world's second largest proven oil and gas resources. Third, is the Americans' real strategic aim of helping and serving the Jews' petty state called Israel. Washington's basic endeavour is to control all important States of the region like Iraq, Saudi Arabia, Egypt and Sudan and turn them into paper statelets which will guarantee Israel's survival and the continuation of the brutal crusade occupation in the Arabian Peninsula."

"But I still maintain that you should arrive at some sort of understanding with the Americans and implement the principle of live and let live."

"You are entitled to your opinion though I don't know why you are so insistent on this point of view."

"Because if there were division of territories, you would not have to receive messages from human couriers on mule back."

Amaso looked at Mehmood Mian. The latter looked so furious that he would serve Dhruv's head to his master on a platter instantaneously, if only the master were to give a signal.

"This is a typical intelligence act you indulged in – snooping around. But let me tell you, I appear more convinced now that you are not an intelligence guy."

"What makes you feel that now?"

"Because no intelligence spy would be foolhardy enough to trumpet an important observation like this."

"What more I have to do to convince you one hundred percent that I am not an intelligence guy?"

"You have to tell me two more stories. We begin Round Two tomorrow morning."

As usual, everybody began the day with a thorough review of the weather. The only relevant question was whether the bad weather would last two more stories. The consensus was that the weather was likely to remain both sides' ally for the next 48 hours at least.

"What is the title of this story?" Amaso was genuinely curious. For him the title of the story mattered as much as winning or losing the toss in a day-night one-day cricket match.

"The title of the story is literally borrowed from you."

"That's heartening to note. I hope that you don't forget to write this."

"I will be able to do so only when we reach home alive," Dhruv said.

He realized that Amaso and company had chosen not to react to Dhruv's remark. He knew he had unwittingly breached the unwritten code of conduct in the present predicament: that he should earn his freedom, not beg it. Making such remarks was a sign of being unsure and should be avoided, he told himself.

Then Dhruv remembered Amaso's question about the title of his next story. "You had, during one of our conversations, used a phrase pregnant with all kinds of meanings. You put it in any condition, against any backdrop, with any characters and the phrase has a new meaning. You had mentioned how even a white bird had a black shadow. That is the title: "White Bird, Black Shadow". It is for you and the posterity to decide how well or badly I have treated the subject. So here I go."

12

White Bird, Black Shadow

Dr Braham Prakash was a harried man. He was urgently required to be with his father but could not do so. His office phones had not stopped ringing ever since the fresh post mortem case had arrived in the morning. The phone calls had started coming as soon as the dead body of an old man was brought to the hospital and the men accompanying it demanded quick action.

The old man appeared aristocratic. The body had turned blue. Apparently, he had been poisoned.

The same caller called repeatedly and appeared confused. The first time, he asked whether the body had been received and how soon Dr Braham Prakash would be conducting the post mortem. When the doctor demanded to know the caller's identity, he hung up.

Ten minutes later, the caller phoned again, apologised for severance of the phone connection and blamed it on "network trouble", identified himself as one Suresh Ram and asked about the doctor's prima facie findings. Braham

Prakash politely told him that he was yet to conduct the post mortem.

While he was busy poring over his father's radiological test reports, the same man was once again on the line. The doctor gave standing instructions to his staff that he was not available to the man called Suresh Ram.

Just when he was about to rush out to meet his father, a strange looking man entered. He held a small towel in his hand with which he was intermittently wiping his face. Seeing a man perspiring in December when New Delhi was reeling under a cold spell was unusual.

"Hello Dr Braham Prakash. I am Suresh Ram."

"What do you want?"

"The post mortem report. And you should write that the old man died of natural death."

Before the doctor could evict the man and threaten to call the police, he noticed that the man had a small revolver hidden in his towel.

"Please sit down. I will not harm you as long as we talk like gentlemen," the unwanted visitor said, while making himself comfortable in a chair. The revolver was no longer visible in the folds of the towel.

"The old man was my father. I poisoned him. It was a slow poison that I had been personally administering him over the past several weeks. To cut a long tale short, the old man was worth tens of millions. I had to devise a way to incapacitate him mentally after I discovered two months ago that he was consulting lawyers to prepare a new will to transfer his entire businesses and properties to my younger brother. I did not mind my only brother to get his due. How could I tolerate an unfair deal and become a pauper in my fiftieth year? Can you get me some water please?"

Braham Prakash knew he had no option. Moreover, he wanted to be through with this psychotic character as soon as possible to be with his father.

The visitor quickly emptied the glass, cleared his throat and began as though he were addressing the nation.

"I did not want to kill him. My limited goal was to destabilise him mentally so that the new will could not be prepared. I conducted intensive research on poisons. In fact, as a law student I had written a dissertation on "Poisons and the Law". That paper was published in a leading law journal of London and I was encouraged by my professors to hone my academic skills further. My father's business empire was booming and he was fond of me then. Where was I?"

Braham Prakash was now convinced that the man was insane. Or probably it was Suresh Ram's tactic in order to command an undivided attention to his monologue. "You were talking about your limited goal to mentally destabilise your father."

"Thanks. I shortlisted half a dozen slow poisons. Let me not waste your time in going into the technical details of these poisons. I selected one whose properties were rather peculiar: it will work on the target slowly but effectively, give him hallucinations, weaken his memory and, over sustained usage, lead to an irreversible damage to the brain. That's precisely what I wanted; nothing more, nothing less.

"But there was a damned rider. One of the properties of this poison was that a slight overdose, particularly on a 60-plus old man with cardiac trouble and high blood pressure, could be fatal. As long as the man was alive there would be no discernible effect of the poison, but in case of death the body would start turning blue four to six hours after death.

"The old boy fitted the bill as far as the warnings were concerned. He had had a heart attack five years ago and had been hypertensive for decades. I was encouraged by the controlled results of my experiments. Therefore, I continued. Even the best of his lawyer friends did not agree to his repeated demands to draft a new will and advised him to wait until his health had improved.

"Ever since I started my experiment, I made it a point to meet my father before he retired for the night and then first thing in the morning. I would also look him up once in the middle of the night. I took all precautions just in case the old boy were to pop off in the middle of the night, turn blue by the morning and put me into trouble.

"The inevitable drama took place this morning. I could not take any of my usual precautions because I had to go for an important cocktail dinner that continued well past midnight. I overslept. I was woken up by my younger brother – I forgot to tell you we are a joint family – who told me dad was not breathing and he had called in the family doctor. The doctor arrived within minutes, examined dad and concluded that he was no longer alive. He also said he saw some symptoms of poisoning and advised us to get a post mortem done.

"I rubbished the idea, citing Hindu reservations in cremating a dissected body but by that time things had gotten out of hand. His lawyer friends supported the doctor's point of view and I could not oppose the post mortem any longer without attracting suspicion.

"That's why I am here. I want the damn thing over before the poison starts making its manifestations." Suresh Ram stopped but kept his dagger-like gaze fixed at Braham Prakash.

"The manifestations are already there. The death must have taken at least six to seven hours ago."

"It doesn't matter. Give me a favourable report and I will pay you your weight in gold. I have taken so much of your time and not hidden anything from you because I am a straightforward man. The law may find me a criminal but none can say I am a cheat. I will deliver on every promise. Name your price."

Braham Prakash knew that he was being sucked into a whirlpool and he could not keep his own father waiting when they mattered most to one another. He had to do some quick thinking to get out of the clutches of this revolver-toting, patricidal psychopath.

"I will do your job. I will have to consult my seniors. It will take minimum of two hours."

"But what about the body turning blue?"

"That you leave to me. When the post mortem report gives an all-clear signal, who will question the colour of the body? In many cases, cardiac patients' body turns blue after death."

"Thank you. And how much do you want?"

"I am not a greedy man. We will discuss that later. First let me get your work done."

"Give me your cell number. I will be in touch with you on your cell phone from now on."

Without batting an eyelid, Braham Prakash took out his visiting card, with his mobile number printed on it, and slipped it into the sweaty hands of Suresh Ram.

Braham Prakash attended to urgent official matters for about 15 minutes and then left his office to be with his father. The first thing he did while walking to the parking lot was to switch off his cell phone. Just when he was unlocking his car, somebody tapped him on the shoulder. He turned back and his face turned pale.

"Where are you going?" Suresh Ram demanded to know.

"To an ice cream parlour to have a Softie?"

"What do you mean?"

"What kind of a silly question is this? If you were to keep tailing me like this, how will I do your work?"

"Wait. I have changed my mind."

"So you don't want the post mortem report?"

"No. I don't want the post mortem report any longer."

"Good. Let me go, then."

"No, I have thought of another plan."

"Come out with it."

"I want the body to disappear."

"What?"

"Yes. And you will help me in making that possible."

"And why do you think I will do that?"

"I will give you a million rupees in lieu of this job."

"I am not interested."

"Two million? Three million?"

Now Braham Prakash snapped. He slammed his car door and shouted, "If you don't leave this place within two seconds, I will call in the police!"

"You can't do that. Your wife came to the hospital, along with your son, to meet your father. My men have told her everything and taken charge of your son. She is very understanding and far more mature than you are. She herself will explain everything to you. She is coming in this direction now," Suresh Ram said, pointing to Sheela, who was running towards her husband.

"Keep this phone with you. You must keep it switched on at all times for the safety of your son. The body must disappear immediately. You are appointed as my sole agent to make it happen," Suresh Ram ordered like a don and walked away.

Braham Prakash's colleague, Dr Zakir Hussain, looked grave.

"I have been waiting for you for the past hour and you were busy with that post mortem case."

Before Braham Prakash could say anything, Hussain held him by his coat, took him out of earshot of a visibly distressed Sheela and whispered something into his ear. Braham peeped into the room his father was in, saw him enjoying a serene sleep, and returned to Hussain to discuss urgent business. The two doctors had animated discussions for about ten minutes. Hussain could sense that Braham Prakash was in agony but his face was inscrutable.

Hussain and Braham Prakash were batch mates in college and had been thick friends for many years. Hussain was well aware of the old man's dead body that had arrived in the morning for a post mortem.

Braham Prakash said, "I need total privacy for about half an hour. No one should come and disturb me during this period. I will be back in twenty minutes. Please ask the staff not to touch anything. You take care of Sheela and take her home."

"Okay, as you wish. I will leave necessary instructions," Dr Hussain said.

Prakash returned in less than twenty minutes, a suitcase in hand. He bolted the door, emptied the contents of the suitcase on the bed and mumbled, "Papa, these people don't understand anything, but don't worry. I will take you to all your favourite places once again. Just give me a few minutes."

First, he undressed his father. "You have always loved massage papa, isn't it? I'm sure you like it," he said as he took out an oil vial. He massaged his father with the odourless oil. Then he applied a thick layer of a body ointment.

After the exercise was over, he whispered to his father, "Papa, this is special oil which will evaporate within minutes and is good for body ache. Besides, it will keep your limbs supple so that you can walk at ease. Now let me dress you up in your favourite suit."

Then he took out his father's suit, shirt and tie, deep blue in colour, and dressed him.

"Now you can sit. Let me put your muffler around your head. After all, you have to face the chilly winds of December. You have to wear gloves too. Not an inch of your body should be exposed to the wind. Yes, now it is alright. Oh, damn it! How can I forget your spectacles? How will you see?"

Prakash stuffed the unused things back into the suitcase: some vials and a pair of rollerskate frames he kept in his small bag. As he looked around the room, he noticed his father's shoes. He noticed how heavy his father's shoes were. These were surgical shoes, made to order two years back after he had recovered from a bus accident. The skates fitted very well under those surgical shoes.

"Okay, let's go now."

Braham Prakash opened the door and, virtually holding his father in his arms, proceeded towards the parking lot. He could have brought his car to the point where his father was but he wanted the old man to walk. His father was not very tall but was heavy. Braham Prakash was not a strong man but was strong willed.

"Papa, this is your car. Just have a look. It's brand new. You always dreamed of being driven in your own car.

At the Police Headquarters in the heart of the city, a distraught young woman was pleading for help.

"Sir, we are not saying he has committed any crime. We have come here to seek your help," said the young lady, tears rolling down her cheeks.

"At best, we can register a 'missing' report," said Additional Commissioner of Police Vikas Yadav. "And that too with regard to Dr Braham Prakash. But what do we do in the case of his father?"

"All I want you to do is to alert your force to be on the lookout for my brother and father. My brother has not returned home since last night. My sister-in-law is traumatised. Our relatives have started arriving from outside Delhi. What do we tell them?"

"Okay. Please leave the photos. I will do what I can."

Braham Prakash opened the door of the car and took his father out. "Papa, see. We are in Ghaziabad. This is the Hindon River. You used to bathe here in your childhood. Let's sit by the river. It's a bright sunny day. I'm sure you will enjoy basking here for a while."

After resting his father against a rock, Braham Prakash said, "I'll be back in two minutes. Let me get some Coke. For coffee, you will have to wait." He came back with two cans.

"Last night must have been pretty bad for you because of the mosquitoes. Imagine mosquitoes in a cold, December night! I'm sorry I couldn't take you to your native house in Bulandshahr last night. We'll try tonight. Will it be of any use, though? Will anybody recognise you after 38 years?

"Mr Yadav, this is Surabhi, sister of Dr Braham Prakash."

"Yes Surabhi. Dr Prakash's photo has been circulated to every police station. I have your numbers. I will get back to you whenever I have any information. What else?"

"Sir, my brother called up last night. He didn't say from where he was speaking. He has switched off his mobile phone. He only said that he and Papa were fine and we shouldn't bother."

"Really? He said he and his father were fine! What else did he say?"

"He told me to ask you to get in touch with Dr Hussain on a top priority basis and said your conversation with Dr Hussain would explain everything."

Some people found it a bit strange when they saw a well dressed but odd-looking old man on skates going towards the Coffee House in Connaught Place, a landmark in New Delhi. A jean clad young man had his arm around the old man. The two appeared to be engaged in an intimate conversation, oblivious of the surroundings. The onlookers quickly ignored the two men. After all, who had time for an odd pair like that on Christmas day?

Prakash chose the first corner table. There were hardly any people on that chilly morning. The waiter arrived and took the order without giving the old man a second glance.

"Papa, I'm sure you will be happy with your outing. This is the penultimate leg of our excursion. How did you enjoy your evening in Nangia Park yesterday? The stroll in Kishanganj the previous day? Fantastic? I can see your eyes nodding in agreement."

The waiter returned after a few minutes and placed two cups of coffee on the table. He was about to leave when Braham Prakash gave him a hundred rupee note.

"There is no hurry, sir," the waiter said.

"I know. We would not like to be disturbed. You can keep the change."

The waiter bowed to Braham twice and said, "You won't be disturbed. Thank you, sir." Then he bowed to the old man. "Have a good day, sir," he mumbled and left without waiting for a response.

Additional Commissioner Yadav was sitting in Braham Prakash's well-furnished house. "This is really amazing. In thirty years of my service I have not come across such a case," he said to Prakash's anxious relatives.

"But how has he managed all this all these days?" said V Kumar, Prakash's brother-in-law, a computer expert.

"He is a brainy chap; a forensic doctor," Yadav commented. "But are you sure that he has called you to the crematorium at four?" He asked, checking his watch. It was ten minutes to noon.

"Yes."

"And he also said that he is coming with the body?"

"Yes."

Yadav's mobile rang. Dr Hussain was on the line. The police official took copious notes and got up after the conversation concluded five minutes later.

"What happened?"

"Some urgent business. Your information is correct. See you at the crematorium at four."

Dhruv stopped here and cast a glance at Amaso. He had been listening to Dhruv's tale intently.

"I am sure this guy Suresh Ram is going to meet his nemesis in Braham Prakash. He will be arrested and charged with murdering his father. He panicked and committed a mistake by approaching the forensic doctor for a favourable post mortem report. His best bet would have been to let the law take its own course and then he could have played on the legal fault lines."

"But what is your explanation for Braham Prakash's unusual disappearance?"

"I think that is to give him time and room for manoeuvring till cops zero in on Suresh Ram and recover his son."

"That's all. You see nothing more in Braham Prakash's unusual conduct with his father?"

"I see nothing more."

"Okay, you will see for yourself now." Dhruv resumed his story.

"Look papa, this is Delhi University Central Library, your place of work and the last stop of our excursion. I won't be able to take you inside because you can't walk up to your first floor room. So, admire it from outside only."

Then with moist eyes, perhaps for the first time all these days, he asked softly, "Tell me Papa, why did you do this to me? I know we never got along. If only you had scraped the ice to find the warmth underneath... Papa, I really admired you, respected you... Why did you do this to me...? Anyway, I hope you found these days fulfilling to your soul... No father and son on earth could have interacted the way we did all these days... There was none else, only you and me. Your last destination has come, Papa."

Prakash's car pulled in at the Nigambodh Ghat parking at the promised time. The entire family was waiting.

All of them froze when they saw Braham Prakash walking towards them with the well-dressed old man on the skates.

"Where?" he asked.

Like a robot, Surabhi gestured towards the newly laid funeral pyre and followed Braham Prakash. Everybody trooped along, like charmed rats following the Pied Piper.

Braham Prakash made his father lie on the pyre. He kissed his face for the last time and then put logs over the dead body he had been carrying over the last four days. All friends, relatives and family members were in a trance, a trance that broke when they heard Braham Prakash weeping like one possessed.

As his wife took a few steps towards him, Surabhi stopped her and counselled, "Let him cry his heart out. He has been holding back these tears all these days."

There was a sudden activity of men in khaki at the crematorium. Several police vehicles whizzed inside the complex. Additional Commissioner Yadav came out from a car, with Prakash's five-year-old son in his arms. Dr Hussain was also with him.

Sheela immediately took custody of her child. Yadav told Braham to come towards the main gate of the crematorium as another body was being offloaded from a police vehicle. Several policemen had formed a circle around Suresh Ram, who was handcuffed.

A police officer handed a document and a pen to Braham Prakash. It was the post mortem report of Suresh Ram's father, which had been signed by Dr Hussain. The post mortem report identified the cause of death as slow and sustained poisoning over a period. After putting his signatures along side Dr Hussain's on the report, Dr Prakash joined his wife and took his son in his arms.

The police officer handed the document to Yadav, his boss. Yadav looked at Dr Hussain and remarked, "I really wonder how Dr Prakash roamed around with his father's corpse all these days."

Dr Hussain pointed towards the skates, which Dr Braham Prakash had tied on his father's feet.

"But that is hardly enough to make a corpse walk around," Yadav remarked.

"I will tell you how my friend made it happen," Dr Hussain said. "First, he applied an anti-decay solution on his father's body, which we forensic scientists use to preserve dead bodies for some days. Then he tied his father's forearms with wooden strips. He repeated the exercise with his father's legs. He put a wooden strip on the dorsal surface of each leg, covering the area from knee to toe and tied each leg tightly with a thin nylon rope. To steady the neck, he used a collar, which is normally worn by patients with injuries to the cervical vertebrae."

Yadav listened to Dr Hussain's account patiently and then surprised him with a question, "Has your friend been to Sri Lanka?"

"Yes he was posted there for one year in the 1980's. He formed a part of the medical team that went to Sri Lanka as Indian Peace Keeping Force. But why do you ask?"

"Dr Prakash has used the same modus operandi which Miller, a revered figure among Tamil Tigers, used in the LTTE's first-ever recorded suicide operation," Yadav said. Then, noticing the raised eyebrows of Dr Hussain, the police officer said, "I am not comparing the two incidents which are as similar and yet as different as chalk and cheese."

"I don't understand. Can you explain?" Dr Hussain inquired.

"Miller launched his operation on July 5, 1987 at the Nelliady Sri Lankan army camp at Vadamarchi, thirty kilometres off Jaffna. Vadamarchi used to be an LTTE base, but it had been captured by the Sri Lankan army, who had been using it as an ammunition depot. It was very important for the LTTE to recapture the camp that had been made virtually impregnable by the Sri Lankan army. Miller volunteered to do the job single handedly. It was an operation that meant certain death for him."

Dr Hussain saw from out of the corner of his eye that Braham Prakash had just lit his father's pyre. He prodded Yadav to continue with Miller's story.

"Miller's reconnaissance of the targeted area yielded a vital detail. There were several security barricades manned round the clock by the Sri Lankan troops. There was no way one could pierce through all the barricades and reach the destination alive. However, there was a catch. From the point of the first barricade to the camp that was to be recaptured, the road was metalled and straight, without any curves or bends.

"Miller asked the fellow Tamil Tigers to pack a truck with explosives and then sat behind the steering wheel, tied to the driver's seat, his one foot tied to the accelerator and hands tied to the steering. Wooden sticks were used in such a manner that he could not move an inch even if he wanted to. The Tamil Tigers then turned on the ignition.

"The truck hurtled down the road, piercing through barricade after barricade. Sri Lankan soldiers sprayed the truck with bullets and Miller was dead as soon as he crossed the very first checkpoint. Nevertheless, the truck rolled on and finally, it rammed against the camp and exploded. The entire structure was blown to smithereens. Limbs of soldiers guarding the camp were found strewn several hundred metres away. The Tamil Tigers videoed the suicide operation, which they show to trainee suicide bombers to date." Yadav quickly finished his narration as he noticed Dr Prakash walking towards him.

"Thank you very much Mr Yadav for everything you have done," Braham Prakash said.

"You should thank your friend Dr Hussain, without whose help we could not have recovered your son and arrested Suresh Ram. Of course, the mobile phone Suresh Ram gave to you for his operation came in handy for us. It was because of this phone that we not only tapped his threatening conversations with you, but also tracked down his exact location," Yadav said as he ordered his men to take away Suresh Ram.

Dhruv cast an inquisitive look at Amaso as he concluded his story. Amaso remained quiet.

Dhruv said, "This is a story which has been close to my heart for years. It relates to two starkly different father and son relationships. One son is so upset by the death of his father that he anoints the body with preservatives and lives with it for days as though his father was alive. Another son abuses the science of medicine to plot his father's death. This is what I mean by white bird, black shadow. The two plots move parallel to keep the reader (in this case, the listener) guessing."

"When did you write the story?" Amaso said, finally breaking his silence.

"I wrote the story of Braham Prakash's father some five years ago, but the Suresh Ram plot was conceived yesterday only.

"What is the result of Round Two?" Mili asked Amaso directly.

"Looks like, we share the points equally again, 5-5." Amaso said. What do you say Mr Dhruv?"

"I tend to agree."

"Which means that the points tally at the end of Round Two stands at 10-10 with the third and last story of ten points remaining to be told," Mehmood Mian remarked.

"Yup," Dhruv said.

13

The Woman in Black

Dhruv and Mili had already lost count of the days and nights they had been captives. The only thing they were bothered about these days was whether the weather continued to be bad or not. It was one of those absurd philosophies wherein bad was good, and good was bad.

Dhruv had realised by then that Amaso would not be an easy conquest. Moreover, Amaso was challenging him on his home turf! It was like Dhruv daring Amaso in a gun-wielding contest. They began the day with a fervent prayer that Dhruv score a decisive victory in his last story and they go back home at the first available opportunity.

Mili was quite upbeat. For the first time, Dhruv had given her a broad outline of the story. He had woken her early in the morning and asked whether she wanted to know what he was going to narrate to Amaso, and she immediately consented. Dhruv noticed that she could have gone on an ego trip, said "no" and gone back to sleep. She did no such thing. The woman had changed in the past week.

To her credit, Dhruv admitted that Mili was not a dumb doll. She had helped him in significantly enriching the story. As a leading heroine of Bollywood, she had a vast experience of listening to hundreds of stories and screenplays and she drew on her film experience, bringing about new twists and turns in the story. He also had a nagging feeling that if he had given up his vanity and roped her in since the first story; he might have already emerged as a clear winner.

The two left their room at the scheduled time for the deciding round. As they were walking through the corridor, their hearts leaped into their mouths. The snowfall had stopped, though the sky was still overcast. The words of Mehmood Mian were ringing in their ears: that the Supreme Leader will not stay for one minute after the snow storms stopped.

Sullenly, they walked on. The place gave the impression that the Supreme Leader was still around. The security guards were firmly in place outside the door, which opened into the huge drawing room. The room was already full. They were the last entrants. Amaso was seated alone on his special mattress. Mehmood Mian and Javed were seated on the mattress on the Supreme Leader's left side. Dhruv and Mili sat opposite Amaso. To their surprise, the fourth mattress was occupied for the first time since the unusual contest started.

A young, beautiful woman, dressed in black, was seated on the fourth mattress. She had fixed her penetrative gaze on the two of them ever since they entered the room. Never for a second, had the woman in black taken her eyes off the pair. Dhruv and Mili found it rather strange to see an exceedingly beautiful and polished woman in the company of jihadis. Even more shocking was her dagger-like gaze that was still fixed on both of them.

"Are we late?" Dhruv asked.

"No, you are on time. We have been sitting here well before time," Amaso replied.

"Enjoying the weather?"

"Yes."

"At our cost?"

"Do you find me so unfair?"

"In fact, it is to the contrary. We were quite baffled to still find you here even after snowfall stopped."

"Weather, Mr Dhruv, is nobody's friend. We are here because we have reason to believe that it is a deceptive calm. This calm phase may not last more than an hour. You can't go far in an hour when there has been an unabated snow storm for practically more than a hundred hours."

Mili found the gaze of the woman in black so piercing that she turned her attention somewhere else and made it obvious to the woman that she was not welcome. The woman also understood Mili's feelings towards her instantaneously. Women are past masters in the art of communication and they do even better when it comes to body language. When two individuals don't like each other, they sometimes convey the point in seconds. Women, on the other hand, have the weird capability of conveying their mutual dislike in nanoseconds.

In fact, while the tea was being served, she seized the opportunity by telling Dhruv to ignore the existence of the obnoxious woman. To Mili's amusement, Dhruv replied, "Yes, boss." The man was finally becoming romantic, she told herself.

"Are you ready with your magnum opus?"

"Yes. And indeed it is my magnum opus."

"What is the title?"

"Sting in the Tale."

"I must say you are an expert in finding catchy titles."

"Expert only in titles? Not in stories?" Dhruv protested again.

"You are an expert in that field as well. It is really remarkable that you have not lost your literary flourishes and good dramatic narrative technique even under the most dire circumstances of your life."

"But who says it is the worst? On the contrary, this has been a springtime in our lives. Both of us have got new offshoots from our trunks, new buds on the old offshoots, new leaves, new flowers, new everything. And it is largely because of you."

"Are you trying to win me over through unfair means, bypassing the ground rules?"

"Ground rules do not put a bar on statement of facts. The fact is that we two have become more complete human beings in the past week than we ever were. Or shall I say three of us?"

"Three of us?" Amaso asked in half amazement.

"If I can dare to include you as well," Dhruv said, knowing fully well that the ball had gone into the goalpost with lightning speed.

Amaso did not make any comment.

"Yes," Mili butted in. "I would go to the extent of saying that this period of captivity has produced a dramatic effect on me. It has purged me of my vanity and taught me how to assess complicated people like Dhruv and you."

"So, you have assessed me?" Amaso asked Mili. Now it was Dhruv's turn to enjoy direct discussions between Amaso and Mili. The protagonists were changing!

"Yes. And let me tell you my observations are always very uncanny and different from the rest of the world."

"Let's have a demonstration of such uncanny observations of yours," Amaso said, enjoying his rapport in the making with the heroine.

"Okay. Now the rules of the game. You ask a specific question. I give a point specific answer. But the condition is that you do not get upset with frank answers."

Amaso had no doubt that the woman whom he had forcibly made Dhruv's room partner had the potential to go the distance to becoming Dhruv's life partner as well.

"I will not be upset with frank answers. Here is my first

question. In case you lose this contest or it remains tied, how do you fancy your chances of your safe release?"

"We are upbeat. In any case we are going to win because he has a twister of a story for you this time."

"How do you assess me as a man?"

"Well, I find you extremely fair, level headed and courteous towards women."

"What do you think is my relationship with this woman over there?" Amaso said pointing in the direction of the woman in the black.

Amaso stunned everybody in the room with this unexpected question. Another very important development took place just then. It started snowing heavily and there was darkness in the morning. A fierce snow storm, much stronger in intensity than ever before, had started raging. Amaso's network, which obviously included local weather experts, was indeed vibrant and effective. Dhruv's eyes were shuttling between two targets – the woman in the black and the scene outside.

In one stroke, the woman in black lost the halo of mystery that she had plastered around herself. Suddenly she looked ordinary and vulnerable.

Mehmood Mian and Javed, who had been ill at ease since the woman had emerged on the scene, looked at Mili entreatingly, as though they were telling her to seize the opportunity and put the cursed woman in her place.

Dhruv had quickly made his own assessment about the woman. She did not belong here. She was an outsider. Moreover, he had a gut feeling that Amaso was aware of all this. Is that why he had called her here this morning?

Before the woman under microscope discerned, by her womanly empathy, that Mili was about to speak, she got up and said, "Excuse me, Supreme Leader, can we go to the Tiger's Den for two minutes please?"

To say that Mehmood Mian's eyebrows were raised would be an under statement. He was appalled by the suggestion and the import of the meaning that went along with it.

Amaso violently gesticulated, ordering the woman not to get up. "Stay where you are. Nobody is going anywhere from here." Then turning to Mili, he said: "Mohtarma, what is your response to my question?"

"You have no relationship with this woman. Primarily because people like you cannot have any relationship with such women. You don't seem to have known this woman for long. More importantly, you do not trust her," Mili replied, trying her best to copy Dhruv in making her sentences as short and hard hitting as possible.

Dhruv was completely bowled over by the way Mili handled this question. Mehmood Mian and Javed started looking at Mili with different eyes from there on.

As for Amaso himself, he knew that his gamble had paid off. The only one in the room who was in disarray was the woman in black robes.

"Gentlemen, thank you all for coming here at a short notice on a public holiday," the ISI Chief said.

"I will make my brief introductory remarks and after that the floor will be yours. The idea is to get the maximum productivity out of this day. Today's topic: Amaso's movement in Azad Kashmir region and the case of the Indian heroine's kidnapping."

General Mir Qasim did not show any signs of the pillow fights he had had with his beautiful wife early in the morning. Their youngest daughter was leaving for advanced studies to Harvard this morning. The wife had forewarned the General that this time, come what may, both the parents would go to see Nikhar off at the airport. As always, he had said yes, only to break the news of his urgent official business on her shortly before 6 in the morning.

The hardest available thing were pillows, and she had lost no time in using them as missiles. One nearly knocked off the General's branded glasses. But being a war strategist, the General had beat a hasty retreat, locked his domestic boss in the room, came to the glass window, showered her flying kisses and left the house after profuse apologies. He had a long grind ahead of him before the meeting that was to begin three hours later. While getting behind the steering wheel of his latest luxury car, the General wondered: Why could his silly wife not understand that he worked inside a pressure cooker called Inter Services Intelligence, Pakistan's premier and most formidable intelligence organisation!

"Well gentlemen, the reason why you are here early in the morning, braving your respective pillow fights, is to discuss the fast developing situation on the Amaso front. The President was briefed on the Amaso issue a fortnight ago. Within days of the kidnapping, the President's Amaso briefings became daily. The Prez himself is in the driver's seat now, and he is getting briefed on the situation as it develops, which on certain days, worked out to 18 times in 24 hours.

"We have kept a strict vigil in the Azad Kashmir area since the beginning of the century's worst snow storms. You know one of our reports suggested that Amaso could be behind the Indian heroine's kidnapping. We have made our own discreet inquiries. The purpose of this meeting is to share these findings with you.

"Nothing could be more ludicrous than to believe that Amaso is currently in Azad Kashmir. The reason we are certain is that our agent was with Amaso himself in Karachi until yesterday. Before that, Amaso was in NWFP and before that in Baluchistan. On each of the two occasions, the same agent was present and she herself certified that Amaso was alive and active in those respective areas."

"It only shows that Amaso is actually hyperactive and he is all over Pakistan," the chief of IB, a relatively much less important organization than ISI, remarked.

The ISI Chief ignored the jibe and gave his assessment of the situation. He also said the signals emanating from the

Green Jihad leadership were : don't trouble us and we won't trouble you.

The ISI Chief was personally aware of several things that could not be discussed at an omnibus meeting where the majority was the authority. He called the meeting to a close and just when everybody was dispersing, he signaled Brigadiers Ali and Osman of ISI and Pakistan Army respectively to stay behind.

After a while, only the three of them were left in the room. Any stranger in the room, who had watched the trio for just two minutes, would have concluded that they were very close-knit indeed. It was common knowledge in Pakistan's military circles that General Mir Qasim doted on the two Brigadiers as his younger brothers and the Brigadiers consulted Qasim on anything and everything.

"So, what is the latest, Brigadier Osman?"

"I have no news."

"And you, Brigadier Ali?"

"I have given instructions to my field staff in Azad Kashmir to begin ground patrols as soon as the snow storms have stopped."

"That's very thoughtful of you, Brigadier Ali."

"But not half as thoughtful as you are, General Sahib." On a questioning glance from Qasim, Brigadier Ali said, "I have only ordered ground patrol. You have ordered a house to house search in the entire area after the storm stops."

Brigadier Osman had some burning questions. "What is your take on reports that Amaso is in our part of Kashmir?"

"That's good for us. The hunter himself is close to be hunted," General Qasim said.

"General, thanks for your computer simulated presentation ˜Operation Hasina Part Two". I have a question, if you permit," the Indian Foreign Secretary asked the Army Chief.

The General had just finished his audio-video presentation before the top brass of the Government of India in the Defence Ministry's War Room. The Chiefs of IB and RAW, India's premier internal and external intelligence agencies, Military Intelligence, Military Operations, the Home Secretary and the National Security Advisor were also present in the War Room.

"Please ask your question," the Army Chief said to the Foreign Secretary.

"What is our information regarding whether Amaso is still present in Occupied Kashmir? Is he involved in the kidnapping of the Bollywood heroine? And what is the status of our two hostages?"

"We have reasons to believe Amaso is still present in Occupied Kashmir. He is probably involved in the kidnapping of the Bollywood heroine. As for your third question, we have nothing which leads us to believe that our hostages have been harmed; at least not as yet."

"What is the basis of your confidence? How reliable is your information network when I believe we have not heard from our best operational man on the ground, Inspector General Dashamlav, for the past eight or ten days?"

"These are operational details which I cannot share with you. Suffice it to say that our intelligence network is alive and kicking. Any more questions?"

The Foreign Secretary shook his head briefly, picked up his file and looked at his colleagues to see if they had any questions. He and the NSA had to go straight to the Prime Minister after this meeting.

"I have a question for you," the Army Chief said to the Foreign Secretary.

"What are our American friends saying with regard to Amaso?"

"General, our American friends are in constant touch with us. Nothing is very clear as of now because of the extremely bad weather conditions in Occupied Kashmir over the past six days or so. I think everybody is waiting for the storm to run its course."

"Are they interested in a joint military operation or do they want India to launch the operation on its own? What are the indications?"

"Nothing is confirmed at this stage, General. As they say, we will cross the bridge when we come to it. Wait for the weather in Occupied Kashmir to clear up."

The weather gods were at their fiercest best. Dhruv could sense the all-out efforts which Amaso's men must have been making to clear the snow. Assured on the weather front, he was now focused on the bizarre things that were happening inside the room. The woman in the black, who looked like a dagger soaked in poison until some minutes ago, was now crestfallen.

Mili had just finished giving her assessment of Amaso's "relationship" with the woman in the black, as directed by the Supreme Leader. Now everybody was looking at Amaso.

Amaso gestured to Mehmood Mian and he immediately approached the Supreme Leader. Amaso whispered directions to Mehmood Mian who kept glancing from his boss to the woman. He got up, asked Javed to follow him and disappeared.

The woman's discomfiture had now become apparent. Soon, Mehmood Mian and Javed returned. The latter was holding a bundle of thick rope. The woman's face turned ashen at the sight.

Javed pushed her mattress towards a pillar, tied the woman to the pillar, pulled out a piece of cloth from his pocket and fastened it around her mouth.

"Javed, don't tie her up so tightly. Tie her up like a dog – I am sorry, like a bitch – with a long rope so that she can change her position and sit comfortably. After all, I want her to listen to Mr Dhruv's story. Just make sure that she is tied loosely to the pillar and she is not able to pounce upon any one of us and take us by surprise."

After Javed had followed these orders, he looked at the Supreme Leader for further instructions who signaled him to come back to his seat. Once everybody was seated at their respective places, there was a pin drop silence in the hall; the continuing snowfall and sounds of picks and shovels were distinct. All eyes were on Amaso, who did not seem to be in a hurry. He was enjoying the biggest tale with a twist, which he was in the process of enacting.

It seemed almost an eternity had passed when Amaso started speaking.

" All of you must be quite foxed by the turn of events in past half an hour, intrigued by this woman and must be wondering why she is being punished like this. I will reveal all. Mr Dhruv, you noticed the other day how I still keep in touch with the rest of the world despite this inclement weather and at the same time, I don't leave a trail.

"Yes, I receive my mail through human couriers who travel by mules and ponies in this part of the world. I have evolved a highly complicated web of courier network, which delivers information to me in coded language from places that are sometimes hundreds of kilometers apart.

"Let me tell you another thing about me which many people know but hardly any believe. I have several body double Amasos. I learnt this trick from Saddam Hussein, who used it successfully for years. I wouldn't tell the number because that is an operational detail. However, let me tell you that I have enough of my look alikes to be at several different locations at the same time to keep the enemy engaged.

"This woman, this bound and gagged woman, who is in front of you, is a top level operative of the Pakistani ISI. It was a few months ago only when the ISI had put her on to me. I could see through the booby trap they were laying for me. When I came into this region about a week or ten days ago, I came to know the redoubtable loyalties of Pakistan government and the ISI, which swung away from me and towards the Americans. I don't trust the Pakistan government or any Pakistani establishment because I know there are many people who would like to exchange me for diplomatic or economic benefits from America.

"But they don't know that I have my dedicated friends at every important Pakistani establishment. This woman did not know this. That's why I made her meet my doubles in places like Karachi, Peshawar and Quetta in the last week. The intention was to tell the Pakistanis, and through them the Americans, that I was not in Kashmir. She took the bait, but she did not realize that spies could also be spied on. We were in this room half an hour before you two came. I had crossexamined this woman in my own way and found her to be a security risk."

"Sorry to interrupt, Mr Amaso," Dhruv said. "Though I have no locus standi to ask this question, I am still curious to know how she was a security risk for you and how you managed to find it out. I will not mind if you were to choose not to answer this question for fear of giving away operational details."

"Let me tell you, Mr Dhruv: the biggest secret of my organization's success is that we spy on the spies. That is my aggressive style. Before coming here, she told her people to be ready for a signal from her after which they could launch house-to-house search operation, followed by combat operations. That is something I have already taken care of."

"If her charge is as grave as what you are saying then why don't you proceed against her, instead of making her sit here in front of you?" Dhruv asked. He could again feel the steely dagger of the woman's gaze piercing through his bones.

"Her fate will be decided later. Why is she here? Because I want her to listen to your story. She has been telling my look alikes in Karachi, Peshawar and Quetta in the past week that I should either execute both of you or hand you people over to the ISI for some operational and diplomatic leverage."

"Why do you want her to listen to my story? What's so great about it?"

"Because I want her to see for herself that Amaso does not spend days with insignificant ants. Somebody has to be extra special to be able to spend days with me."

"There is a practical problem which I am facing as a story narrator," Dhruv said, coming back to the crucial business of his and Mili's passport to safety.

"What's that?"

"I no longer have a level-playing field."

"What do you mean?"

"The stakes are much higher for me now with this dangerous woman becoming my audience. What is more, the post-match scenario has also become confusing after your disclosure that she has ordered a search and combat operation for us after the storm gets over. Under the circumstances, how will I be able to concentrate on my job?"

"Mr Dhruv, what you are saying perhaps is right, but the mettle of a man is known only in challenging situations like this. I can't help you there except to remind you that when the going gets tough, the tough get going. You had better start your story because this time the weather is going to open to us a larger window, which I may be inclined to use. What is the title of your story?"

"It is 'Sting in the Tale'."

"Oh, yes, you already told me. Sorry, I forgot. Are you ready with the story?"

"Yes, Mr Amaso, here I begin my third and last story."

14

Sting in the Tale

The D day had come. No, it was not the Doomsday for the world. It was the Day of Decision for him. The world could go to hell; he cared not at all.

It was December 31, 1999, the eve of new millennium. Amarnath had been preparing for this for the past six months. Today he would kill himself. He had ensured weeks ago that he could remain alone at home on the chosen day. He had purchased tickets for a gala dinner in a five star hotel for his wife Manorama, son Kinshuk and daughter Kriti. He could sense a mood of wild happiness sweeping the entire household when he got home that night with the tickets. He felt remorseful at this stroke of divine tragic comedy.

At six in the evening, Manorama shouted, "Come on kids, time to start getting ready." It was loud enough that Amarnath heard it clearly in his study.

Amarnath squirmed and shifted in his chair. From subsequent conversations, he could make out that Kriti was on the phone, a conversation she had just started and her mother's guess was that it was not going to end before half an hour.

Kriti had just entered college and being a sensitive girl with a literary turn of mind, she had opted for English literature. She had been very attached to her father, but for the last year or so, she had gradually withdrawn herself from him. Manorama had told him some months before that she had become friends with a boy and a girl of her class whose fathers too were drunkards. She had found common cause with them.

Amarnath also learned from across-the-house shouts that Kinshuk was watching a football match that had just started. Football was a passion with Kinshuk. Perhaps the last common ground between the father and the son. He too had drifted away from his father. It had not taken him his MBA studies to realise how and why his father was on the verge of becoming a failed businessman. The man had just lost initiative, drive, and the will to succeed. Moreover, if such people were to take to gambling, as his father had, then it was a poison draught. He detested gambling.

By 7pm, Manorama had achieved two things – she had herself got ready and successfully weaned away her young kids from their respective addictions.

"Where's your dad? What is he doing?" Manorama asked Kriti.

"Where else but in his study?"

"He must have started hitting the bottle already."

"For once you are wrong, Mom. Because Dad is listening to Yanni's music and is reading a book."

"Really, I can't believe it. And hasn't he finished that damned book yet?"

"Come on mom, haven't you read certain books several times? Why do you fault him if he is reading it for the second time?"

Manorama headed straight to the study. Kriti was right. She stood there at the door for a while.

He could be changing. That is why he had booked for us the exorbitantly expensive New Year's Eve tickets weeks in advance in such difficult financial times as these. But, old habits die hard, she thought. She was about to close the door when something happened that had not happened in years.

"Manno, wouldn't you come in and sit with me for a little while the children get ready? I can see you are already decked out and dressed to kill."

Manorama's feet had turned heavier than lead; they did not want to go to Amarnath.

"You have not started drinking yet?" She preferred this routine, mundane question to being entangled with him when he was in a strange mood.

Undeterred, Amarnath asked, "Are these the only issues left between us?"

Her silence was defying.

"Anyway, you will not see me now drinking."

"Let me tell you something before you go any further. You are like a cheat cloth merchant who measures more and cuts less cloth."

Amarnath would have become furious had it been some other day. He knew his past deeds had done nothing to give him the "khul ja sim sim" code for opening the Manorama cave. On the contrary, he seized both her hands, kissed them and said: "I love you, Manno."

Manorama disengaged her hands, got up, went to the door, looked back once and went out without closing the door.

It was around 9 pm that all three finally left home. Kriti peeped into the study before leaving. She was surprised that her dad had not begun drinking yet.

Amarnath was alone. It was a decisive moment. It was exactly on June 30 that he had decided to kill himself on December 31, giving himself a clear six months to review his resolve and test his will power on a daily basis. Each day had only reaffirmed this one. In fact, from the day he had bought the Gala Dinner tickets – December 1 – he had started considering that if he could display the same steely attitude and steadfastness in his business, he would not have been tottering on the brink of bankruptcy in the first place. Despite his financial constraints, he made sure that he paid his hefty life insurance premium in time.

He had decided to move legally so that his family members were not harassed. He had obtained a prescription from his doctor friend to take a sleeping pill of 20mg every night to get to sleep. He had calculated that from July 1 to December 31, there were 184 days. This meant that he would have 3680 mg of ammunition on the D day. This cold mathematical calculation became his strength.

Amarnath took another care. Every time he bought the sleeping pills, he made sure that he would rid them of the metallic foil and store them in empties of other much-used medicines like aspirin. Soon after everyone left, he started on his last mission. He started to consume the tablets one by one. He chose this longer route deliberately as he wanted to test his will power and patience. Moreover, it would be a good game to play when he had all the time in the world to play it. After all, life had been a game for him. He could watch himself dying, slowly.

He had loved adventure sports during his youth – riding, rafting, hang gliding and mountain climbing. He had met Manorama at a riding school and had fallen for her vivacious and bubbly personality. Her beauty was the perfect icing on the cake.

Amarnath's wooing skills, perseverance and ready wit made sure that the maiden fell, true to the script. And in one stroke, Amarnath, a poor officer in a nationalised bank, became the heir to a multi-million dollar Piramal empire.

Amarnath loved his bride like one possessed. Manorama frequently had to tell him that he was neglecting the business for her. On each occasion like this, Amarnath would grin sheepishly, go back to work but would come back on other such opportunities, when he could combine business with pleasure. For years, Amarnath kept his business on the rails.

As luck would have it, his business started to go downhill after his children were born. By the time they went to college, they saw the household waging a losing battle with finances. Partly because of inept administration and partly because of his new found diversions – wine and women – he kept sinking in the quicksand of financial difficulties.

Properties and premises were pledged to the banks. With each passing year, the list of mortgaged properties grew longer and longer. However, not a single property could be redeemed.

In the next phase of his downhill journey, Amarnath began selling the properties off one by one. Amarnath's name had already been struck off the list of successful industrialists. He was fast hurtling to the stage where his flagship industry and his mansion at a premium location in Bangalore threatened to go into the red zone.

He did not know what happened to him after reaching the highest point in his life's graph: his marriage with Manorama. When he took to drinking initially, it was occasionally during parties on the weekends. First weekends became longer. Then the glasses got bigger. There were times when he would finish half a bottle of spirits in one extended session.

As his drinking became a concern for the family, another drastic change appeared in Amarnath: he turned a hardcore atheist. So much so that he would consume more meat and liquor on Mondays and Tuesdays – the days on which Hindus did not usually permit themselves such indulgences – than on any other day. He also got involved in physical relationships with several women, though never emotionally.

For several years, he lived his life as though it was a rented flat. The worst was his gradual alienation from his family members. In a year, his concerns had drifted from mundane things to larger, existential questions. What is life? What will come of it? Is life worth living? Why suffer this monotony of repetitive lifestyle? What more he had to see in this life? Why should he go through the motions until an unknown, unseen force – known as God or Nature or Destiny or Death – pushed the off button?

The final change came some six months ago, when he read that book and decided that time had come for him to bid adieu to this planet called Earth, which he had been visiting for the last 45 years.

The pills had started showing their effect. He was getting drowsy though he had not even consumed one-third of his stock of pills. Were the pills too strong or was he hallucinating? After all, this was the first time he was attempting suicide.

To divert his attention from his messy past, Amarnath took to his only passion: internet surfing. He had acquired amazing skill and speed in finding newer and newer websites for game shows, puzzles, quizzes, gambling and online lotteries.

His mobile phone rang. Naushad Azhar was calling. Amarnath's business partner was a man of few words. True to his nature, Naushad spoke for just ten seconds. "Go to ˜khuljasimsim dot com" without wasting a single minute. A jackpot of a hundred million dollars is waiting to be won. Go. Get it. Wish you all the best."

As Naushad hung up, Amarnath acted immediately on his friend's instruction. He always took Naushad seriously. He had known Naushad since his courtship with Manorama began. Naushad belonged to an aristocratic family. He used to visit Manorama's house frequently and chat with Manorama's father for hours. Amarnath had a lurking fear that Naushad was in love with Manorama, though he never uttered a word about it.

When Amarnath's business started sinking, Naushad bailed him out by putting in substantial funds. After a couple of years, Amarnath, still unable to repay Naushad's loan, offered him business partnership as an honourable way out. Naushad accepted the offer reluctantly.

Soon, the laptop screen was filled with a red-lettered banner that screamed how a gamer could win a whopping 100 million US dollars through a newly invented unique method. As Amarnath read further, he got interested in the format of the game. The game comprised of ten levels and had to be completed in 30 minutes. The personalised clock would start ticking on top right of the player's computer screen after the contestant pushed the "START" button, the "Rules of the Game" section informed. The first three levels were comprised of variants of some well known video games which he had played – and reasonably well – a decade ago when he had started internet surfing. The next three levels were quiz rounds, each having one multiple choice question. The player had to tick off one correct answer out of four choices.

After clearing these six rounds, the player would reach another quiz round for three more levels, but this time much more difficult. Each of these three quiz rounds would consist of a single question and there would be no clues or choices. Finally, there would be a mindbender round where a mathematical puzzle would be set. The last round would have to be compulsorily completed in ten seconds, no matter how quickly the player had completed his earlier nine rounds. After successfully negotiating all the ten rounds, the player would have to press the "SUBMIT" button. All this would have to be done within the stipulated time limit of 30 minutes.

Amarnath had suddenly become as watchful and alert as a tiger on the prowl. His drowsiness had gone. He was aware of the dichotomy of his mental state between now and some minutes back. It set him wondering, thinking.

Life is nothing but an extended mind game. As long as a man is in command of his faculties, he is in a can-do-it mode. When the spark is gone from his life, he becomes a rudderless boat.

He was itching to play, but he thought it prudent to learn more about the rules of the game, first. Ten rules were listed.

1. Remember this is a jackpot edition of the game show, which promises to fetch the winner a sum of US$100 million. For the last ten months, no one has claimed the monthly prize money of US$10 million. This unclaimed prize money has been clubbed to make it the biggest-ever and the richest game show in the history of the world.

2. Our earlier editions had a ticket of US$100. Since this is the Jackpot, the ticket this time costs US$1000.

3. If this Jackpot is unclaimed, we will revert to the US $ 10 million prize money from next month. The organisers reserve the right to announce the date of the next Jackpot, if at all such a decision were to be made.

4. The ticket money is payable by your credit card. We accept all leading international brands of credit cards. (See list.)

5. Each game is to be completed in 30 minutes.

6. Each of the ten levels of the game show is a death match and has to be compulsorily cleared. For example, if you lose in round 9, then you have to play the game anew.

7. You can play as many games you want but every time you play, you must purchase the ticket afresh.

8. Please do not waste your time and money in copying the questions in the hope that you may improve your next game results. Our IT engineers have developed the software

in such a way that each time you play you get a different set of games and quizzes and puzzles. The chances of an individual getting the same set of questions or games or puzzles are extremely remote.

9. Remember the deadline for this jackpot is 18h30 GMT, December 31, 1999.

10. Please do not forget to press the "SUBMIT" button after completing the game. If you have successfully completed the ten levels but have not pressed the "SUBMIT" button, you will not qualify for the prize money. Start now. Good luck.

For the last ten minutes, Amarnath had not swallowed any more of the pills. He read Rule 9 again, which gave 18h30 GMT as the deadline for the contest to end. This meant that the contest was to end at the millennium's last midnight. It was already 11.30 pm IST. It meant that by the time he started the game after filling in his credit card details he would have less than thirty minutes to complete the game.

Amarnath did not waste any more time and clicked on "START". The web site asked for his credit card details that he filled in quickly. In a few seconds, the screen flashed a message that his credit card had been accepted and he could start the game now. He took barely ten minutes in clearing the first three levels of games. He had resumed popping sleeping pills at regular intervals.

As he reached Level 4, the screen flashed the beginning of the Quiz Round. The first multiple choice question appeared on the screen.

"Who discovered Greenland?"

The question was followed by four options:

(a) Columbus (b) Vasco da Gama (c) Eric the Red (d) FaHsien.

Amarnath took several pills at a time. He did not know the answer. He was an instinctive gambler. He invoked the time-tested elimination method. After his graduation, he had prepared for the Indian Civil Services examination, though he never cleared the examination. He remembered by heart that Columbus had discovered America in 1492 and Vasco Da Gama had reached the Indian coast in 1498. As far as he could remember, he did not recall these two great explorers having ever been associated with Greenland. FaHsien had come to India in circa 400 AD and he too did not seem to have anything to do with Greenland. He had never heard of Eric the Red. Without wasting any more time, Amarnath clicked on option "C".

Bingo. He had hit the bull's eye. The answer was correct. He was given an option of reading the detailed answer or move to the next level without wasting time. He saw the computer clock which showed that he still had 18 minutes more in which he had to complete six rounds of which the last round had to be compulsorily completed in ten seconds. He knew that he had enough time for seeking detailed answers.

"Eric Thorvaldsson, better known as Eric the Red, came to Greenland in 982 AD. The Icelander had been exiled from Iceland for three years for killing a man. He returned to Iceland after his explorations and as he wanted settlers to go to this extremely cold land where hardly a blade of grass grew, he gave it an attractive name: Greenland."

The Level 5 question was even more difficult for Amarnath. The question and the four options that filled the screen were:

"What is Leonardo da Vinci not associated with?" The four options were: (a) Painting (b) Sculpting (c) Architecture (d) Mathematics."

Amarnath had recognised the name of Leonardo da Vinci as a celebrated artist who painted the world's best known paintings like "The Last Supper" and "Mona Lisa". He had no idea about da Vinci's forays into such spheres as sculpture, architecture or mathematics. He told himself that Option 'd' was the odd one out in the list of options and clicked on "d".

A congratulatory tone signalled that he had successfully negotiated Level 5. Nevertheless, he was hungry for a detailed answer that read as follows:

"Perhaps none in history achieved so much in so many different fields as Leonardo da Vinci. Leonardo was an outstanding painter, sculptor and architect. He also designed bridges, weapons, highways, costumes, scientific instruments and even weapons. He invented the diving bell and tank and designed flying machines. He also made important discoveries about the structure of the human body by dissecting corpses to find out how the human body was put together. He became an expert in every field that interested him."

Quickly, Amarnath had covered half the distance and more than 16 minutes were still left. With the game's deadline of 18h30 GMT he wondered briefly if there were 14 minutes left or 15 till the deadline.

The Level 6 question brought a smile to Amarnath's face. He continued taking pills and read the question and the options.

"A human neck has seven vertebrae. How many vertebrae are there in the neck of a giraffe?"

Amarnath quickly went through the options: (a) 7 (b) 14 (c) 21 (d) 28 and clicked 'a'. He had learnt it by heart as a student that all mammals share certain characteristics: like giving birth to live young and having seven vertebrae in their necks. He went for the next level, not opting to know the elaborate answer.

Amarnath felt his head had started spinning, though he was still in control of his faculties. He continued to take the sleeping pills. Level 7 began with a question that he thanked the website for putting in its data bank.

The question was "Who invented the Zero?" He confidently typed out the answer: "Aryabhatta". He knew that though Aryabhatta's invention was made long before the birth of Christ, the Indians had invented a far better number system than the Europeans had. The Indian number system, including the zero, was brought to Europe in circa 900 AD by Arab traders.

The computer stopwatch showed he still had more than ten minutes left and he had already reached Level 8.

It took him less than a minute to clear Level 8. The question transported him twenty one years back. His father-in-law had surprised Amarnath and Manorama both by giving them tickets to Australia for their honeymoon. As the newly-weds roamed around the continent sized country and savoured the Australian cuisine, they delved into Australia's history. Manorama surprised him with her knowledge about Australia. Amarnath remembered how profusely he had thanked Captain James Cook and hearing this, Manorama, had angrily asked who was James Cook and why was he thanking him. Amarnath seized the opportunity and said, "If Captain Cook had not discovered Australia, I would not have been able to rediscover my Manorama."

The Level 8 question was, "Who discovered Australia?"

He looked at the computer clock. Still more than eight minutes to go and he had only two more rounds to clear. The only problem was the sleeping pills were beginning to show their impact. Less than twenty pills were left.

Amarnath wanted to finish the game as fast as possible. The Level 9 question, which came up on his screen, did not stump him but he had to make an effort to answer it. The question was, "HTML is a computer programming language. It was adopted in the 1990s for the creation of World Wide

Web documents on the Internet. What is the full form of HTML?"

The pills' impact was clearly discernible now. His memory was failing him. He knew the answer. Just a couple of months ago, when his office engineer was repairing his personal laptop, Amarnath had instructed him to ensure that all his files were saved. The engineer had told him that all his files were in HTML format and had been saved. It was out of sheer curiosity that he had asked him the meaning of HTML.

After he kept thinking for about five minutes, the answer came to his mind like a flash. He lost no time in typing out the answer: "Hypertext Markup Language".

He was jolted out of his stupor by the musical congratulations that announced that he had reached the final round. He trained his eyes on the screen. The letters on the screen had begun to float around. He tried hard to concentrate and fixed his gaze at the screen.

A red lettered "IMPORTANT NOTE" informed Amarnath that though he still had more than four minutes left to complete the game, the tenth and last round was a mathematical puzzle and had to be completed in ten seconds.

Amarnath went ahead with Level 10. The Question read as follows:

"Type out a 9 digit figure and make sure its numerical value is 8 only."

Amarnath had been following numerology for more than three decades. He knew that for expediting numerological calculations, the letter 9 could be ignored because the numerological value of this letter is zero. He quickly wrote out his answer: "899999999"

He could barely keep his eyes open now, but he did hear the congratulatory music. His screen showed that he had successfully completed the game and the "SUBMIT" button began to flicker. He could not count how many pills remained on his desk: four, six or nine. But the number of the leftover pills was definitely below ten. He was hardly conscious when, he thought, he pressed the SUBMIT button. Then his head lolled on one side of the table.

Naushad Azhar was very watchful when he entered Amarnath's house shortly after midnight. He got out of his imported car, opened the main gate, parked the car in the driveway and closed the main gate. It was more than a month ago since the main gate was unguarded, as Amarnath had terminated contract with the security service that provided six guards for keeping round the clock vigil. Wasteful expenditure was the reason given by Amarnath to the security service for terminating the contract.

Naushad had a trim body that belied his age. Though he was on the wrong side of his forties, he appeared to be not older than 35. He came to Amarnath, observed his pulse for two minutes and then finally got down to the main task he was supposed to handle.

Naushad picked up two of the seven unconsumed pills and pocketed these. He was wearing surgical gloves. He took care to put Amarnath's wallet in his pocket after checking that it had Amarnath's business cards as well as a driving license. Then he lifted his business partner, put him in his car and sped away.

Manorama and the children returned home around 1 am. She headed straight to the study while the children went to their respective rooms. Kinshuk and Kriti ran out of their rooms when they heard their mother shrieking: "Where is your father?"

The children searched every nook and corner of the house but their father was nowhere to be found. They returned to the study where their mother was sitting on the floor beside her husband's favourite chair.

"I had warned you that he is up to some thing. And we should not leave him alone in this state of mind for long," Manorama said, tears rolling down her cheeks.

"Relax mom. Why are you imagining the worst?" Kinshuk said. "You know that I had come home secretly around 11 pm. I had told you that he was swallowing those tablets one by one and working seriously on his laptop. He was not drinking. I told you all this when I returned to the hotel. Dad must have gone out."

"My worry is only five pills are left on the table. Which means he consumed 179 of them."

"How does it matter when you know we had replaced the sleeping pills with similar looking vitamin pills," Kriti said.

"Why do you forget there were 20 sleeping pills in that stock of 184?" Manorama said chidingly.

"That's right; there were 20 sleeping pills. Why do you forget that each of those 20 pills was point two five milligrams potency, only? Even if he consumed all those, only five milligrams of sedatives would have gone inside his system, which is not lethal."

"But then he should have gone off to sleep. Why is he missing? Where has he gone?" Manorama said.

"For a man who has been consuming more than half a bottle of whisky every day for years, five milles of sleeping pills can hardly make him feel sleepy," Kriti stuck to her ground. "Let's find out from his friends."

"No point," said Kinshuk, who had been working on telephone for past several minutes outside the study. His face looked grave.

The mother daughter duo looked at him questioningly.

"We all know he had only four friends with whom he used to spend his evenings. I have already called each one of them and none of them is aware of Dad's whereabouts."

"Did you speak to Naushad uncle?" Kriti asked her brother.

"Of course, he was the first one I contacted. But he said he had not talked to Dad for two days."

There was silence in the house for some time. Then, ominously, the telephone rang. All three looked at one another. Manorama took the call. The children saw their mother's facial expressions changing from that of concern to anxiety to alarm.

"What happened? Who was it?" Kinshuk and Kriti asked.

"Your dad is in the Intensive Care Unit of the government hospital at the end of this road. He is in a coma."

"But what happened to him? Why is he in a coma? Has he had an accident?"

"He is in coma after consuming a high dose of sleeping pills. The doctors have already flushed his stomach.

But... Let's go."

Dhruv stopped here and cast a confident glance at Amaso.

"I invite you to make your guess at this stage."

"Your story is full of possibilities. I think the hero of your story is going to die. And he is not going to get any money even though he has won the jackpot."

"Can you elaborate?" Dhruv said.

"There may be some technical or legal hitches in getting him the jackpot money. It is a tragic story you have conceived this time."

"And what according to you is the sting in the tale?"

"I just told you. The hero does not get the jackpot money even after winning the contest. Your final sting can relate to Naushad, whom you are trying to build up as a villain."

"You don't think that Naushad is a villain?"

"I certainly don't view Naushad as a villain."

"You are free to change your guess now because once I resume, I will stop only after concluding the story," Dhruv offered.

"I have played my cards. I don't want to change my guess."

Dhruv resumed his story.

Inspector Nagraj was listening intently to Manorama's version. It had been more than twelve hours since she and her children had been camping in the hospital. They had had him transferred to a reputed private hospital, where Amarnath remained in ICU in a serious condition.

Manorama told the policeman how her husband had been purchasing sleeping pills once a week and had been storing them in his study at home for the past six months. She told the Inspector that while cleaning up the study, her daughter had stumbled upon the huge pile of pills some three weeks back. One pill was taken as a sample piece to a test laboratory and the tests confirmed it to be a sleeping pill of 20 mg potency. She also told the police inspector about the book her husband had bought more than six months ago. The book was about a young girl who decides to commit suicide because she did not find life worth living any more. Finally, Manorama told Inspector Nagraj about the counterplan prepared by herself and her children under which all but 20 sleeping pills were replaced by harmless vitamin pills.

"You are saying that out of Mr Amarnath's stockpile of almost two hundred tablets, only twenty were finally sleeping pills, the rest having been replaced by you with vitamin pills?"

"Yes."

"And that each of those sleeping pills were only of a very mild potency?"

"Yes."

"But how, then, did the doctors flush out more than fifty milligrams of undigested sedatives from his stomach? The doctors also suspect that, as much dosage of sedatives, if not more, had already been digested by Mr Amarnath," a suspicious Inspector Nagraj said.

Manorama and her children did not know what hit them.

"Did anyone, apart from you and your children, know that Mr Amarnath had been stockpiling sleeping pills and you had been replacing them with vitamin pills?"

"No."

"When you were away from home from nine last night till one this morning, did anybody visit your house?"

"What kind of a question is that Inspector? When we were not at home, how could we know whether anybody came?"

"I mean, did he talk of some appointment at his residence? Or are you aware of any friend of his who can drop in without appointment?"

"No, he did not talk of any private appointment. As for your second question, he has at least four such friends who can drop in any time without prior appointment. My son has spoken to all four of them and none of them was with my husband last night. But why are you asking all these questions, Inspector?"

"Because we have evidence that some body visited your house in your absence last night. The visitor has to be well known to your family because he or she brought the car inside your driveway. We have picked up tyre prints of this car and these are different from your car's tyre prints. But surprisingly, there are no finger prints of the mysterious visitor."

Manorama was shocked. "What do you mean, Inspector? My husband is fighting for his life in the ICU and here you are telling me that you have been snooping around in my house, lifting tyre prints and fingerprints. I will speak to the Police Commissioner!"

"Madam you can speak to the Police Commissioner, but let me tell you I am not from your area police station. I am from Special Branch."

"You may be from any branch you like, but what business do you have to snoop around my house?"

"Because I suspect that some body attempted to murder your husband."

"What! Murder! What for?"

"One hundred million US dollars."

"And who had that kind of money? My husband didn't."

"Your husband won a hundred million US dollars jackpot offered by an online game show."

"When?"

"Last night, when all of you were away."

"How do you know this?"

"Your husband's laptop was on. The screen was displaying the message: "Congratulations. You have won our game show's jackpot of one hundred million US dollars. We will be issuing necessary instructions to your bankers in due course."

Early next morning, Kinshuk and Kriti came to the hospital with tea and breakfast for their mother. She looked tense.

"How is dad?" Kriti asked.

"Still not in the clear."

"Have you heard anything from Inspector Nagraj?" Kinshuk asked.

"Speak of the devil and the devil appears," Manorama nodded towards the hospital's main entrance where a police jeep had just parked.

"Good morning madam. How is Mr Amarnath?" Inspector Nagraj asked. He seemed to be in an upbeat mood.

"The doctors are going to monitor him closely in the next twenty four hours. But his condition continues to be critical."

"I am sure the God Almighty will take care of him."

Manorama did not know how to respond to that. "Would you like to have some tea and sandwiches?" Manorama asked the Inspector.

"No. Thank you, madam."

She again fell silent. No one spoke for a couple of minutes. Inspector Nagraj continued to watch Manorama and her children very closely. She could sense that the Inspector wanted to say something.

"How is your investigation progressing?" Manorama asked.

"We have made a breakthrough."

"What is that?"

"We have arrested Mr Amarnath's business partner, Mr Naushad Azhar."

"On what charges?"

"There is a lot of circumstantial evidence against him."

"Such as?"

"He visited your house on that night. He was the one who took your husband to the hospital in his car. We have matched the tyre prints picked up from your house with his car's tyres and yet he lied to your son. In any case, Mr Naushad has admitted that he visited your house on the midnight of December 31 and January 1."

"What made you suspect Naushad?"

"We investigated your husband's mobile phone call records. Naushad was the last man to call up your husband. Yet he lied to your son. This was enough to probe him further."

"Has he admitted to making an attempt to kill my husband?"

"He denies that. On the contrary, he claims that if your husband were to survive, it would be only because of him."

"That's absolutely right. The doctors here told me that if my husband were to be brought to the hospital ten minutes later, his chances of survival would have been zero."

"Mr Naushad has told us that he had been protecting your husband for weeks."

"How?"

"That, he refuses to elaborate right now and says would tell his story at an appropriate time."

Another day passed.

Inspector Nagraj had been conspicuous by his absence for the last 24 hours. Manorama and her children did not know whether it was a good or bad sign.

Amarnath was still in the ICU. The chief doctor was to examine him at 10 am and then his medical bulletin would be released to the media. More than a dozen television channels had been camping in the hospital premises for the last day, since the news leaked that Amarnath had won a $100 million jackpot.

The hospital's cashier had prepared a demand note asking Amarnath's family to deposit Rs 75,000 immediately. When he saw television reporters coming to the hospital in hordes for the VIP patient, he thought it wise to consult the Financial Director before handing the demand note to Amarnath's family. The Financial Director shredded the note.

Dr Desai, the chief doctor, walked up to Manorama shortly after 10 am.

"I have good news to give to you. Your husband is out of danger and fully conscious. You can visit him for five minutes."

Manorama could not have been given happier news. She hugged her children. All three were ecstatic. None of them was in a mood to involve outsiders in their quiet celebrations. Inspector Nagraj would have been the most unwelcome creature on earth at this time. Yet, as luck would have it, the Inspector, who had not made an appearance in a day, emerged on the scene. Obviously, the hospital authorities had informed him about the patient's recovery.

Manorama broke into tears as she looked at her husband who was visibly pale and weak. Kinshuk and Kriti stood on the other side of the bed and looked at their father with concern.

"Why did you do this?" Manorama demanded to know.

"Because I could not take any more failures," Amarnath replied.

"Where did you fail?"

"I failed on every count; as a businessman, as a husband, as a father and perhaps as a human being too."

"Even if you failed on all these counts as you are saying, what right did you have to attempt suicide? Is your life your own only? Do we have no right on your life? Do you have no right on our lives?"

"I thought I was not wanted."

"You are wrong, Dad," Kriti said.

"And who says you are a failure, Dad? You have shown that you are perhaps the most successful man in the world," Kinshuk said.

Amarnath looked genuinely puzzled with his son's remark and looked at him questioningly.

"Do you remember that you were playing an online game on your laptop that night?"

"Yes, I think that I completed all the levels but I am not sure whether I pressed the "SUBMIT" button in time."

"You did, and you won the hundred million jackpot."

Amarnath swooned.

Doctors told Manorama and children to leave the ICU immediately. Inspector Nagraj stayed put.

The next morning, Amarnath was moved out of the ICU into a private room. The doctors found his recovery phenomenal. Such was the power of money, they joked.

Amarnath was in a chirpy mood. The doctors had disappeared. Inspector Nagraj's threatened visit was still an hour away. Manorama and the children had broken loose to go shopping.

Amarnath never felt so happy and contented. He even joked that his failed suicide bid meant a rebirth to him and he thanked his extreme action for this blissful state. His family life, which days ago seemed to be like a Sisyphean labour, was now imbued with a new meaning and purpose. He had rediscovered his loving wife and doting children. It was not just love but their rejuvenated respect for him that he valued most. He knew it was not just money. It was much more than that. In any case, the money had still to come.

The Amarnath family talked away to glory. The happy days were here again. He gave a blow-by-blow account of his online conquest of the game show. His wife and children listened to him in a state of stunned disbelief. All three lustily clapped as Amarnath gave details of how he negotiated each of the ten levels of the game show. His children wondered how their father was in control of his faculties even while he was gulping down tablets after tablets of sedatives.

Then Inspector Nagraj arrived. He came with Naushad who looked a bit ruffled after spending a night in the police station. Suddenly, the atmosphere became sober and businesslike. However, two people seemed more confident than the rest to negotiate the current storm – Amarnath and Naushad.

Amarnath came to the brass tacks immediately. "Why have you arrested my friend Naushad, Mr Nagraj?" he asked.

The Inspector explained the case against Naushad. Amarnath laughed and said, "Inspector, nothing could be further from the truth than your theories and suspicions." Then he told the Inspector the story to which only he and Naushad had been privy.

Amarnath explained how one night he was sleepless and actually felt the need for the pills he had been storing. He went to his study, took a double dose and returned to his bed. Twenty minutes passed and he did not get a wink of sleep. The next half an hour, he repeated the exercise thrice over, but with the same result. The first thing he did in the morning after that sleepless night was to get a sample of two pills tested in a laboratory. He was told that they were vitamin pills, not sedatives. He knew that his family had discovered what he was up to.

He discussed the matter with Naushad who had from the very beginning given his quiet acquiescence to the suicide plan without contesting it even once. Amarnath found it a bit strange but thought that perhaps his suicide suited Naushad. However, Naushad had other plans. Naushad volunteered to replace the fake pills with genuine sleeping pills.

At this stage, Naushad butted in and said, "I consulted experts and replaced every tablet with a sleeping pill of a mild potency. At that time, the total number of pills was one hundred and fifty, and that meant that the total dosage was less than forty milles. I was told that this dosage was hardly lethal to a hale and hearty man who consumes a glass of liquor every day." Naushad gave the names and telephone numbers of the three experts he had contacted. Inspector Nagraj noted down the details.

Amarnath then finished his story by reporting the sole new development. For the next 30 days, he started stocking his 20 mg sleeping pills in his bookrack while not disturbing the location of the original stockpile of 150 or so tablets.

Naushad then told Inspector Nagraj that he knew that Amarnath would definitely require mild medical attention but he had no idea that his friend would be landing in ICU in a critical state. Naushad told the Inspector that he purposely reached Amarnath's house at the stroke of midnight. This was to give Amarnath time to complete the internet game. He wanted to spring a surprise on Amarnath's family and that is why he took all those precautions which he did; such as using surgical gloves, putting Amarnath's wallet in his trousers' pocket so that his identity could be established by his business card and driving license, and took him to the hospital.

A grateful Manorama looked at Naushad and thanked him. "I never believed in your theories Inspector Nagraj. I always knew that Naushad is a do-gooder, not a villain."

The Inspector knew he could no longer keep Naushad in his custody. He left Naushad in the room and instructed his subordinates to keep vigil until he returned from his field investigations. Inspector Nagraj did not announce his decision to set Naushad free until he had recorded statements of the three experts whom Naushad had contacted. The Inspector also spoke to owners of the ten chemist shops from where Naushad had purchased 150 sleeping pills of 0.25 mg potency. All corroborated Naushad's statement.

After lunch, everybody was relaxed. Manorama was at her husband's bedside. The children were busy talking to themselves. Naushad was leafing through a magazine. The Medical Superintendent entered the room.

"How are you feeling now, Mr Amarnath?" he asked.

"Better."

"The Managing Director of American Express Bank is here and wants to see you immediately. He says it is an urgent official matter. An American reporter from TIME magazine is also waiting to interview you. Besides that, reporters from a dozen odd television channels have been camping here for the past several days and they are getting restive to talk to you, now that you are out of danger. Who would you like to see first?" the Medical Superintendent asked.

"Let the banker come first," Naushad said. Amarnath concurred.

The banker was ushered in five minutes later. The bespectacled, balding man in his late fifties was immaculately attired in an expensive suit. He looked worried.

"Hello, Mr Amarnath. I am Satish Santiago, the Chief of India operations of the American Express Bank. Congratulations for winning the jackpot. We would like to feature you in our new ad campaign. We will offer you very attractive terms. I have come here personally to seek your unofficial approval. The details can be worked out after you are discharged from the hospital and have fully recovered."

"But why me? I am not a celebrity."

"You are the newest celebrity in this celebrity hungry country. We are particularly pleased to know that you have been our customer for last nearly two decades, and what is more, ours is the only credit card you have ever held. This is precisely what we want to highlight in our ad campaign," the banker explained.

Naushad intervened and said, "I think he should be up for it. Right now, though, he is not too well. I am sure I can tell you in my capacity as Mr Amarnath's business partner that he would consider your offer with an open mind. Can we do anything else for you, sir?"

"Er, there is something disturbing and I seek your indulgence, Mr Amarnath," the banker said, coming to the sensitive part of his mission.

"What is it?" Amarnath said, puzzled.

"Sir, if you remember, on 31st December, you used your American Express card to make two payments. One was for Rs five hundred thousand in favour of the Life Insurance Corporation. I believe that this is your annual premium that you have been paying for the last several years towards the "Key Man" policy that your company has purchased for you. I am told this was the last day for making the payment or else it would have entailed a heavy penalty. Hours later, you made the second payment of one thousand US dollars to an

American company, the world leader in online game shows. Unfortunately, your credit limit at that time was Rs five hundred thousand only and only one transaction could have been honoured."

Everybody present in the room suddenly realized the magnitude of the problem.

"Eventually only one transaction was honoured?" Amarnath asked incredulously.

"Yes sir," the banker replied and bowed his head.

Amarnath could see the world collapsing before him. Obviously, the bank would have cleared the LIC payment. One, he had been paying his insurance premium through his credit card every year. Two, as the banker was saying, the bank officials were aware that dishonouring the LIC related transaction would have inflicted financial loss to Amarnath, their old customer. That is why the bank's top boss was there personally, trying to sugarcoat their gross error with an "attractive offer" of an ad campaign.

Being a businessman himself, Amarnath was aware that the American company would be well within its right not to release the jackpot money if the purchase of entry ticket, the very basis of eligibility, were to be invalidated.

"Your suspense is killing, Mr Santiago. Tell me which transaction you did not honour – the one relating to the American company?"

"No sir. Our junior staff committed that mistake. Your second payment of a thousand dollars was honoured and the other one was not. But I assure you that our bank will bear whatever penalty is imposed on you by the LIC for late payment."

Amarnath and family hardly bothered to hear the second part of the banker's statement. They hugged one another. They were bursting with joy. The banker silently watched the celebrations, completely bewildered.

There was a knock on the door. It was the Medical Superintendent again. Apparently he had come running and was out of breath.

"Mr Amarnath, the Chief Minister is holding line on my office phone and wishes to speak to you to personally congratulate you on your win. Besides, a senior official of the American company is here to deliver to you the banker's cheque of one hundred million US dollars. Scores of media people have surrounded him and are demanding that you come out onto the hospital lawns so that they can telecast the event live. What is your call?"

A beaming and confident Amarnath got up from the bed, placed his arms on the shoulders of Manorama and Naushad and told his children, "Let's go for a walk."

Dhruv stopped here and announced that his third and last tale was over. All eyes were now on Amaso, curious to know his verdict.

"Who won this round?" Mili asked Amaso.

"Obviously Mr Dhruv has won this round. He gets ten out of ten," Amaso said.

Mili cheered lustily and was about to give Dhruv a tight hug when she checked herself at the last moment.

Outside, the storm was continuing, though with depleted force.

Amaso then looked at the woman in black and said to Mehmood Mian, "Take her away. I will tell you later what is to be done with her." Then turning to Mili and Dhruv, he said, "We disperse now. Let's meet after half an hour to discuss some important matters."

15

The Hurly Burly

Mili could not have been happier. She did not waste a second after reaching the room and started showering kisses on Dhruv. His entire face underwent, what Mili called, an ESI therapy. By this weird term, she meant kissing Every Square Inch of the target, which often meant the face, but could sometimes also mean the entire body.

Mili had told Dhruv during one of her numerous ESI therapy sessions with him that she had reserved her ESI therapy for his entire body for "the big day". He never inquired what she meant by "the big day"; and she, on her part, never volunteered the information.

Dhruv invariably turned silent after every ESI therapy session. This time was no different. He was in deep thoughts.

"What are you thinking?" Mili asked, still not releasing Dhruv from her grip.

Dhruv did not reply and kept brooding while Mili continued to bombard his face with kisses. Finally, she released him from her embrace and repeated the question. Dhruv's facial muscles twitched as he spoke.

"I am thinking about the mysterious woman in the black."

"What about her? Are you besotted by her beauty?" Mili teased him.

Dhruv ignored the broadside and said, "I think, we need to be wary of her. The woman is as dangerous as she is sexy."

"What do you mean?"

"I don't know. I am just sharing my gut feeling."

The storm had stopped. Their promised appointment with Amaso, probably the last one, was still fifteen minutes away. Then there was a loud thump on the door. A man shouted from outside that the Supreme Leader wished to see them at once.

A minute later, Dhruv and Mili were in the hall where Amaso was already standing. It was an unusual sight to see Amaso standing. There was an air of urgency.

Amaso took Dhruv's hand in his and after shaking it vigorously, he said, "Mr Dhruv, I must say that I am always going to cherish the memory of the past few days I have spent with you and the mohtarma. I had fixed another meeting with you two to discuss your third story. But I am afraid, I will have to leave immediately because the weather has cleared. I wish to inform you that both of you will be set free. I have instructed Mehmood Mian to personally escort you people to your territory, but you will have to wait for a few hours."

Then turning to Mehmood Mian and Javed, who were standing by his side like alert sentries, Amaso said, "Please make sure that our guests' stay here is comfortable. Inform me after the guests are escorted to their land safely."

Amaso again shook hands with Dhruv, nodded goodbye to Mili and rushed out. After Amaso's exit, the hostages felt something was amiss. Who said terrorists were not human?

A few minutes later, Mehmood Mian and Javed returned to the hall. The former left none in doubt that he was the boss now. He clapped his hands to summon the cook, ordered him to prepare tea for four and asked Dhruv and Mili to sit on the mattresses. Dhruv noticed that Mehmood Mian sat alone on the mattress where Amaso used to sit. Javed sat on the mattress where he and Mehmood Mian had sat. Dhruv thought that it was not just military men who were sticklers for hierarchy; terrorists also believed in it.

Mehmood Mian called for the woman in the black to be brought before him immediately.

"So Mr Dhruv, how are you feeling now?"

At first, Dhruv did not understand the query and then realized that the question's thrust was "now". "Now" could have two connotations: one, after winning the contest; and two, after Amaso's exit.

As Dhruv was still debating the real import of the question, Mehmood Mian shot another one. "I know you must be feeling damn relieved. But tell me did you feel nervous while you were preparing the third story?"

"Yes and no. Yes, because it was a question of life and death. No, because this time I took her help," Dhruv said, signalling to Mili.

Two men brought the handcuffed and chained woman before Mehmood Mian. Her hair was unkempt. She was wearing tight trousers and a top that displayed the contours and curves of her figure. As she walked into the room with a lot of effort, her forehead showed beads of sweat. Her hair flew into her face, enhancing her raw sex appeal. Mehmood Mian noticed the prisoner's presence from out of the corner of his eye, but he continued with his speech.

"Let me tell you some thing, Mr Dhruv, the Supreme Leader could have easily won the contest. Probably, he didn't want to. I have never seen him so tense and anxious about his personal safety as in the past few days. It is indeed creditable that though he got regular feedback every four or five hours on how his trusted friends were plotting to engineer his capture for personal or national gains, which allowed him little or no concentration, he listened to your stories intently."

"On what basis do you say that the Supreme Leader could have easily won the contest?" Dhruv asked.

"What to talk of the Supreme Leader, even I could have easily defeated you. I also like thrillers. Unlike the Supreme Leader, who likes to read books, I like watching movies."

"Mr Mehmood, there is an old saying in India: who sees if a peacock dances in the woods?"

"What do you mean? You think I am boasting?"

"I didn't say that. What I mean is ..."

"No need to explain, Mr Dhruv," Mehmood Mian said politely. Dhruv and Mili noticed the change in him. "There is still some time left. Both of us can play the similar game for one story only. At stake will not be your freedom because that you have already won. Honour will be at stake for both of us. What do you say?"

Mili nudged Dhruv. He knew that she would not be happy with another stake out.

"I am sorry, Mr Mehmood. I am very tired. Besides, I don't have a story plot coming to my mind immediately," Dhruv said.

A disappointed Mehmood Mian looked around and saw the handcuffed prisoner. For the first time, he addressed himself directly to the woman: "You must be feeling very uncomfortable, aren't you?"

"You bother about your own discomforts which are going to befall you shortly," the woman said with a poisonous sneer.

Mehmood Mian flew into rage with this reply from the prisoner. "Take her out! Tie her to the roadside electric pole and hang her!" Mehmood Mian ordered.

The guards started to drag the woman out of the mansion.

Dhruv shouted, "Stop!" The guards stopped in their tracks. "Wait, Mehmood Mian. Does Islam permit murder of a spy, particularly if the spy happens to be a woman?"

Dhruv noticed the expression on the woman's face changed from cruelty to gratitude.

Mehmood Mian did not have a ready answer for this question. As he brooded for one, there was a commotion outside.

Guns roared, grenades blasted, fighters ran from one place to another. The noise of rapid fire from assault rifles came nearer every second and before Mehmood Mian and Javed could take combat positions, several armed men entered the hall like a gale. They were dressed in Pakistan Army fatigues. They quickly disarmed Mehmood Mian and all his men and huddled them together in a group.

Mili was petrified. She had been instinctively holding the arm of Dhruv when a soldier nudged her ribs with the gun's barrel. She disengaged her hand from Dhruv's arm. The soldier did not remove the gun's barrel from her chest and pressed her ribs until it hurt. She got the hint and threw her hands up. Dhruv followed suit. Two soldiers came forward and tied the hands of Dhruv and Mili.

Another man dressed in army fatigues entered the hall and saluted the woman in black, who by now had regained her composure.

"Hope we are not late, madam?" the man, who seemed to be a leader of the raid party, asked.

"If you had come a few minutes later you would have found me on a public electric pole. What about the obstacles outside?" she asked.

"There were just six; all have been taken care of. Their bodies are lying outside. Most of them have just one hole in their bodies. It shows they were taken completely unawares," the raid party leader explained.

"It also shows your men's marksmanship," the woman in the black said.

"That goes without saying, madam. After all, these are elite commandos of the Pakistan Army who are the best in the world."

"What is to be done with these men?" the team leader asked about the security guards who were dragging her out a few minutes back. She looked at them. There were two of them. One man could not cope with the woman's angry look which resembled a King Cobra in flight as it pounces upon a wounded dove trying to fly and swooned. She now turned her gaze to the other guard.

He was of stronger mettle; he kept standing but wet his pants.

The woman laughed on seeing the man's urine forming a small puddle on the floor. Mili had seen such maniacal mirth only in films.

"Take them away. You can use them for constructing roads or digging tunnels. Subject them to hard labour for 16 hours a day for a year and if their behaviour is good, release them. Or else, you know what is to be done."

Dhruv was right, Mili thought. The woman in the black was indeed dangerous. She was powerful, combining powers of an army commander as well as a judge.

"And what about this Bollywood heroine and the mole?" the team leader asked, referring to Mili and Dhruv. "Kill them and bury their bodies here only so that the Indians cannot even say that their kidnapped nationals were taken to our territory?"

Mili was scared stiff.

"No. Don't be so harsh. After all, this man showed the guts in challenging their decision to hang me. We will see later what is to be done with them." The woman cast a coquettish glance at Dhruv while speaking.

"Finally, what about these two?" the leader asked about Mehmood Mian and Javed. "Pack them along with the guards and use them for building roads and digging tunnels?"

"No, they have completed their quota of breath." She snatched the leader's assault rifle and pumped dozens of bullets into Mehmood Mian and Javed. Dhruv noticed that not a single bullet missed its target. Mili watched the live horror show dumbstruck and fainted.

Mili regained her consciousness in a dark room. She looked around but could not crane her neck beyond a point as the back portion of her head flared in pain. She wanted to press her head but a rope tied her hands. She remembered the chain of events before she came to this high-ceiling room, which had just one small ventilation grille.

Mili noticed that the rope had loosened. With some efforts, she freed her hands, which instinctively went up to that portion of her skull that was hurt. She touched her tangled hair at a particular point. The skin underneath pulsed a warning pain. She remembered that she had fainted and while falling down her head must have landed on the floor or on some sharp-edged object. She felt the dry cakes in her hair, which was her own blood.

Mili wanted answers to many questions: Where was she? Where was Dhruv? Were they safe? Who was this mysterious woman in the black? Her head ached.

Dhruv had studied the wily woman very carefully ever since she had acted as a firing squad for Mehmood Mian and Javed. The two close lieutenants of Amaso had been killed like mosquitoes.

He tried to analyse the three sets of people whose fate the woman had decided: the security guards, Mehmood Mian and Javed, and Mili and he himself. Despite her poisonous traits, the woman was different indeed, Dhruv told himself. Here was a woman who knew how to square the circles and how to count the ants on earth while aiming for the stars. Her response in respect of the three sets of people was different and perhaps justifiable from her sick point of view. However, why had she separated him from Mili? Where was Mili? How was she?

Dhruv did not have to wait long. The gates of his dungeonlike cell, which let in very little sunlight, creaked open and somebody walked in. He did not attempt to look up to see who had entered the cell. The entrant, obviously, did not like the indifferent attitude. Dhruv was startled when the entrant spoke.

"Have you got so resigned to your fate that you don't even look up to see who has come in? It could have been your sweetheart Mili also!"

Dhruv was suddenly alert. The woman in black, whom he had always seen in masculine dress, was now wearing a sari, a dress peculiar only to the Indian subcontinent. She looked ravishing in jetblack with lowcut, tight blouse of the same colour. She had not tied her long hair.

The woman was the lone entrant into the room. She took her own time to walk from the door to the cemented platform where Dhruv was sitting. She stopped in front of Dhruv and stood, deliberately ignoring the fact that part of sari that was supposed to cover her breasts had fallen to the ground. As a result, her curvaceous figure was on display.

"How are you, young man?" the woman asked.

Dhruv ignored the question. Instead, he fired his own question, "Who are you?"

The woman smiled and then responded slowly "If you did not know this earlier, by now you must, my dear. You must be thankful to be alive. You have no rights and privileges, but only duties and compulsions. It is I who have the right to ask you questions, stupid man." The woman was no longer smiling, but was shaking with anger. She adjusted her sari to cover her halfnaked breasts, which were threatening to burst out of the blouse.

Dhruv realized that he probably needed this reality check. Quickly, he composed himself and said, "Let it remain as it was earlier."

"Let remain what?" the woman said, surprised.

"I mean, why are you covering these two very beautiful little mountains with your sari?"

The woman was nonplussed at Dhruv's sudden change of gear. Dhruv took further advantage of the situation and cooed another question, "What is a fairy like you doing in this world of demons?"

This question had the desired effect of mellowing her down. "What if this fairy is only a demon?" she breathed down over his neck as she posed the counter question.

Dhruv wanted to ward her off but could not as he remembered that his hands were tied. The woman noticed his predicament, sat beside him and began unravelling the knots of the rope. Soon Dhruv was unbound.

The woman came very close to him and looked straight into his eyes. Dhruv weighed the pros and cons. He knew what mattered most at this moment were not emotions, morals or principles but operations. He did not take his face away. The woman understood the signal and put her lips, burning with desire, on his lips. Dhruv still did not budge from his position. The woman did not appear to be in a hurry to take her lips off. Dhruv was already feeling the burning sensation of her breasts rubbing against his chest as she continued with her kiss. Dhruv hugged her tight, changing position by shoving her down onto the cemented platform as he gave her one long and hot kiss.

A minute later, he got up and sat some distance away from her. The woman readjusted her sari and sat upright, knowing that Dhruv was about to speak.

"You are a strange woman. A short time ago, you killed two men in cold blood. Now here you are with your prisoner, making love. Is there some method in your madness? Who are you? Where am I? Where is Mili? What do you intend to do with us?"

"To answer your last questions first, you are in Azad Kashmir. Your girl friend is also here and safe."

"She is not my girl friend. I am nothing to her. She is a superstar. She is like the sun. I am like a firefly. Billions of fireflies cannot challenge the sun. But what do you intend to do with us?"

"I will play with you like a cat plays with a mouse before eating him up."

"So you will kill us?"

"I never use such a reprehensible word."

"Reprehensible! It is interesting indeed to hear from a person such as yourself the use of such a word!"

"What do you mean by "a person such as yourself"? Do you know I am Oxford educated?"

"Thank you for giving some information about yourself. Tell me something more about yourself. What is your name? What do you do? Why are you in this kind of milieu? Of course, Oxford does not breed jihadis!"

"I can't tell you my life history, nor is it necessary. It should be sufficient for you to know that I am here on an important mission."

"What are we in this important mission of yours – pawns or key pieces?"

"Your role was purely incidental. You started as pawns. But now, I must say, you have graduated to become key pieces."

"Now tell me what brought you to this room and that too without any aides? Obviously you did not come here to have sex with me."

"Let me tell you, I have had sex with scores of men. On all these occasions, it was an operational requirement. Sex is neither a taboo nor a passion with me. I came here for no operational reasons, though. It is sheer curiosity which has brought me."

"What kind of curiosity?"

"I have seen how you won over Amaso and how a Bollywood heroine, who is the heart throb of millions, has fallen in love with you!"

"She is not in love with me!"

"You would be a fool or a blind man not to see this. Anyway, the point I was making was that I was curious to touch and feel the person who has bowled over two important persons, so different from one another. Obviously, you would not have liked me to kiss you in front of your girlfriend."

"And still you will kill us?"

"That I have not decided yet. I am waiting for certain instructions from my bosses."

The woman got up and turned back to leave. She was surprised to see Dhruv hold her hand. "Even you have a boss?" Dhruv asked.

"What do you mean? Am I above being commanded?" She said as she sat close to him.

Women like you actually are, Dhruv wanted to reply. He checked himself and substituted his statement with a question, "Will I be beheaded if I were to kiss you?" Dhruv was at his charming best.

"No. You will be rewarded, in fact. For every kiss you will get two back."

Dhruv worked on her body for the next couple of minutes. In between, he looked towards the door. She told him not to worry as nobody dared to enter the room without her permission. When Dhruv became more probative about her breasts, she whispered, "Let's go to a proper room."

Dhruv rejected the suggestion, saying, "So far, you have done it for operational requirements. Now you will see it happening to you naturally. Look at the situation, the ambience and the spontaneity. This cement platform will add to the ambience. You will never forget this experience."

She acquiesced. Fifteen minutes later, she was in a delirious state. Dhruv was right, she thought. She would always remember the unusual ambience in which she had been taken by him. She quickly recapitulated all her sexual encounters and tried to remember when she had had sex with a man who did not even know her name. She could not remember a single instance. Finally, she got up from the cemented platform and dressed.

"Can I get a cigarette?" Dhruv asked casually, his demeanour suddenly reflecting more confidence than ever before.

The woman ignored the demand and the synthetic intoxicated voice in which it was made. Instead, she took his hand, as a police officer holds a convict, and said dryly, "Let's go."

She was careful to leave his hand as they stepped out of the cell.

Dhruv observed his cell as he stepped out. It was situated in a huge open area. He also noticed another cell at some distance where, presumably, Mili was lodged. The woman was leading him to a double storied house. The ground was covered with snow. They were moving along a tiled walkway that had been cleared of snow.

The entire place was well guarded. He saw more than ten armed men in army fatigues deployed all over the complex.

The guards saluted the woman as she walked past them. She took him to a big well furnished room on the ground floor, which had a huge bed, a sofa, two chairs, a table and an attached washroom.

She seated herself on the sofa. Dhruv walked to a closed window. He opened the window and peered out. The window opened onto another ground. He was surprised to see a helicopter. The motor was off but he could see two pilots seated inside.

"Close the window and come here," the woman instructed politely.

"Where is Mili? Is she alright? Can you tell them to bring her here?"

The woman frowned and got up. "You are not here on a picnic or on your honeymoon. If you want to remain alive, you are not going to mention her name again."

"Have you killed her already?"

"No. And I am not going to answer any more questions from you."

"But I insist. I want to see her."

The woman pressed the bell. A sentry came in running.

"Listen. If this man wants some thing to eat or drink, get it for him. If he does not behave like a prisoner, hit him. If he still does not listen to you, kill him. How is the actress doing?"

The sentry hesitated to answer and when he noticed the stern looks of the woman, he said, "She is not well."

"Describe her condition in detail."

"Her head is swollen from some injury which did not occur here. She is running slight fever. She is hungry and thirsty. As per your instructions, she has not been given any food or water ever since these two were shifted here."

"Good. When is the television team coming?"

"They have already left for this place and will be here in the next ten to fifteen minutes."

"Inform me as soon as the television team completes its task. After they leave, you can give her food and water. Get her examined by a doctor as well. Remember that under no circumstances should she be able to see this man. Is that understood?"

"Yes madam."

"Good. You can go now and don't forget to fetch him a pack of cigarettes."

Dhruv looked at her angrily but did not speak a word. The woman went to the washroom.

He could not help but think of the frailty whose name was woman. He had read Shakespeare during college. It was only now that he understood the real depth of the bard. Dhruv had thought that a man could conquer a woman if he satiated her in bed. He realised the bankruptcy of that thought. He pondered over his well calculated gamble on the cemented platform and his frank self assessment was that though his conduct was in accordance with the copybook standards, he had failed to achieve a strategic victory over the opponent.

She came out of the washroom after a few minutes, dressed in army fatigues. She took army boots from a cupboard and sat down on the sofa to don the heavy leather shoes.

"I am leaving for an important meeting. I should be back late in the evening. It would be better for you if you behave. Or else ..." she hissed and got up to leave.

She came back from the door and said, "By the way, you were right. I would never forget what we did in the cell. You were also right that it happened naturally, perhaps for the first time, as far as I am concerned. Just as you did it for the first time. If you thought you could win me over like that, then you are highly mistaken."

Without waiting for Dhruv's response, she went out. A few minutes later, the helicopter took off. The inference was obvious. Only key officials could have the luxury of a helicopter or an aircraft standing by for them; she fitted the bill.

Dhruv was brooding over the fate that had befallen him and Mili. A proverb came to his mind that summed up their current predicament: out of the frying pan, into the fire. He knew his last ditch effort of trying to win her over through non-combat means had come to naught. In the process, he had lost his virginity, which the clever woman did not fail to notice. He chided himself why he did what he did. Again and again, this question would leapfrog from the back lanes of his mind to centre stage and each time he would unsuccessfully try to convince himself that he did it to buy their freedom.

Dhruv could somewhat understand the macabre game that was being played. The non-state actors were out; the state actors had taken over. The terrorists had not made any demand for releasing the prisoners. The demands were going to be made by the Pakistani intelligence now. They were using Mili for issuing an appeal to the Government of India. That is why the relevance of the television team. Importantly, the television team could not have been summoned earlier because Mili had to look like a hostage and a traumatised victim.

He knew too well that if he and Mili ever faced a serious threat to their lives since their kidnapping more than a week ago, it was now.

16

The Final Challenge

In a room in New Delhi's South Block, where the Prime Minister's Office and the Foreign and Defence Ministries are situated, nine wise men were in the middle of a serious conference. The room was that of the National Security Advisor. The Cabinet Secretary, the Foreign Secretary, the Home Secretary, the three Services chiefs and the chiefs of IB and RAW were present at the meeting.

The NSA rubbed his hands together and brooded as the chiefs of IB and RAW just finished their presentations.

"Gentlemen, it is a most extraordinary situation. I have to inform the Prime Minister immediately. I am certain he will have to call a meeting of the Cabinet Committee on Security to take a decision on the matter. Please wait here. I will not take long."

The Cabinet Secretary picked up the television remote and switched it on. He clicked from one news channel to another. All were giving breaking news. For the first time since the kidnapping of Bollywood heroine Mili and another man named Dhruv, the Lashkar-e-Toiba had claimed responsibility for the act and had made known its single-point demand for releasing the kidnapped couple: safe passage for notorious terrorist Mulla Zahoor, who was in the custody of the Indian authorities.

The Cabinet Secretary remarked, "It does not matter which television channel you put it on. All are having discussions or phone-ins with experts thrown in between news, profiling Mulla Zahoor."

Experts called the two-for-one swap offer a master move of the LET. It showed that the terrorists were serious, did not jack up their demands and made it appear feasible. It showed that the LET were very clear in their thinking and priorities. It also showed the stature of Mulla Zahoor among terrorists. Probably no single terrorist had spilled so much blood in Jammu and Kashmir as Mulla Zahoor.

Another expert pointed out that terrorism in Kashmir had gone up dramatically ever since Mulla Zahoor was arrested a year ago. He also went on to cite "rumours" that Ghazni Baba, who had been tormenting the Indian security forces for past six months, was a half-brother of Mulla Zahoor.

The NSA walked in. The Cabinet Secretary switched off the television.

"We have 15 minutes more, gentlemen. As I told you, the PM has ordered to convene a CCS meeting immediately. All the members the Home Minister, the Defence Minister, the

Foreign Minister, the Finance Minister and I are in town. Luckily, all officials concerned are also here. Therefore, the CCS meets in fifteen minutes with a single agenda: the Kashmir kidnappings. Let's complete our work in this period," the NSA said.

"But what about our meeting? Will that be after the CCS meeting?" the Home Secretary asked.

"Yes indeed. I had a couple of points to discuss with you all. Now that this CCS meeting is scheduled, it makes better sense to hold our meeting after that only. We meet here immediately after the CCS meeting," the NSA said.

"Who gave you the authority to kill Amaso's top men?" the ISI chief shouted, his face red with anger.

The mystery woman, who always dressed in black but was today in army uniform, was seated opposite him. There was no one else in the room.

"If I had not killed them, they would have raped and killed me," she lied.

"They had been overpowered and disarmed. They did not pose any threat to you. You killed them in cold blood," General Mir Qasim said.

The woman did not reply.

"But for the good work you have done, you would have been in a soup."

"Which good work you are referring to?" she asked inquisitively.

"Let me inform you Miss Gulnar Butt; the President is pleased with your neat operation of hijacking the kidnapped Bollywood heroine. He also appreciates your work of sending the heroine's appeal to news agency offices in Srinagar. This has given us a huge leverage."

Gulnar was fully alert now. She sensed a kill here. She had always dreamed of becoming the ISI chief. She would be the first ever woman intelligence chief in the world. She knew how to climb the ranks. That is how she had attained such a senior position when she was not yet forty. She had kept her body fit. Her skin was flawless, her face radiated raw sex, her eyes reflected a maniacal charm, and her breasts, waist and hips were shapely enough to put actors and ramp models to shame. She looked at least a decade younger than her actual age. At parties and informal get togethers, she would invariably be the star attraction. Such was her persona that at several parties she stole the thunder from even leading actors.

"It takes lots of guts and planning to hijack Amaso's prisoners, General," she said.

"That is the only good thing you have managed to do in this particular episode; otherwise, your performance sheet is full of black marks."

"What else is being held against me?"

"Where was the need for you to have sexual intercourse with Dhruv?" the General asked with a straight face.

Gulnar was awestruck as the full import of what the ISI chief had just said sank in. She remained tongue tied for some time. She had indulged in much more brazen behaviour in the past; but not even once had she been caught with her pants quite literally round her ankles, as she was now.

The General understood what was going on in her mind and said, "Yes we have been spying on you, but that's the rule of the game. I should not be shocked if even I am under the scanner. Rather, I would be surprised if I am not."

"But what wrong did I do? It was an operational requirement."

"Your act with Dhruv is on record, and the record does not show how it was an operational requirement for you. Instead, it shows you enjoying every bit of the act and eventually making a confession to Dhruv that it was not your operational requirement; in as many words."

Gulnar knew she had lost the game. She was still wondering why she had been summoned and why she had been instructed to come in uniform.

Gen Qasim was reading her like a broadsheet. He told her to wait in the visitors' room until he came back from an urgent meeting with the President – his fourth since the morning. He also advised her to keep herself mentally ready to meet the President, a former army chief, if he so wished. Then she understood why she was told to come in uniform.

The General returned forty minutes later and went straight to the Visitors' Room. He looked perplexed. During the two-minute-long walk to his office, he told Gulnar what the President wanted. After reaching his office, the ISI Chief instructed his PA not to give him any calls and asked for tea and biscuits.

The PA smiled as he passed on the instructions to a peon and said to a curious colleague, "I have worked with three ISI chiefs, apart from the present one. All bosses are alike: they want to talk to this woman, Gulnar, only in strict privacy, seated in cushy sofas and sipping tea."

The PA's observation was wide off the mark. The ISI chief had indeed sunk into his sofa while Gulnar was seated opposite him, but he was not looking at the curves of her body. He had serious things to discuss with Gulnar, who looked aghast.

"How can the President do this? How can he call off combing operations for Amaso? Is he not bothered about the nation's future, considering the promises made by the Americans?"

"Look here, officer. The President is primarily considering his own future. Amaso is a life insurance policy for the President. As long as Amaso is a threat to the Americans and he is at large, our President is safe."

"Why?"

"Because he would outlive his utility and become a liability for the Americans after offering Amaso to the Americans on a platter. Remember the fate of Zia ul Haq; what happened to him after the Afghan war was over. Zia died in a mysterious plane crash. If the present President has to be politically relevant in the international scheme of things, Amaso has to be alive and kicking. You should thank your stars that the President did not punish you, unlike those two Brigadiers."

"Which two Brigadiers?"

"Brigadier Ali and Brigadier Osman who ordered combat operations and door-to-door search for Amaso."

"Don't you think it would make our President much more relevant and powerful in international politics if Amaso were to be in our custody, secretly of course?"

"Don't even in your wildest dreams harbour such thoughts," General Qasim cautioned. "Can you contain the fragrance of flowers? Can you arrest the wind? You must be out of your mind to think that any one can catch Amaso alive in the first place and then keep it a secret."

"And why do you think the President has not taken action against me?"

"This is indeed baffling. Your offence was far more serious. You killed Amaso's closest aides in cold blood. I think, besides the fact that you are a Special Operations officer, what saved you was your master move of getting a televised appeal from the Indian heroine to the Government of India and laying the blame on the door of Lashkar-e-Toiba. Importantly, for you, the LET claimed responsibility for the act."

Qasim's RAX phone rang. He rose from the sofa, slowly walked towards his desk, sat on his chair and picked up the receiver, "Hello," he mumbled into the mouthpiece.

Suddenly, the General jumped up. The receiver nearly fell from his hands when he heard the caller's voice.

"Gentlemen, as you have seen and heard yourself at the CCS meeting, tomorrow is the D day. I hope that this Kashmir kidnapping episode will come to an amicable resolution tomorrow," the NSA, T R Raghvan said.

"I have my own reservations, Mr Raghvan, which, as you know, I shared at the CCS meeting," the Army Chief said. "The Prime Minister's decision will go a long way in giving a boost to terrorism in Kashmir which we have brought well under control after hundreds of our men and women laid down their lives. This man Mulla Zahoor, whom we are releasing tomorrow in exchange for our two hostages, is single-handedly responsible for killing more than a hundred army personnel."

"But what could the PM do when the Chief Minister of Maharashtra put his foot down and told him categorically that he would withdraw his party's support to the PM's coalition government if the LET's demand was not accepted immediately?" the NSA explained. "You know very well that the Maharashtra CM's regional party has 40 members in the Lower House of Parliament and withdrawal of his support would reduce the government to minority. In this situation, is the PM left with any option?"

The Home Secretary agreed with the Army Chief and said, "Our problem is that we don't have a national policy on kidnapping of innocent citizens by terrorists even though we have been grappling with the menace for more than two decades. Ten situations bring forth as many kinds of responses from our political leadership."

The NSA realised that his colleagues were getting into polemics. He reminded them that they were not there to participate in a debate on the political executive's perceived sins of omission and commission. Finally, order was restored and the nine wise men started preparing the roadmap for their individual departments to make sure that the prisoner-hostages exchange would go off smoothly the next day.

The NSA noted that the CCS spent at least ten minutes in discussing with concern the issue of Inspector General Dashamlav's "disappearance".

"Good afternoon, Qasim. This is ..."

"Very good afternoon, Mr President," the ISI Chief cut short the President as he recognised his voice.

"I called to tell you a couple of things."

"Shall I come over, sir? It will take me just ten minutes."

"No. I have to give you two directions only, which can be

done by phone as well; why waste each other's precious time?"

"Tell me, sir."

"But before that I would give you some information."

"Please go ahead, sir."

"I just received the Indian Prime Minister's telephone call. He was all sugar and honey during our conversation. He said his government was committed to normalising relations with Pakistan and resolving all our bilateral disputes amicably. The interesting part came in the last forty seconds of the conversation when he informed me that his government had just decided to release Mulla Zahoor in exchange for the two Indian hostages held captive by the LET."

"But what kind of help can we give to India when our official stand is that no anti-India terrorist activity is going on in Pakistan?"

"That's why he did not ask for any help. He just informed. The fact that he himself telephoned to give this information was enough to convey the level of importance the Indian government is attaching to the Kashmir kidnappings. Ten minutes later the US Secretary of State called our Foreign Minister and said the Pakistan government should ensure that the LET does not harm the Indian hostages."

"That's very clever of the Indians. They are firing from the American shoulders. Now what are your instructions for me, sir?"

"First, the two Indian hostages should be released safely at the appointed time and place tomorrow. Second, your Special Operations specialist, Miss Gulnar, should disengage herself from the two Indian hostages as early as she can."

Gulnar was fuming during her helicopter journey from Islamabad to Azad Kashmir. Her mission was a success. None other than the President himself had appreciated it. Yet, there was a contra side: the modus operandi she had decided upon for the final act would not be allowed. Instead, the two Indian hostages were to be released immediately and she was not entitled to any role in the final drama. She thought of a plan as her chopper landed in the complex where the hostages were kept.

Gulnar's caretaker had been extra careful. He had understood the need for a doctor examining Mili as early as possible. By the time Gulnar returned, Mili was back to her normal self, though her solitary confinement remained unchanged.

The first instruction Gulnar gave after landing related to Mili only. After that, she headed straight to Dhruv's room in the approaching dusk.

Dhruv did not bother to give her a second glance after Gulnar entered the room. She sat down in front of him but Dhruv did not take his eyes off the magazine he was reading. He heard some steps approaching the room and was surprised to see Mili walking in. She looked pale and terrified. Her head was bandaged. She ran towards him, but the alert sentry was quicker and held her back. Gulnar waved her hand and signalled the sentry not to bother and to leave the room.

"You are free Miss Mili to go to Mr Dhruv and do whatever you please," Gulnar said.

Mili looked at her suspiciously, slowly walked towards Dhruv and sat by his side, clenching his hand tightly.

"I am sorry Mr Dhruv for whatever inconveniences that you have faced here. I am happy to announce that both of you are to be released."

Mili could not believe her ears and could no longer suppress her emotions. She hugged Dhruv and seconds later, remembering her recent hardships, sat properly facing the woman whom she was seeing for the first time in army fatigues.

"I think, now I should introduce myself to you. I am Gulnar Butt. I am with the Pakistan Army," she said and shook hands, first with a shaken Mili and then with a suspicious Dhruv. She got no response from the hostages. Undeterred, she went on to address them.

"Miss Mili, you will no longer remain in the cell. You can share this room with Mr Dhruv or you can...!"

"I will stay here only. Can I, please?" Mili asked.

"By all means."

"You are with the ISI or with the Pakistan Army? What do you do? What is your background?" Dhruv spoke for the first time since Gulnar returned from Islamabad.

"You ask too many questions," Gulnar said, trying not to sound irritated. "I can't answer all your questions, but suffice it to say that I have studied English literature at Oxford."

"That's why Amaso wanted your presence when I narrated my last story. When are we going to be released?" Dhruv asked.

"Tomorrow. We leave before dawn."

"What do you mean by "we"? Are you going to accompany us?" Dhruv asked.

"I have replaced Mehmood Mian for you and will personally escort you two to your territory. Whatever was agreed between you and Mehmood Mian will now be valid between you and I."

"What agreement you are talking about between me and Mehmood Mian? I don't understand anything."

"Mehmood Mian threw a challenge which you accepted."

"You are referring to an informal story contest."

"Yes, it will be a friendly one-day cricket match between us. There will be no stakes, just as you had agreed with Mehmood Mian. Only the honour will be at stake."

A plan flashed in Dhruv's mind.

"What kind of story you would like me to narrate to you?"

"A whodunit story where the protagonists are

intelligence personnel and cops on the one hand and terrorists on the other."

Dhruv thought about it a while and then said, "Now that we are going to be released, will you be indulgent enough to hand over my cell phone?"

"What cell phone? I don't have any cell phone of yours."

"No, not you. Mehmood Mian had. He always kept it in his pocket."

Gulnar went out after hearing this. Dhruv looked at Mili smugly.

"What are you up to?" Mili asked.

"Wait and watch."

"Don't try anything silly with this dangerous woman. Let us get out of here. Forget about your cell phone. What is so ..." she cut herself short as Gulnar entered the room.

Dhruv knew she had gone out to give instructions to her men to dig up the place where they had buried Mehmood Mian and search his body for the cell phone. Dhruv had seen her eyes sparkling, not unlike a tigress when she sights a potential kill. He knew what Gulnar would be thinking: that his cell phone could be a storehouse of information.

"Let me see, Mr Dhruv if we can get your cell phone. However, what is so special about your cell phone? Miss Mili also wanted to ask this, I believe?"

"It will act as a neutral umpire for our friendly match."

"How?" Gulnar asked, puzzled.

"I need time to think of a story. The earliest I can tell you the story is tomorrow morning when we would be travelling."

"Where does your cell phone figure in this?"

"How long do we travel from this place to the point of our release?"

"At least an hour, which includes a jeep ride, as well as trekking on foot."

"This means I would only have time to tell my story while travelling. The cell phone will come in handy as I will store the clue to the twist in my tale in my cell phone."

Gulnar paused to think. Her mind had already started racing when Dhruv talked about his cell phone. The small contraption could be her last chance to bounce back and salvage her lost honour. Her sexual act with Dhruv had been secretly filmed and she was on record confessing that she was doing it for personal and not operational reasons. She hoped that Dhruv's cell phone would yield some information about him. He might have made and received some calls. Besides, the phone book could have phone numbers of Dhruv's contacts.

A man entered the room just then. Before, he could speak, Gulnar signalled to him to wait for her outside.

"That's quite a novel idea, Mr Dhruv. However, let us see whether it is doable," Gulnar said and went out.

Mili looked at Dhruv with a quizzical expression. He took her hand and pressed it gently his two to assure her that he knew what he was doing and he was in command of things. Gulnar darted inside after a minute.

"Mr Dhruv, your cell phone has been located. It should be here in half an hour," Gulnar said with a degree of smugness in her demeanour.

"I think it should be earlier than that," Dhruv replied without batting an eyelid.

"I beg your pardon! Is that an observation or a demand?" Gulnar said, her voice trembling with anger.

"The former, obviously; because the phone was purchased the day I was kidnapped. It does not have a single incoming or outgoing call and its phone book is empty, simply because I could hardly get any time to feed any telephone numbers into it."

Gulnar gave him a defeated look. The same man appeared at the door and Gulnar went out. This time she took longer to come back, fortuitously so because Mili could no longer restrain herself from planting a passionate kiss on Dhruv's lips. Mili felt rejuvenated to some extent by the time Gulnar returned.

"You are very clever indeed, Mr Dhruv. You read the minds of people very well," Gulnar said.

"Especially when these are the minds of the intelligence people."

"Your confidence in yourself is amazing. Amaso always suspected you to be an Indian intelligence agent. Amaso was wrong. A person as recklessly confident as you can never be a successful intelligence operative."

"It took me three stories to convince Amaso that I am not an intelligence man. Thank you very much indeed for giving me a certificate even before you have heard a story from me."

"If that is a challenge, Mr Dhruv, I accept it."

"An intelligent woman like you would do that precisely, Miss Gulnar Butt."

Dhruv gave Gulnar a hard stare as he uttered these words.

"Weave your story well, Mr Dhruv. This challenge is a matter of honour between us. Good night folks," Gulnar said dryly and walked out of the room.

Mili flung herself into the open arms of Dhruv as Gulnar slammed the door closed behind her. It was supposed to be their last night in captivity, after all.

Dhruv and Mili could not sleep that night. They were too anxious about their impending release. They had a lot to share with each other in terms of their experiences of solo captivity. Moreover, they had a job to do: one last job of preparing a story for Gulnar. It was the final challenge and a matter of honour for both.

Dhruv treated the upcoming challenge as a joint venture. He was no longer hesitant in discussing his story ideas with Mili. Both understood that they were no longer individuals in tackling their final challenge. They were to swim or drown together.

However, Dhruv deftly evaded Mili's queries about his plan. She asked many questions about his cell phone about which Dhruv was so particular. Dhruv silenced her by stating that the phone was of sentimental value to him. His father had gifted him the phone that morning when he flew from New Delhi to Srinagar. Dhruv was not trying to hide anything from Mili. He was being extra cautious, as he suspected their room to be bugged.

A little before six the next morning, a security guard came in and gave them a message from Gulnar that they were to leave within one hour. The man also brought two pairs of salwar kurta, two pullovers and two pairs of woollen socks for Dhruv and Mili. He said "Madam" had sent new clothes, as she did not want them to be wearing soiled, crumpled and torn clothes at the time of their release.

Around 7 o'clock, both captives were ready. The weather was good, though the sun was too feeble to pierce through the cloud cover. Gulnar entered the room. A lingering feminine fragrance wafted across the room, testifying that Gulnar knew how to use her charm even though she was in a profession that was a bastion of patriarchy. She was dressed in blue denims and a black top. She was wearing branded sport shoes.

She looked like a tourist – and an attractive one.

"Are you ready?" she asked cheerfully.

They nodded affirmatively.

"Your story, too, is ready?"

"Yes, but where is my cell phone?" Dhruv asked.

"It's here with me," Gulnar said, showing Dhruv his cell phone.

"Got any information from the phone?"

"No, did not even try."

"I find it difficult to believe that you did not even open the phone."

"I opened it just to see whether it is functioning or not and whether its battery needed charging, but the battery is okay," Gulnar said.

Dhruv had no means of finding out immediately whether she was lying or telling the truth. However, when she said she had operated the cell phone, he was relieved, though he did not show the feeling.

Gulnar observed that Dhruv was in deep thought. At that moment, she had neither the time nor the inclination to think and analyse the reasons for Dhruv's pensive mood. She had charted a dangerous path for herself. It was a gamble; and she had always been a great gambler when it came to taking decisions at crucial junctures. Today was yet another such example. She had put herself in the role of the chief choreographer of the denouement of the now famous Kashmir kidnappings.

Gulnar told herself that she had to defy the President's explicit orders for three reasons. One, this way she had a chance to salvage her lost honour. She was still hopeful of stumbling across some information, which could once again turn the tables. She had an idea that strategically the order of importance of the two captives was just the reverse. She had no evidence to prove to her country's leadership that Dhruv was more important than Mili. Two, if she were to fail in this, she could at least win an intellectual battle over Dhruv by challenging him in his own field of expertise: story telling. Three, in the unlikely event of her failing in either of these two scenarios, a bonus point was waiting to be won by her as she could personally receive Mulla Zahoor in exchange for Dhruv and Mili.

Gulnar came out of her brief reflective mood and said to Dhruv, "I have done away with the jeep. Instead we are travelling by a bullet proof car."

"Why? A bullet proof car is heavier and less manoeuvrable, especially in hilly terrain," Dhruv said in a matter-of-fact tone.

"That's right."

"Do you envisage a threat from certain quarters?" Dhruv asked.

"No, but a jeep is noisy; a bullet proof car is not. You need a quiet vehicle to tell your story, isn't it?"

Dhruv got the logic, but kept quiet.

"What is the title of your story?" Gulnar asked.

"I have not given any title."

"Why?"

"I leave it to you to think of one."

"Still, there should be some title. A story without a title is like...!"

"A baby without a name; a rose without fragrance; an oyster without a pearl! Is that what you mean?"

"You said it; rather lyrically, I suppose."

"This story is the denouement of this kidnapping drama. You can title it "The Denouement", if you like."

"That seems to be a good enough working title. Let's start our journey. You can start your story now."

Dhruv, Mili and Gulnar were on the back seat of the bullet proof car. Gulnar instructed Dhruv to sit in the middle. An armed security guard was on the front seat along with the driver. At five minutes past 7 am, the driver started the vehicle. Compared to the past few days of blizzards and snow storms, the weather was pleasant. Their final journey to freedom had begun.

"Please give me my cell phone for a minute," Dhruv asked Gulnar.

"Why?" Her tone made it evident that she was suspicious of Dhruv's demand.

"I need the phone to type a one-line message giving the climax of the story. I will save the message in the inbox and return the phone to you. We had agreed to use the cell phone as a neutral umpire between us, Miss Gulnar Butt. Hope you remember?"

"Yes, I do remember. I didn't realise that you would enter the message before you begin the story," Gulnar said and handed Dhruv his cell phone.

Dhruv opened the phone, typed out the message while an alert Gulnar watched, switched it off again and handed it back to her. The whole exercise took less than a minute.

"Kindly pay attention, Miss Gulnar Butt. Here I go with my story. It is an out-and-out cops and terrorists drama."

"I am listening, Mr Dhruv," Gulnar responded.

17

The Denouement

Ahmed Qureshi cursed his fate as he read the one paragraph "Top Secret" secret note that rolled out of his secure fax. He had just arrived in his office that afternoon, a Sunday, after the Director of Intelligence Bureau personally called him at his residence in Srinagar and told him to go to his Gupkar Road office in fifteen minutes to receive an urgent fax.

Qureshi was due to retire a month later. As Deputy Inspector General of Jammu and Kashmir Police, in charge of intelligence matters, he was a repository of secret and sensitive information. His 35-year record of policing was flawless, but because of his habit of calling a spade a spade and doing only what he thought was right, he never inspired confidence among his seniors and the political masters. That is why in the first 25 years of his service he had been transferred all over the state as many times. It was only in the past ten years, ever since insurgency began in Jammu and Kashmir in a big way, that he was not moved from the primary intelligence wing. Within the first six months of his taking charge of intelligence as Superintendent of Police, he proved his mettle and the Central Government in New Delhi did not fail to notice.

This became Qureshi's main source of strength. He quickly became a key police official from New Delhi's point of view and the state government could no longer transfer him or deny promotion to him without giving a long and credible explanation. He had endeared himself to the Central government, as he was bold, honest and had a vibrant network of informers. With the Central government that had come to office two years before, his equation was extremely good and as a result, his influence went up enormously. So much so that it was an open secret that New Delhi's top ministers and bureaucrats dealt with him directly, bypassing his seniors.

Qureshi was a man of average height and looks. He was diabetic and was prone to high blood pressure. He was a family man, fully devoted to his wife and his two children, a son and a daughter. He had married his daughter to an IT professional, while his son was pursuing higher studies in New Delhi.

The rigours of his intelligence job in the last decade had taken an additional toll on his health. He had had a mild heart attack three years before, but after a month of bed rest, he returned to his grinding schedule. The Director General of Jammu and Kashmir Police had told him only the day before that after the two high profile visits were over, he would be promoted to Inspector General of Police and given an extension of three years. Qureshi had thanked him for the much delayed promotion, but declined the offer of extension. He had cited the obvious health grounds and explained that he wanted to lead a quiet retired life.

Qureshi read the Top Secret fax again.

"Agent 11B reported this morning that terrorists have smuggled into Kashmir two highly sophisticated waist jacket bombs. The devices were smuggled into the country from India-Nepal border. It is believed that the waist jacket bombs are to be used by fidayeen groups for targeting HM and UNSG."

It was a RAW report that the IB Chief had faxed to Qureshi. He knew it was not very often that India's external intelligence agency, Research and Analysis Wing and internal intelligence agency, Intelligence Bureau, worked in close coordination, and that too so promptly. The IB Chief had already told him to get cracking immediately after receiving the fax.

The Indian Home Minister was due to arrive in Srinagar three days hence, on Wednesday, to assess the ground situation and review security arrangements for the first ever visit to the Kashmir valley by the United Nations Secretary General the next Saturday. These officials were the potential targets of "fidayeen" groups as the RAW report mentioned.

Nobody understood the importance of the top UN official's visit to Kashmir better than Qureshi. The Indian

Foreign Office had created a flutter by announcing the visit of the UN Secretary General to Kashmir a few days ago. It was indeed a ground breaking development. It signalled the Indian government's supreme confidence in its diplomacy, and that it was prepared to throw open Kashmir valley not just to foreign diplomats but also to the top official of the UN. New Delhi's smugness was galling to those who dreamed of wresting Kashmir from the Indian Union. The Indian government had approached the UN decades ago, seeking the world body's intervention for resolving the Kashmir dispute between India and Pakistan. However, shortly afterwards, New Delhi realised its diplomatic blunder in internationalising a dispute that could best have been resolved bilaterally between India and Pakistan. From the Indian detractors' point of view, the ideal way to demonstrate the disputed status of Kashmir was by targeting the UN Secretary General.

Wednesday arrived all too quickly. Qureshi had mobilised his entire personal network of informers. He was in close touch with all relevant security agencies of the state as well as the Centre. He had barely slept in the last three days. This was largely because of his standing feud with the political establishments in Srinagar and New Delhi.

The Union Home Minister, Brij Bihari Mishra, better known as BB, wanted to unfurl the national flag at Lal Chowk, the congested downtown area, infamous for a high number of terrorist attacks. He vehemently opposed the Minister's wish. He argued that the Minister would be a sitting duck for terrorists. Even if the security forces were to pull off an incident-free flag unfurling ceremony, the exercise was unnecessary and could compromise on security arrangements for the UN Secretary General's visit. When his attention was brought to similar protests from several other security agencies and the fact that the Home Minister still wanted to go ahead with his programme at Lal Chowk, Qureshi said the Minister could very well do so but not until he, Qureshi, was in charge. He articulated his stand through an official note. The Minister blinked.

However, Qureshi could say nothing when the Minister's revised itinerary reached his desk. The Minister had cleverly roped in another public function. This time he wanted to inaugurate the newly constructed surgery wing of a government hospital. The wing had been operational for the last three weeks. Moreover, the state's Health Minister had inaugurated it. The reason given by the Union Home Minister's office for "inaugurating" the already inaugurated and fully functional surgery wing of the hospital was that the Minister wanted to make an important announcement with regard to treatment of those who lost their limbs in landmine blasts.

Qureshi had seen enough of rapacious politicians. This time he did not oppose it, though he wished the Union Home Minister would go away after the only important engagement the routine review of law and order arrangements at Srinagar's most secure address: Raj Bhavan, the official palatial residence of the state Governor.

BB was not a reckless politician. He was a strategician, a cerebral politician. His own party colleagues privately joked about his labyrinthine brain, saying that if one were to drive a nail into his forehead and then pull it out, the nail would come out as a screw. He knew all along that a police officer like Qureshi, whom he admired a lot, would never allow such an atrocious plan as unfurling of the national flag at Srinagar's Lal Chowk.

What the Home Minister probably did not know was what was in store for him at his only public engagement in Srinagar. Qureshi was better informed.

Dhruv stopped his narration because their car came to a halt at a security checkpoint. Alert security personnel quickly surrounded the car from all sides and had a good look at the occupants. Twenty seconds later, the barricade was removed and all guardsmen saluted the vehicle.

Gulnar was used to such acknowledgement. Nobody had demanded to know her identity. Her face was enough. For Pakistanis, she was a celebrity, one who was better known, and respected, than glamour dolls of the country's film industry. She gestured Dhruv to continue with his story.

Qureshi was made overall officer in charge of all security arrangements for the two high profile visits. All civilian and paramilitary agencies had been told that Qureshi's orders would have to be obeyed. It was the first time that Qureshi had been given such unbridled powers. His seniors and detractors were envious of him.

The Union Home Minister's visit was on and progressing well. His motorcade was heading to the government hospital for his public function, after which he was to go to the airport to catch his charter plane back to New Delhi. Qureshi changed the route of the minister's motorcade at the last minute.

The VVIP motorcade passed through the Boulevard Road that was closed for traffic at the last minute. Qureshi led the motorcade in a bullet proof jeep and watched the roadside buildings carefully all through the journey. Just when the minister's convoy entered the hospital, Qureshi received a message that terrorists had hurled a grenade at a passing luxury vehicle in a marketplace two kilometres away and five people had been injured.

The Minister was introduced to the hospital brass and was taken around the new surgery block for a few minutes. Then he proceeded to the OPD hall, which had been readied as a makeshift indoor venue for the minister. BB Mishra noted with satisfaction that all the chairs were occupied. His PA promptly told the Minister that there were 220 chairs in the hall. The Minister started with his speech.

When he was detailing steps initiated by his government for ameliorating the lot of the masses, there was commotion at the main gate. Qureshi, who was standing just behind the Minister, moved a few steps away and inquired from his walkie-talkie what was happening. He was told that a man had sustained injuries in the grenade attack and his attendant wanted to take him to the operation theatre. The way to the operation theatre was through the OPD where the minister was making a speech. The guards told the injured man's attendant to take him to the old building in the same hospital complex but he insisted on taking him to the new surgical ward, which he said, was better equipped.

Qureshi darted to the main gate. First, he demanded to know from police officers on duty how the man managed to reach the new surgical ward where the entry was restricted. On his instructions, the surgical ward had been sterilised, a term used for a security cleared place. The answer he got was that the security personnel in charge of the outer gate had allowed the ambulance in after seeing an unconscious man who was bleeding profusely from the stomach.

Qureshi stepped forward to see the injured man. The young man was lying on a stretcher on his stomach and his clothes were smeared with blood. Qureshi asked the attendant to turn him over so that he could see the extent of the man's injury.

The Minister had lost patience by this time and came to the main gate. Qureshi observed that the injured man, lying unconscious all this while, shuffled slightly on the stretcher. The DIG noticed something protruding from the injured man's back. In a flash, he kicked the stretcher with full force and the stretcher started wheeling down the corridor. Barely had the stretcher covered a distance of twenty feet, when there was a huge explosion.

The whole building shook with the impact of the blast. The stretcher was thrown into the air, hit the ceiling and fell down in a mangled heap. The blast severed the head of the bomber which rolled towards the main gate where scores of hospital staff and security personnel were present. The Minister had come to the main gate and was standing close to Qureshi. Rather dramatically, the bomber's severed head stopped its directionless journey right at the feet of the Minister.

Luckily, the builder of the hospital's new surgical complex had used heavy stone for construction, instead of ordinary bricks. Even more fortunately, the long corridor was empty as the OPD hall was the centre of all activities. The sidewalls and the ceiling of the corridor, made of solid stones, bore the brunt of the explosion. As a result, no one was killed and there were no serious injuries. Six people, four from the hospital staff and two security personnel, received minor shrapnel injuries.

The Union Home Minister was dazed, but safe. The bomber's accomplice, who came as an attendant, tried to flee. Before Qureshi could bat an eyelid, two police officers opened fire on the fleeing man. Two bullets hit him in the back, felling him instantly. Qureshi ran to the bomber's accomplice and felt his pulse. He was wearing a locket.

Qureshi knew the significance of the locket. He pressed it in the middle and it opened. A cyanide capsule was hidden inside. The young man was too raw or inexperienced or perhaps had lost his nerve. He did not even try to bite into the cyanide capsule.

Qureshi quickly pocketed the locket. He asked an inspector to fetch a hearse and whispered some instructions into his ear.

Within minutes, all TV networks were airing the breaking news: "Union Home Minister escapes a suicide bomb attack in a Srinagar hospital. Suicide bomber and his accomplice killed."

The Minister returned to New Delhi safely. The first thing he did after reaching New Delhi was to run off two official letters: one to Qureshi, appreciating his professional skills and thanking him for saving his life; and the second to the chief of Jammu and Kashmir Police, recommending Qureshi's double promotion.

Qureshi received the Minister's letter of thanks the next morning. He also got an official intimation that he was promoted as Additional Director General of Police with immediate effect.

Qureshi telephoned his wife to give her the good news. However, she and her children already knew, as did the entire television watching population of the country.

There was still a lot of work to be done. Qureshi was now focused on the investigation of the hospital incident. He was sure that the suicide bomber had set off a waist jacket bomb, but he had to await the forensic report.

The forensic report that arrived that afternoon confirmed Qureshi's suspicion. The investigators had recovered several parts of the explosive device from the blast site a Singapore-made 9 volt battery, two on-off switches, wires and belt shreds. A special team of Central Bureau of Investigation, the premier Indian investigating agency better known by its abbreviated form CBI, was rushed to Srinagar by a special plane to carry out the investigations, as there was not much time left for the UN Secretary General's visit. The investigators raced against the clock and in less than 24 hours confirmed that the suicide bomber was wearing the highly sophisticated waist jacket bomb.

The conspirators had packed no less than half a kilogram of C1, C2, C3 combination explosives, and an equal weight of pellets, together in the specially made pockets in the suicide bomber's jacket. They chose the "Claymore effect" to inflict maximum damage by stuffing hundreds of tiny spherical pellets of 2mm uniform size in the plastic explosive tied to the suicide bomber's waist. This was the first terror attack in the Kashmir valley in which terrorists had used iron pellets in an explosive device. It showed how the terrorists were increasingly becoming more and more hi-tech. Investigators used a powerful magnet to collect hundreds of iron pellets.

The investigators concluded that the assassin had worn a vest jacket and a waist belt with the explosive charge on his back. The jacket was intended to keep the explosive intact until he triggered the detonator. The two on-off switches picked up from the blast site were the detonators. The bomb was designed to eliminate a specific target and that is why the quantity of explosives packed into the device was not very high. If the quantity of the explosives were high, parts of the bomb like battery and switches would have burnt or melted.

The 8 cm wide and 65 cm long abdominal belt, similar to the one used by patients suffering from spinal problems, had steel ribs for support. Three ribs had been removed to accommodate gelatine sticks. This explained why the explosion severed the bomber's head.

The investigation thus established beyond doubt that one of the two waist jacket bombs had been used up. It was now time to find the whereabouts of the second such bomb from the bomber's accomplice who gave his name as Qadir.

Qureshi went back to the hospital. Qadir had survived twin bullet shots that missed his vital organs by millimetres. Qureshi had already resorted to an age-old intelligence tool : disinformation. He used the media effectively by planting the news that the suicide bomber's accomplice was shot dead as he tried to flee.

Qadir was fully conscious when Qureshi entered his fortified room. Qureshi's junior staff had already informed him that Qadir was willing to cooperate. Qadir began to sob when Qureshi sat on a stool close to his bed.

"Sir, I will tell you whatever I know. I am not a hardcore jihadi like Anwar was."

"The suicide bomber's name was Anwar?"

"Yes sir. Those people recruited me two months ago. I was in search of a job when I met Anwar. He gave me ten thousand rupees and then sent me on a four-week training course some place. I was taken to the training camp blindfolded. They promised to look after my family if I were to die in an operation. Honestly, I did not want to become a jihadi. I wanted to get a job that could keep me financially afloat and also allow me to pursue my further studies."

"If you are not a hardcore terrorist then why were you carrying a cyanide capsule?" Qureshi asked.

"They thrust it upon me and warned me that if I were to be caught alive by the security forces, they will wipe out my entire family. They said a more important operation was coming up and my getting caught alive could jeopardise that operation."

"We know about the coming operation. Tell us who was your and Anwar's boss?"

"I took my instructions from Anwar only. However, I heard him talking to one particular person several times, who clearly must have been the boss."

"What did you hear during Anwar's conversations with the boss?"

"That the second attack was to be made on the UN Chief on the coming Saturday and that the boss would be personally present on the spot to ensure that everything worked smoothly."

"Anwar must have addressed his boss by some name?"

"Yes, he did once and was warned not to do it again."

"By what name Anwar had addressed his boss?"

"Ghanti Baba."

Gulnar ordered the vehicle to stop. Dhruv was surprised as no security checkpoint was in sight.

"What was the name you said?"

"Whose name?" Dhruv asked, puzzled.

"The name of Anwar's boss."

"Ghanti Baba."

"Oh, Ghanti Baba! I could not hear properly because of the running vehicle's noise. Please carry on with your story."

Qureshi's talk with Qadir was useful. He had full 24 hours to prepare to take on the final challenge.

The UN chief initially wanted to visit the Kashmir valley for two days. Besides, he desired to have as many as six engagements, which entailed his travelling outside Srinagar as well. However, in view of the attempted assassination of the Indian Home Minister, the UN chief's office readily agreed to New Delhi's request to change his itinerary. Now, according to the revised itinerary, the foreign dignitary was to have only a day-long visit of Srinagar and two engagements: an all-party meeting at Raj Bhavan and inauguration of a rural electrification programme. The revised itinerary was a tightly held secret.

Qadir's information that Ghanti Baba was to personally oversee the attack on the UNSG could have demoralised any police officer, but Qureshi was different. He saw a ray of hope in the fact that Ghanti Baba was to be the chief architect of the terrorist operation against the UNSG. There were several reasons for this.

Ghanti Baba had been an enigma to security personnel ever since he had wreaked havoc in the Kashmir valley. No one had ever seen Ghanti Baba. Fantastic stories of his appearance and personal likes and dislikes floated around like folklore. There were as many stories about him as there were tongues; and not even one was authentic. According to one account, he had an apparition like existence. He was a glib talker and a master of disguises. Several times, he had been stopped at security checkpoints in the Valley but each time he talked his way out of a potentially messy situation.

One version claimed that there was one thing he could not disguise – his unusual height. His six foot five inches tall frame was unmistakable.

Yet another account credited Ghanti Baba with being a weird man. He was forty, had a strong libido and unlike hardcore Islamists, he had a weakness for alcohol. He was said to be in touch with "madams" who supplied him girls. Ghanti Baba's close confidantes were known to approach madams, asking for girls for their boss. The modus operandi was such that the "madam" would send six or seven girls, of whom Ghanti Baba would keep one or two for the night and send back the rest, though he would pay for all.

He commanded a 700-member strong jihadi network in the Valley and loosened his purse strings rather liberally. He was very fond of women and moved in company of women and children, posing as a patriarch of a large joint family. This facilitated his unimpeded movement across the Valley.

Whatever the truth was, there was no denying the fact that Ghanti Baba was a brutal person whose group kidnapped security personnel and local Kashmiris perceived to be police informers. Not a single person kidnapped by his group returned alive.

In the maze of fantastic stories spun around his persona, there was one fact that shone like a feeble sun from behind a thick cloud cover. All his major acts of terrorism – bomb blasts or executions's – bore his signatures: a metallic, miniature "ghanti" (a bell) that was deliberately left at the spot. This explained why the person was known as "Ghanti Baba".

This fact led to more fiction. The most interesting, though unverified, aspect of his personality was that he wore a "ghanti" around his neck all the time. He never removed the "ghanti", not even during sex.

For the past month, Qureshi had kept Ghanti Baba at the top of his hit list. He had even formed an ultra secret unit to keep a tab on the elusive terrorist's movements and neutralise him when the appropriate time came. The time had come now, he told himself. A young, dynamic officer by the name of Aftab headed this unit. Aftab had won Qureshi's confidence completely. Aftab had the uncanny ability of coming to him with bits of information about Ghanti Baba's whereabouts that proved to be dead accurate. At least thrice earlier, Qureshi nearly caught Ghanti Baba after raiding the place identified by Aftab. However, each time, Ghanti Baba was a step ahead of the raid party and had left the place a few minutes earlier.

It was Friday evening. The UNSG's arrival in the valley was barely 15 hours away. Qureshi had embarked upon an ambitious plan and, from his side, dealt his cards very carefully for a pre-emptive strike. He knew that by tonight his quarry would be in or around Srinagar to be able to personally oversee the attack on the UNSG. He had activated his network of informers and fanned out his special team members to different places in and around Srinagar.

His efforts were beginning to yield dividends. Aftab called him on his office telephone to say that he had just met a woman and she wanted to see him immediately for some urgent matter. Aftab also said that he had reasons to believe that the matter could pertain to Ghanti Baba, though the woman had refused to say anything on why she wanted to meet Qureshi.

Twenty minutes later, the woman was seated in front of Qureshi in his office. Aftab had escorted her in and sat beside her, but she did not utter a word until Qureshi signalled him to leave and wait outside.

Qureshi observed the woman in detail. She was stern looking, in her mid thirties. Her demeanour suggested that she was not overawed by the fact that she was sitting in front of a powerful police official. She was carrying an expensive leather purse.

"What can I do for you, Miss?"

"On the contrary, I can do something for you, sir," the woman spoke politely, but firmly.

Qureshi looked at her inquisitively.

"I run a boutique in downtown Srinagar. Several young and beautiful girls work for me. All of them are poor but come from god fearing families. One of them is a call girl. I came to know this fact today only when one of the girls Gul Bano told me that Ghanti Baba's men approached this girl in question, whose name is Mumtaz. In the evening, after the boutique closed, Mumtaz left with Ghanti Baba's men. Before leaving, she told Gul Bano in confidence where she was going. I can tell you the place, provided you are interested."

For the next five minutes, the woman explained to Qureshi the location where Mumtaz had gone. Qureshi took copious notes. He thanked her, thinking that she had finished; but she had not. She took out her visiting card, borrowed a pen from Qureshi and wrote out a number on the card.

"This is my mobile number. I will be glad to be of any help to you," she said while handing the card to him.

Qureshi took the card and thanked her again. He gave her a card in return.

"What is this, sir?"

"This is a special security cleared card. You can come to my office any time without going through security checks and without a prior appointment. I am giving this to you in recognition of your valuable services that you have rendered suo motu."

"But sir you have not even found out yet whether my services are useful to you! You have not even asked my name?"

"Your name is there in your visiting card. Moreover, I am satisfied by your conduct. Thank you very much indeed for all your efforts."

However, the woman still did not get up.

"Anything else?"

"Yes sir. Mumtaz also told Gul Bano that one of your key officers is Ghanti Baba's mole in your establishment. I am giving the address of Gul Bano to you. I am sure you would like to talk to her yourself about it, but please keep this meeting of ours a secret."

The woman wrote Gul Bano's address and got up.

Qureshi summoned his Superintendent of Police, Riaz Ahmed, immediately after the woman left. Ahmed sat on a chair in front of Qureshi and then suddenly jumped up.

Something had bugged him as he sat on the chair. It was a small metallic bell. Aftab had sat on this chair twenty minutes before.

Dhruv stopped here. No one spoke for a few moments as the vehicle was approaching a security barricade. Beyond the barricade was a mountainous path, which was not navigable by car. The occupants of the bullet proof car were asked to get down. Gulnar browsed through some documents, signed at two places and after a few minutes told Dhruv and Mili to follow her.

"From here we have to trek for ten to fifteen minutes. You can continue with your story, Mr Dhruv," Gulnar said.

A dozen armed security personnel followed them at some distance.

"I stopped because I have come close to the climax. You can make your guess now about the climax," Dhruv said.

"I don't see any twist in your tale. It is fairly simple ..."

"Sorry to have interrupted you, but can you give me my cell phone?"

"Again? Why?" Gulnar protested.

"I need to add an all important word in my clue which I have stored for you. You will appreciate that newer and newer ideas keep coming during a creative process."

Gulnar thought for a moment and handed Dhruv his cell phone. Dhruv opened the phone, went to the message inbox, added a word to the message, saved the message and switched off the phone.

Mili sat on a rock to rest as Dhruv worked on the phone. She was panting. Gulnar kept standing and surveyed the area. The Line of Control that divided Pakistan-held Kashmir from Jammu and Kashmir was less than half a kilometre away. She spotted that Pakistani troops had already taken positions, hiding behind rocks, ready to intervene if something went awry. She appeared fully confident of herself.

"Please go ahead with your guess," Dhruv said as he returned the phone to her.

"It is clear. Aftab is Ghanti Baba's mole in the police establishment, if not Ghanti Baba himself. Am I right?"

"Wait for the denouement which is about five minutes away."

"Alright then, proceed with your story," Gulnar said.

Qureshi asked his PA to send in Aftab immediately.

"Get hold of that woman. Fast," Qureshi ordered as Aftab stepped in.

"But sir, you let her go. She climbed into a rickshaw and went away. It is more than five minutes since the driver sped off."

"Don't worry. I have given her a card, which I said was security cleared and could get her access to me in my office any time of the day. Actually, that card had nothing but a chip with which you can track her movements in a hundred kilometre radius. Use plainclothes men only. Ask another small team to follow you at a discreet distance. Inquire from her about the waist jacket bomb and ask the team following you to recover it. Also, ensure that she does not gain access to a locket that she might be wearing. If she is wearing one, it may well be in the shape of a "ghanti", Qureshi said as he picked up a phone.

Aftab sprinted out. The SP's mouth was half-open, as though he were Alice in Wonderland.

About an hour later, the woman was produced before Qureshi in his office, her hands tightly tied. Sparks were flying from her eyes, but she said nothing.

"What about the waist jacket bomb?" Qureshi asked Aftab.

"Sir, she says she knows nothing of such a thing."

"Where are the rickshaw and the driver?"

"I tracked her from my GPS system and soon our vehicle overtook the rickshaw and blocked its way. Sub-inspector Arshad and I approached the rickshaw from either side. Arshad handcuffed her before she could understand anything. The driver tried to flee, but our people caught hold of him. The driver is in our custody and the rickshaw is parked in our office compound," Aftab replied, standing upright.

"Good job. Have you searched the rickshaw?"

"I am afraid not yet, sir. I will do it personally and get back."

Qureshi worked on the phone for the next five minutes. In the meanwhile, the SP had called two policemen to keep a strict watch on her. The woman was secured to a chair placed in the far corner of the room.

Aftab came running into the room a few minutes later, waving a waist jacket.

"I have got it, sir. It was hidden inside the rear seat of the rickshaw. Arshad was with me during the search operation. He has done an advanced diploma in explosives and he confirms that it is a very sophisticated bomb."

"Get the explosives experts on it and make sure that thing is safe," Qureshi ordered Aftab. Then, turning to the SP, he said, "Send a crash message to our headquarters and DGP's office that Ghanti Baba has been arrested. Take her to our usual place for interrogation. Henceforth, Ghanti Baba's bell will not toll for any innocent person."

The UNSG's Srinagar visit passed off smoothly the next day. Another minor development also took place. Qureshi agreed for a three year extension of his tenure.

18

The Hour is Nigh, The Moon is Split

Gulnar was ashen-faced as Dhruv completed his story. They had just crossed the Line of Control. The sun shone brightly and it had become rather hot suddenly. She had spotted a grove of trees from some distance. It was now barely twenty metres away. Like a robot, she walked towards the grove.

"Are you here with us or have you floated out of your body like a yogi, Miss Gulnar Butt," an upbeat Dhruv asked when she did not speak for a while.

"You are indeed a master storyteller, Mr Dhruv. Now I understand why a man like Amaso kept your company for several days."

"Thank you for the compliment, but would you not like to see the clue which I stored in the cell phone."

"Sure," she said and switched on the phone. They had reached the grove. There was no sign of Mulla Zahoor, the terrorist who was to be exchanged in lieu of Dhruv and Mili.

They had arrived half an hour before the scheduled time for the exchange of the captives.

She read out the saved message loudly, "You won many a battle but have lost the war, GB, the woman."

She was startled with the enigmatic message that hardly looked to her like a clue to Dhruv's story. Before she could air her thoughts, she saw some movement from the other side of the grove. Dozen-odd armed Indian troops were approaching them, with Mulla Zahoor in the centre. Gulnar's armed men were alert, but even they were surprised when armed commandos suddenly emerged from nowhere and surrounded them. They were hiding atop trees from where they jumped down and took control of Gulnar's men.

Gulnar looked behind to see what the Pakistani troops were doing a few hundred metres away across the LOC. However, the foliage was so thick that she could not see anything. She saw that hundreds more Indian troops in combat gear had quickly taken up positions in their vicinity.

A man dressed in a blue suit stepped forward, taking a deep drag from his cigar. "Welcome to India, Miss Gulnar Butt alias Ghazni Baba," he said.

Dhruv and Mili were dumbstruck, Dhruv even more so, realizing that his fictitious story, which he had spun a few hours ago, was being enacted in reality.

Inspector General Dashamlav ordered his men to escort Dhruv, Mili and Gulnar to a waiting bullet proof Gypsy. The vehicle's engine was running as the three sat on the rear seat.

Two armed guards sat in the boot space of the vehicle. Dashamlav issued some last minute instructions and sat on the front seat alongside the driver. The vehicle sped off. One pilot Gypsy and three escort vehicles, all bullet proof, were part of the small caravan.

Inspector General Dashamlav swirled in his revolving chair, saying nothing. Dhruv and Mili were seated in front of the cigar smoking officer in a huge, well furnished office in the high security zone of Srinagar. Gulnar was at the far end, handcuffed and shackled to a chair.

To Dhruv, Mili and Gulnar herself, the scene was reminiscent of the climax of Dhruv's story.

"Welcome to Srinagar, Miss Mili and Mr Dhruv. You are safe now. I am Inspector General Dashamlav from the IB."

"Can you explain what is happening, IG sahib?" Mili asked.

"I will tell you. I am waiting for an important phone call," Dashamlav said, just as his phone rang.

Dashamlav spoke not at all as he listened to the caller. He muttered "yes" and "hum" several times during the five-minute call after which he replaced the receiver.

"Okay, Miss Mili, now I am at your service. Tell me what you want to know?"

"What exactly happened at the grove? Who was that fierce-looking man who was with your men? Why did I get a feeling that it was a war-like situation and I am returning from a battlefield?" Mili asked, trying her best to emulate Dhruv to put pointed questions.

"It was indeed a warlike situation and you can surely tell your family, friends and future generations that you came back from a battlefield," Dashamlav replied. "The only thing is that we won the war without a single shot fired from either side. The man you saw there was Mulla Zahoor, a notorious terrorist who was to be exchanged in lieu of you two. Zahoor is a close friend of Miss Gulnar Butt alias Ghazni Baba."

"Who is Ghazni Baba?" Mili asked.

Dashamlav briefly told them about Ghazni Baba and about the challenge, the terrorist had issued to him. Mili was aghast at the stark similarities between Ghazni Baba's story and Dhruv's tale that he had narrated an hour before to Gulnar. She put two and two together and furiously kicked Dhruv in his left leg. "You cheat! You told me that you are not an intelligence man!"

Dhruv interrupted at that point, rubbing his leg. He told Dashamlav the story of his story. He also briefly touched upon his unusual contest with Amaso and the fate of Mehmood Mian and Javed.

Dashamlav listened to Dhruv's account with rapt attention. Then he spoke, "Mr Dhruv is right Miss Mili. He is definitely not an intelligence man, but let me tell you that he has acted far more deftly and responsibly than the best of my men. I can also say that probably I myself would not have been able to act with such aplomb as Mr Dhruv did. He certainly does not deserve a kick from you."

"Then how do you explain his story which came to be

enacted in real life only minutes later?" a defiant Mili demanded to know.

"That is the hallmark of a creative man. Sometimes the written word is not very different from real actions and this is precisely what has happened here. It was a coincidence, and a stunning one at that," Dashamlav explained.

"One more question, IG sahib. I wondered all along about Dhruv's obsession with his cell phone. Can you explain that mystery to me?" a subdued Mili asked.

"This is one thing which Miss Gulnar Butt alias Ghazni Baba must be ruing. She must be cursing herself that she glossed over a point that a lay person like you noticed. First, you help yourself to some tea."

The tea bearer served tea to Mili, Dhruv and Dashamlav, in that order, and then turned to leave. Dashamlav ordered him back. "She may be an enemy but don't forget your Indian tradition. Serve her tea."

Dashamlav pressed a bell and asked the young policeman who stepped in to free Gulnar's handcuffed hands so that she could drink tea.

"Coming back to your question about Dhruv's cell phone, Miss Mili, it was a godsend for us. We were in constant touch with Dhruv's father, who, perhaps you know, retired as a General in the Indian Army. His father is an expert in espionage devices and worked as a strategist in the army. His advice during the last ten days was very useful to us. He told us that he had presented a cell phone to Dhruv on the unfortunate day of his son's kidnapping. He also told us that it was smart phone, equipped with a functional GPRS technology. We hoped against hope that the cell phone would be operated just once, howsoever briefly.

"It was our luck and Mr Dhruv's resourcefulness that the cell phone was operated not once, but thrice. We had put Mr Dhruv's cell phone number on our tracking system and it yielded rich dividends after more than a week. We could make out your exact location, and that helped us prepare for our commando operation, which you saw in the grove."

Gulnar shuffled in her seat, but did not speak a word. Dashamlav switched on the television. A news channel was giving "breaking news", which said, "Two Indian hostages, including Bollywood star Mili, rescued in a commando operation from southern Kashmir, very close to the LOC. Both the recovered hostages are unharmed. A senior woman operative of the Pakistani ISI, suspected to be behind the hostage drama, has been arrested." Dashamlav let out a sigh of relief satisfied that his phone sessions with his friends in media had borne fruit.

After everybody had finished their tea, Dashamlav ordered his men to take Gulnar away.

At New Delhi airport, a huge, colourful tent was bursting with representatives from the print and electronic media. The Union Home Minister and the Maharashtra Chief

Minister had come to the airport to receive Mili and Dhruv. However, for a change, the media was completely oblivious of the presence of two political VIPs. Their attention was riveted on Mili and the new real life hero, Dhruv.

All TV channels had deployed their OB vans in the vicinity to telecast the press conference live. After a few routine questions about how they were feeling, the reporters picked on Mili for some incisive questioning.

"Would you like to go to Kashmir again for work, Miss Mili?" a prominent English daily's reporter asked.

"Most certainly, yes, but not alone this time."

"Then in whose company you would like to go to Kashmir? Your husband?"

"You guessed it right," Mili replied. She was enjoying the session.

"Have you found your husband, Miss Mili?" a TV channel's woman reporter asked, unable to contain her excitement.

"Yes."

"Who is it, Miss Mili?" tens of voices asked.

"He is there right in front of you," Mili responded, pointing to Dhruv.

"Will you marry Miss Mili, Mr Dhruv?" a seasoned film reporter asked, adjusting his glasses to have a good look at Dhruv.

All cameras were focused on Dhruv. He was too stunned to answer the question. There was complete silence for two minutes. One could hear the distant roar of jet engines, coming in to land. The film reporter, sensing a bigger story, repeated his question to Dhruv.

Instead of replying to the question, Dhruv nervously turned towards Mili and said, "Why do you bring up private matters through the media?"

There was a deafening uproar from the media. The Home Minister and the Maharashtra Chief Minister were enjoying the spectacle and the new unfolding drama. All business and commercial activities had come to a standstill. Hundreds of onlookers had gathered around the open tent, their number swelling by the minute. The word had spread like a jungle fire that a live press conference of Mili and Dhruv was going on. All government and private offices within the airport complex stopped working and the employers and the employees were glued to their TV sets.

The media had taken upon itself the role of matchmaker; and they were determined to get a black and white answer from Mili and Dhruv after the actress went live with her confession. Mili and Dhruv kept looking at each other for a few minutes and whispered to one another.

The journalists protested against the bilateral parleys between Mili and Dhruv and egged them on to speak into the microphones.

A senior journalist came forward, gestured his colleagues to calm down and shot a pithy question at Mili. "Miss Mili, Mr Dhruv has publicly refused to answer the question. Its only interpretation can be that he is not interested. What will you do now?"

There was a roaring applause over the sharp question and then there was a moment of silence.

Then, Mili showed all those present why she was the reigning queen of Bollywood. Suddenly, she dropped on her knees, taking Dhruv's hand in her own, and said loudly, "Will you marry me, Dhruv?"

The media was no longer media by now; it had become a mob. The journalists clapped, whistled and jumped up at the spectacle. Here was a film actress who was going live to the world, without any script or a screenplay and no director choreographing her actions. Smiling and shaking his head, Dhruv kneeled down, helped Mili to stand up and then lifted her in his arms.

"I will marry you, darling," Dhruv shouted at the top of his voice.

There were instant celebrations, inside and outside the tent. Still photographers were busy taking shot after shot. Scores of reels were exhausted in two minutes. The Home Minister and the Maharashtra Chief Minister knew that those shots were going to be displayed on the front pages of every newspaper: Mili on her knees, asking for Dhruv's consent for marriage and Dhruv lifting her in his arms.

After the celebrations were over, a TV anchor demanded everybody's attention and then put her question to Mili. "Will it be appropriate to describe your ten days in captivity as a journey through different stages of hell?"

Order was restored with this question. Everybody waited to see how Mili would respond to the question.

"Who says I was in hell? These were the ten days in Paradise with my Adam; and a Serpent here and an apple tree there."

Mili hugged Dhruv and laughed and sobbed uncontrollably. No one disturbed them. The two then started their slow walk to Mili's waiting Merc.

Postscript

In a tribal mountainous village on Afghanistan-Pakistan border, a feast was in progress. A huge wild boar, killed only a few hours before, was being roasted. The boar was fastened to a metallic frame and a charcoal fire was glowing underneath. A lever jutted out of the metallic frame, which was connected to a long wooden handle. Two tribesmen operated the wooden handle dexterously, ensuring smooth and even roasting of the boar.

Eleven men were sitting around the fire. It was a cold night. The men had covered themselves with thick blankets.

Not far away, fierce looking bearded men, armed with Kalashnikovs, were guarding the Group of Eleven. These guards formed the fourth and innermost layer of armed protection. The third layer of more heavily armed men was two kilometres away. The second layer was five kilometres away from the Group of Eleven. The first, and outermost layer, was ten kilometres away and were armed with anti-aircraft guns and rockets.

Each of the four security units was in constant communication with one another through frequency hoppers and other sophisticated communication gadgets. Apart from the four elite protection units, hundreds of soldiers were on high alert, covering nearly a hundred square kilometres of the area.

If the place were to be attacked by planes or combat helicopters or infantry, these men had instructions to fight to their last breath. These highly indoctrinated and motivated jihadis belonged to The Green Jihad. It was well nigh impossible for the enemy to reach up to the Group of Eleven until the outer layers of protection were dealt with. By the time, these outer layers were neutralised; the topography of the area was such that the Group of Eleven would have virtually disappeared into thin air, courtesy of an intricate network of tunnels cut into mountains.

The chief cook signalled his men to stop rocking the boar, went near the fireplace to inspect the animal. Satisfied that the boar had been roasted in the typical Pashtoon style, the chief cook took out a sharp dagger from his robe and cut a big slice from the boar's rib cage. He sprinkled salt, pepper and other customary condiments on the piping hot meat and served it to a tall man seated in the middle.

After tasting the roasted meat approvingly, Amaso signalled that the food be served to all. The dinner over some twenty minutes later, Amaso cleared his throat to give his brief address.

"Warriors of Prophet Mohammed, peace be upon Him, we meet again after our meeting in that island in the Bay of Bengal. I called this plenary session of The Green Jihad to tell you that it is getting increasingly difficult for us to meet like this. Therefore, I have decided that we will not meet like this in future; or at least until the conditions improve. All of us were present at the last meeting and you would recall that certain decisions were taken at the meeting."

Head of the Green Jihad's Iraqi unit, who had been itching to speak for quite some time, grabbed his chance as Amaso paused.

"Sheikh, I am sorry to interrupt you, but where is our woman colleague who was present at our last meeting?"

"Well, she has met her nemesis in the form of Inspector General Dashamlav of the Indian Intelligence. Coming back to business, I was referring to certain decisions that we had taken at our last meeting."

"Yes, one decision was to start our activities in Kashmir on an experimental basis. You had said that the Kashmir experiment would be reviewed after an appropriate time and a decision would be taken whether to continue with our Kashmir involvement or not," the Green Jihad's Chechen unit head spoke.

"Yes, that appropriate time has come now," Amaso said.

"What is your decision?" the Green Jihad's Malaysian head asked.

"My decision is let us have a laser beam focus on Afghanistan, Iraq, Palestine, Somalia and Southeast Asia. I announce the closure of our Kashmir operations."

The End